THE BLOOD OAK CHRONICLES

Book One : The Mark

Raven *and* Moon Watson

iUniverse

THE BLOOD OAK CHRONICLES
BOOK ONE : THE MARK

iUniverse books may be ordered through booksellers or by contacting:

iUniverse
1663 Liberty Drive
Bloomington, IN 47403
www.iuniverse.com
844-349-9409

Because of the dynamic nature of the Internet, any web addresses or links contained in this book may have changed since publication and may no longer be valid. The views expressed in this work are solely those of the author and do not necessarily reflect the views of the publisher, and the publisher hereby disclaims any responsibility for them.

Any people depicted in stock imagery provided by Getty Images are models, and such images are being used for illustrative purposes only.
Certain stock imagery © Getty Images.

ISBN: 978-1-6632-2442-2 (sc)
ISBN: 978-1-6632-2443-9 (e)

Library of Congress Control Number: 2021911885

Print information available on the last page.

iUniverse rev. date: 06/11/2021

DEDICATIONS

<u>Raven Watson:</u> *I would like to first thank God for giving me the ability of imagination to even consider putting my thoughts to paper. To my Co writer and Husband Moon Watson for inspiring me and believing me. I love you now and always. To Dreame, which is an app for digital books to read. Thank you for igniting my passion to become an Author. And Finally to my Papa and Beanie, your love as my parents always gives me hope. I hope I have made you proud.*

<u>Moon Watson:</u> *First, I would like to thank The Lord for giving me purpose after a stroke and heart attack. To James, never give up. To Gerber, IT Department. To Camden, Don't Eat the Pot Roast. To Nate, Donut. To Dad, I'm hoping I made you proud. Finally, to Mom and Raven, your love and support have made a him into a HIM.*

PROLOGUE

T he first sounds I hear before I enter the light are screams that sound all too familiar. The screams are all I have ever known, my cries drown out the last of those screams. My eyes adjust to my surroundings, a woman lying in front of me, her eyes are closed. I crawl towards her with a familiar scent that gives me a sense of comfort. I know her... She is my mother and she is dead because of me.

It has taken me some time to take my first steps. I stumble at moments. I notice from one of these falls, water coming from above me. I stare into a pool of water, and I see myself for the first time.

My skin is soft, a dark blue hue. There are majestic horns on my forehead, and what appears to be leather-skinned wings on my back. I tumble on what appears to be my tail which is pointed at the tip. Then the pain hits me harder then the fall. It is a gnawing, profound sensation that was never committed to memory, yet feels familiar all the same. It's a longing burn near and inside my belly. I need to feed...

I step out of the opening of the cave that I have lived in since the beginning. I only crawled to the area where the light shined the brightest, but never any further then I have now. I glanced back at the remains of what once was my mother. The wind blows through my hair, which I recall was the same color as the wet substance in my mother's remains. My strong, magnificent wings spread open before I leap into the unknown. My eyes scan the area for what appears to be a larger amount of water and wide stretches of land. So many scents fill my nose that I am able to target what I am searching for. My prey awaits for me, the hunt resumes...

I land in a clearing where the scent lingers the least, before seeing what drives my mouth to water for the very first time. It stands near a modest body of water, drinking thirstily from it. This is what will be my first prey. My prey appears not to have noticed me. I scan this new creature more closely. a graceful, four legged thing with long pointing protrusions coming from its head that branch off in various directions. It is astoundingly beautiful. My breathing is steady, and in an instant I leap upon its back, and I easily throttle it. Holding its head down, my tail becomes taut, and I stab it through its muscular neck. Writhing in pain, I begin to feed on its essence, and I hungrily relish draining its life! Gods, this feels glorious!! It doesn't take long before this beast's eyes gloss over and roll back, showing only the whites. I remember the look my mother gave me as her heart stopped, and her eyes appeared the same. This was a lesson that would never be forgotten, for now my hunger is satisfied and I can return home at last.

With my hunger satisfied for the moment, I enter the cave. It is cold and sends shivers through my body. I grab a cloth my mother used to use to wrap around my body, adjusting it for my wings and tail to get a free range of movement. This is one of the items that I found among my mother's body. The feel of the cloth gives my skin tingles and feels like a warm embrace, as I sit and watch outside as water pours down the falls. My eyes become heavy as I slumber into the familiar dark void.

I am awakened by a sickening odor that burns my nose. I adjust my eyes to detect the presence of this scent. A creature appears in the entrance of the cave, it is larger than my previous prey. With each moment, I see closely the appearance of a different form, a brown coat with white spots on its back. Like my prey it stood on four legs and the sounds it made was that of grunt and growls. I am frozen, this feeling spreads through my body unsure of what to do. All I can do is watch closely to what this beast will do next.

The beast approaches my mother's body, and my heart quickens with each step it takes towards her. I narrow my eyes and ready my frame for what happens, preparing to fight or flee, if necessary. The savage creature chomps down on her foot, stripping the meat off of the bone. I hear deep within my body, the release of a blood curdling scream, and I pounce on the beast relentlessly. The previous feeling was replaced with a sense of unbridled fury heating my body. Clawing at its eyes, It whimpered in surrender. I began hissing while it backed away from us and retreated. It was stronger than I thought it would be, but as quickly as it came, the beast fled.

My breathing slowed down as I closed my eyes, I felt myself trembling from the previous attack, as I turned to face my mother. My wounds are slowly healing, but I know I must prepare soon. I needed to do something before I sought to hunt my next prey. I touched her face. It was as cold as it was when I first climbed out of her. The last sounds I heard were her cries before her heart stopped. I smiled, yet dropped a single tear, because she gave her life in order for my own to begin. For that, I am grateful and have cherished her ever since the first moment I knew of her existence. I know the beast from before will return to consume the rest of her, but I will not allow that to happen again.

I gathered her body in my arms, and inhaled her scent, which gave me strength for what I was about to do. I placed her gently on the earth, as with my claws, I started digging into the earth with ease.

It did not take long before a hole was before me. This was where I would place her, safe from all beasts, which sadly, includes myself. I know that I would be alone once this was done, something that could not be helped. As I stood to my feet, something shimmering caught my eye on her finger. I slowly remove it and place it on my clawed forefinger of my right hand. I felt that I should give her something of me as a strand of my hair fell from my head, then another. The hair danced whimsically as it fell, before resting in my mother's open hand. My mother lied on the earth with uniquely colored hairs of mine in her hands. A final parting gift as I begin to cover her with earth blinded by the tears that welled in my eyes.

Since my first feeding, the hunger aches have returned to my body. Such was the pain, that I could not seem to think clearly at the moment. I track my next prey which is much larger than the last, it is black and white on four legs grazing in a field. It has not noticed my presence and before I can pounce on it, I see a blur. It is another beast that has taken my prey down. I know this scent, and it sends me into a frenzy. Slowly I see a tawny beast with a golden form similar to the previous beast from the cave, but somehow different. It is devouring my prey. I see red, and before it can react, I leapt onto it. Wildly digging into it's skin, I scooped heaps of flesh from its side, yelling in pain as it clawed my flesh as well. I held this beast's life in my hands as it no longer struggled to fight. Its essence is mine as I am healed of my old and new wounds. Overcome with animalistic savagery, I tore the head from this dead thing. I cupped my trophy over my head and unleashed a primal scream. I am more than satisfied and stronger realizing this is what I needed and will always need to survive. I smile as I make my way in search of my next prey.

ACT 1..

CHAPTER 1

As the sun rose, blinding my eyes, I groaned at the thought of having to wake up, and I rolled over in my blanket to welcome more sleep. "Lilly! Lilly! Wake up, you wretched girl!" I heard my father calling me from outside of my room. "Do you hear me child?" he yelled louder, as if he was in the same room. "Yes father, I hear you, I am up." I say. Lifting myself off the bed, I go to wash my face. In my reflection is what I'd consider a rather plain face looking back at me, with blonde hair, green eyes, and a 'heart shaped' face as my mother used to say. I smile at the memories of her. "If I have to drag you out of that washroom by your hair, by all the Gods, I will!!!". My thoughts of her are shattered by his words.

I muster a smile on my face before I enter the dining room where he is sitting at the table with a fork in one hand and a bottle of spirits in the other. This was a familiar scene to yet another day with my 'beloved father'. "Good morning father!" I nervously greet him as I cheerfully walk into the room, studying his mood carefully. He meets my smile with his routine drunken scowl. "What would make it a good morning is if I had my fucking breakfast." he says after taking a long gulp from his bottle. "Father, I am sorry." I say, as I know whatever I say at this point will not calm his temper, and so I begin to prepare his meal. He mumbles a few more insults my way before I sit the plate of food in front of him. With a swift, backhanded motion, his hand slaps me across my face sending me flying into the next room. "Next time the food had better be on my table BEFORE I wake or you will get worse than that!" he roared, before cooling his throat once more with a swig of whiskey. I can only nod as I taste the familiar flavor of copper filling my mouth. I wipe the blood from my nose, lamenting how I miss my mother.

1

"Lilly St. Peter, where are you?" a sweet voice calls out to me. "I'm going to get you!" I giggle as she comes closer to where I am hiding. "I got you!" she declares as she grabs me and tickles me in her arms. This was our morning ritual that I once looked forward to before breakfast every day. "Now go wash up before your father wakes for breakfast." she would always say, as I would nod and hug her tight, burying my head into her ginger hair, which always reminded me of strawberries. Happily I would run, smiling down the hall into my father's arms before preparing for another day with my parents.

The ride to town was always a pleasant one as I sat in the middle while my mother who was singing a song and my father would hum along. It was a sunny day as we approached the edge of the town, my father stepped down from the wagon then helped my mother and I down. "I'm going to go visit Paul the Blacksmith. Why don't you and Lilly go purchase some supplies while I am away?" he said before smiling at her. This is how I learned what love looked like. I dared in my tender young heart to hope someday I might feel this way. My mother held my hands as we went shopping together, After returning home, our night ended with us together outside watching the lights in the sky. My happiest moment was the last moment as I closed my eyes trying to hold on that memory, but nothing lasts forever.

It was raining as I stood over my mother's grave. It happened so suddenly. One day she was happily singing and dancing with me, then the next, she was coughing up blood in bed while breathing heavily and shaking uncontrollably. My father would not let me see her after the town Healer had left. "Your mother is too weak to speak to you Lily, she needs her rest." His eyes were red, welling with tears. He walked away, leaving me numb, on the other side of my mother's door. Pressing my ear against the door, I could hear her wheezing. Each breath sounded so painful to my ears. I placed my hand on the door, not knowing if she could hear me. "Mother, I love you and father is so lost without you. We really need you to get better. You are our everything, a piece of you always connects us. You are what makes this family whole." I pleaded, but to no avail. I listened closely for her breathing, which had stopped. "Father!!!" I yelled for him, but there was nothing more that could be done. Mother was gone.

The marker over her final place of rest had read; 'Gwendolyn St Peter, beloved wife and mother'. All I could do is cry. I stood there knowing that her body now must lie below the earth. I placed flowers on her grave that I knew would have made her smile. I returned to my father who was in their room. I slowly opened the door and saw him on their bed. He had been like this since mother died. I could not stand to see him in this way. As I entered, he looked up at me, holding a bottle in his hand with a tired look on his face. "You look so much like her," he whispered, and sheepishly smiled. "but she is gone, fucking GONE!!" he yells, throwing the bottle against the wall, leaving shards of broken glass about the bedchamber floor. I came around to comfort him, but as I grasped his hand, he flew into a rage. My father smacked me so hard that I lost my breath. He had never hit me before this, and had never laid a hand on my mother. I am on the floor in shock. My thoughts are drowned out by his yelling, covering my head as he continues to hit me. The only comfort I have is a quiet prayer to the Gods that it will soon be over. Mercifully, he soon passes out on the floor in front of me.

So it has been ever since, a never-ending cycle of suffering and pain. In the dining room, I lifted my head, staring at my father who had passed out on his plate of breakfast. I go to the washroom and clean myself before I start my day, walking outside towards the barn to feed the animals. They seem to look forward to seeing me as I hum the song I remembered my mother singing. The sun shines high in the sky as I head towards the field after feeding the animals. I continue with my chores everyday and start the same. Even so my heart becomes lighter, because I am happy to be alive. Once I have finished my chores for the day, I head back to the house to prepare our meal. We are sitting eating our meal together in peace. This is rare for my father and I. It has been a long day and I am too tired to eat on my own. The silence is deafening as I glanced over at his one hand.

One day my father was chopping wood after drinking all night, the axe slipped from his hands and the blade took off three of his fingers. After hearing his cries of pain I ran to him wrapping his hand in the torn hem of my dress. He remained in bed afterwards for seven days. The town Healer gave him some herbs for the pain and fever. This was the reason I had to start working harder inside as well as outside of the house. He was no longer able to work the land, which made his mood only that much darker. He began to drink more from that day and I would receive more beatings.

He noticed me staring. "What the fuck are you looking at, girl!?!" he blurted casually. Startled from my thoughts, I shake my head. Rather than to strike me, or yell, my father smirks at me, sending a chill through my body with fear. "You think me less of a man because of this hand?!" he accused, holding it high over his head. He laughs and licks his lips "I am more than enough man for you!" he bellowed, standing to his feet. He suddenly walks over and grabs my hair, dragging me down the hall. I scream "No, Father I'm sorry!", not wanting to suffer another beating. All I can do is hold on to my hair, trying to pry it from his grip. He kicks open the door to his bedchamber and throws me on the bed, the same bed he shared with my mother, where she died alone, and here I am, alone with this man who does not appear to be my father anymore. He hovers over me as I try to push him off of me, but it's futile. One of his hands is holding my wrists, pinning my arms down far above my head. He covers my mouth with the other hand. The stench of whiskey in his pores makes my nose burn to the point that all I can do is let the tears run down my face.

"I can end your life right here if you continue to fight me, bitch!" he says with a malevolence that I have never known. My eyes are wide at the next move he makes. He removes his hand from my mouth, all I can do is press my lips together. His hand lifts up into my dress removing my undergarments. If I scream I know he will kill me.

I want to disappear, but all I see is his face breathing rancid air closer to mine. His manhood is big and hard as it slams into my body, I feel a sharp rush of pain, starting at my opening, and spreading through my core. Involuntarily, I scream, jerking to get free. He grunts and pushes deeper into me, making me feel as if I will shatter into a million pieces. He rips the top of my dress suckling on my breasts biting me while he grabs the other roughly in his hand. I can only whimper between the sobs, as it feels as if he would never stop. His body suddenly stiffened as I felt a warm liquid coming down my thighs. Finally he said, "Gwenodlyn, how I have missed you so much. I love you." and then he collapses on top of me. The last thing I hear is his snoring, I am numb inside, torn, and destroyed, but I manage to push him off of me. I head to my room slowly, as my body is in so much pain. I lie on my bed, and cry myself to sleep.

From this point onward, I avoid my father as much as possible by making his meals before he wakes. When I hear him approaching, I keep my head down to avoid his gaze. I bear with his insults and beatings without saying a word, only trying to focus on better days, which are far and few between. He is my father and as his daughter. I am obligated to stay and care for him. It is what my mother would have wanted, even if he was not caring for me as a father should. My days seem darker, alone in my room with the door locked as he has come into my room on several occasions. It is during those times, I imagine that I am with my mother as she sings and dances with me in a field of wildflowers. There is no pain, only the sun endlessly shining on us. I hold onto this moment until he is finished and stumbles out of the room. Since then, the door remains locked. He does not bother me when he realizes this, or maybe he is too drunk to care. Whatever the reason, it is the only peace I have before I wrap myself in my blanket and hold onto my own body for dear life.

"Lilly, let's go! We are going to town for supplies!" my father growls at me. It is the first time I look at his face, this stranger who is no longer my father, but rather a stranger that has stolen my innocence and the last veil of my chastity. I nod and go to prepare the wagon for our trip. I look forward to the trips down the hill into town, and to be around other people away from him for a while. We are silent until we reach the town. I hop off of the wagon without saying a word to him. I walk near the market for meats and fruits. I pause when I overhear a group of men talking, "We have to round up the villagers, all the men!" one bearded man says. "We have to protect the women and children!" another man adds. "Old Man Nesbit says we should leave it alone and let God handle it. After all, we are not Hunters." the florist chimed in. "OLD MAN NESBIT'S A FUCKING COWARD!!!" said the Sentinel, with uproarious laughter. "There is a demon out there and if we have to hunt it, that's going to be it for us" the florist cringed as the crowd of men continued to converse. I walked past them after paying for the supplies. A demon... I ponder, I've heard of such tales, but never knew that one existed and was near our village.

My father shouts for me, "Hurry girl, we are heading home!" His tone shows me that he has heard about the demon as well. "If that bastard demon comes near what is mine, I will fucking end it!" he says, waving his deformed fist in the air. I do not respond, as my thoughts are on what this demon is, and what it wants. My father laughs at his own words, "Its damn existence is intolerable. Why can't the blasted creature stay away from us good natured people?" he grumbles in absurdity. Him? A good natured person? I think that person died when my mother died. Once we are home, I start to prepare our meal after tending to the animals. I go into my room for the night, remembering to lock the door and secure it. As I lay on my bed, I wonder what this demon looks like. Is it some evil creature or beautiful illusion? Sleep soon engulfs my senses. "A demon, eh?" I hear myself saying before being captivated by my dreams.

The next morning, I built up the courage to speak to my father about the demon. He looks up at me and in a solemn and hushed tone he begins to tell me the tale. "These creatures come from the darkest part of the forest in the highest mountains where no sun shines, only coming out to hunt, so legend tells it. As a wee lad, I encountered one. All at once I was terrified, yet he chose not to consume me, possibly because I was akin to unripened fruit, but he scared me by raking his claws across my chest." He opens his shirt to reveal a long scar. "I knew then that my days were numbered." he takes a long gulp of his drink as he finishes his story and shakes his head, most likely trying to forget the memory. He gets up from the table and leaves the house with a fresh bottle in his hand. He will most likely pass out in the stable where I will find him in the morning. I clear the table, retiring to my room. If the demon spared his life, I wonder if it is REALLY so evil. I have learned that evil can come in the form you least expect. I lock my door and wonder more about this demon before sleep embraces me for the night.

The next morning, to evade another unpleasant beating, I head to the field instead of the stables. It is harvesting time, and I need to tend the corn fields. It is a hot morning as I wipe the sweat from my brow. I start gathering the corn from the stalks, when I hear a sound near the bushes ahead of me. My curiosity draws me closer to the source. There, a scarlet man with wings on it's back, a tail, and on his handsome face horns that are swirled under his black hair lies near the cornfield. He is so beautiful to me. As I kneel near him, it appears that his breathing was labored, and that he is hurt. I notice the deep cuts in his chest and stomach, and his clawed hands have blood on them. It didn't matter how it came to be, I decided that I must help him. I drag him to the barn where the tools are stored. It is the safest place that I can think of for now. I throw a blanket over him and run back inside the house. "Where have you been, girl?!?" I hear my father from the other room the moment I enter, "My meal is not on the table, I have warned you too many times. I'll have to teach you another lesson." he says with a terrifying stillness. Before I can react, he grabs me and places me on top of the table. As I struggle against him, he stands behind me. I know what is coming and brace my hands on the table. I feel his hands on my backside, and the whack of his hand lands on me. I await for the next one, and with each smack, I think of the demon. I can only say a prayer that I can help him in time. It is all I can focus on during the beating.

After I prepare my father's meal, I realize that I do not have much of an appetite. I do manage to squirrel away a little bit for my secret houseguest. I head to the barn where I have the demon hidden away with fear of how my father would react to his discovery. While obviously not human, the demon did not give off the appearance of a monster. He truly appeared sophisticated and almost fegal. I approached nervously with clean clothing and water. I cleaned his wounds. He has not opened his eyes as I continue to focus on my task. I am still sore, but I begin to clean the blood from his clawed hands. I wonder where this blood came from. Could this be the demon the villagers were speaking of? He looks so peaceful, his skin is crimson with scales on his upper chest that I trace softly with my fingertips. How could something so beautiful be so-called evil? I am jolted from my thoughts when I hear, "Lilly where the hell are you girl?"

Time passes, and the demon still has not awoken. it has been ten days since I first found him. I am worried that my father will discover him, so I cautiously place him in an area where the older supplies are. I carefully lay him in the corner. I wipe his hair from his face and smile.

He does not weigh as much as I thought or maybe I'm simply stronger due to the hard labour that I am used to, which is why I can easily move him. Father and I head into town on this day. As we approach, I see several men in black cloaks. On their cloaks, is the image of a flaming sword, which is the symbol of the Hunters. My eyes widen as I notice more of them as we ride deeper into town.We finally stop, my father grabs my arm and in my ear he whispers in a harsh tone, "Do not go near them. Heed my words girl, and return back quickly." I slowly nod and proceed to begin my shopping. In the town square, I hear a woman say "I have heard that the Hunters have tracked the demon and it killed their comrades." "More Hunters may come if the creature can not be found, and they will even bring in enslaved witches to help." another villager says. "I hope not," the other woman says. "They are more ungodly than the demons. The sooner they find it the better." Both of the women shake their heads. "Young lady are you ready?" the patron asks as he reaches for my supplies. It did not take me long to return back to the wagon. Waiting for my father, my only thoughts were to get back to my friend in the barn. I was conflicted with wanting to turn him in to the Hunters, or keeping him safe. I had no choice, but to help him, who was I to decide to end the life of a demon?

"Why are you so damn quiet and distant?" my father says after we arrive home. I think fast to respond, "The Hunters made me nervous." I lied. "Huh. The Hunters are nothing you need to worry about unless you are a demon." he grunts. I unload the wagon and go to prepare our meal for the night stealing a glance over at the barn. While in town I was able to visit the town Healer before returning back to the wagon. "Lilly it is good to see you." Healer Vincent greets me as I enter his office. I smile as he gives me a hug. "You seem so fragile my girl, is there something the matter?" he asked. Between the beatings and the unnatural incidents with my father, I have not the heart to tell him the horrible truth which has become my life. "Oh no, I've been working hard on the farm as of late, but I have not been sleeping well. Having nightmares about that demon attacking." I say, doing my best to give him my most frightened look. "Poor child," he says, "here is some lavender and chamomile herbs to help you sleep. Just add a few pinches of this either in your food or drink." I listen carefully as he continues to give me instructions. I tuck the packet of herbs in my dress, knowing that I will soon need to use them.

Later that night, I sprinkle a few pinches of the herbs in my father's meal, before hearing him come into the house. I place his food on the table before he sits down, and without a word he begins eating. I slowly start to notice him getting drowsy. I may have put in a little more than a few pinches. I needed to tend to the demon as soon as possible. I look up to see my father snoring loudly as he falls out of his chair. I clear his plate, and I leave the house walking towards the barn. As I approach the barn I hear a noise, and I start to panic. Did the Hunters find him? I rush into the back room, where I see, to my great surprise, that he is awake. I freeze in place, and he hisses at me, baring fangs, as his eyes change to black, I brace for his attack, but he stumbles back holding his bandages. Even after all this time, his wounds haven't healed completely. I slowly walk closer. As I approach, I notice he is still in pain. I place some water to his lips, and he opens his eyes wider. The black eyes from a moment ago are now replaced with green ones staring back at me. "Thank you." he spoke to me, but his lips did not move. "Did you say something to me?" I ask curiously as I remove the cup from his lips. He smiles and I hear in my head gentle laughter. "I said thank you. Is that not the proper response to show gratitude?" the question echoed in my mind. Am I going crazy? I'm more than a little startled by all this. "I am speaking to you telepathically, or with your mind. It is the best way to communicate with a human If I spoke to you verbally, you would not be able to understand, and the frequency of my voice would cause you to bleed to death." I shudder at the thought of his words, but as he noticed my change in mood, he gave me a warm smile. The way he looked at me I could not help, but blush.

"I brought you some food," I say, regaining my composure, I kneel down next to him. "this may help you feel better.". "You are a kind human," I hear him 'saying' "but this food will not suffice.". With his hands he cups my face and kisses me gently on my lips. Despite the recent interactions with my father, this is my first kiss and I give in to him completely. I feel like my head is spinning, and my body is melting. He pulls away from me. I want more, but my gaze travels to his wounds, which have somehow completely healed. "What is your name, human?" he asks. I blink, still adjusting to his voice in my head. "My name? I am Lilly St Peter" I answer. "Lilly St Peter..." he says. OH!! How I swoon at the sound of my name coming from him. He seems deep in thought for a moment, then he stands up, his wings stretching out, touching the walls. His tail begins to coil and sway, back and forth. I can't believe how tall and handsome he is! He notices me admiring him and smiles. Holding out his hand to me, he politely bows, "Well met, Lilly. I am called Jaran" and he places a kiss on my hand.

From that night on, I explained to Jaran that Hunters were searching for him, the rumors of Witches being brought in, and how I have been keeping him safe. I told him about my drunken father, and how I lost my mother. He listened attentively, and for the first time I appreciated someone finally hearing me. With tears in my eyes, he recognized my pain, and wrapped his wings around me. Never before had I felt so safe and secure. I had yearned for so long to be washed with this kind of feeling. He would rub my hair while I continued to cry in his arms. I fell asleep in his arms. In the morning, I heard my father calling me. "I have to go perform my duties. Please do not leave, Jaran. I promise I will return just as soon as I can." I plead. Jaran stays silent, he just smiles and nods. I ran from the barn and entered the door of my home, walking right into a close up view of a disfigured hand. "You stupid fucking girl!" my father growled, as his hand slaps me across my face. I fall quickly to the floor. All I can mumber is my own voice repeating "I'm sorry. I'm sorry..." as I cower from the floor. I'm not sure if I can take another beating, not after the bliss I experienced last night. "Please father, no more!" I shout. "No more? Pleading with me after I give you everything. Chance after chance I give, and you never learn! You no good piece of cunt, I'll teach you a lesson you will never forget." He walks over and grabs the horse whip. "Yes, this will do for a bitch like you..." he says with a snarl, as I scream awaiting the pain with my hands over my head.

The first lash cuts deep in my arm, causing blood to gush from the wound. I place my hand over it instantly. The second goes across my back. This feels like it goes on forever, with such brutality that eventually I pass out. I wake up on the floor, my head pounding.

I am not sure how long I have been out. I look outside to see the sun setting on the horizon. I slowly stand up and go to clean myself thoroughly, wincing as every part of my body aches. I need to check on Jaran. I hope he has not left. My mind fills with a nagging fear, as my father is nowhere to be found. I worry that he may have found Jaran in the barn. No. No, I cannot jump to that conclusion. I open the door to my father's room, where he is passed out on the bed with a bottle in one hand and the horse whip in the other, which still has my blood dripping steadily from it. I unsteadily leave the house and head towards the barn. The animals seem calm tonight, my father must have tended to them after my beating. I enter the back room, noticing him resting. He opens his eyes, which are shimmering in the dark.

He smiles, but it quickly fades as I come closer. Then I realize that some of my blood has soaked through the sleeve of my shirt. He notices it even as I try to cover my arm. "Hello Lilly," he narrows his eyes and furrows his brow before continuing "tell me what happened to you?." For a moment, I can only stare at him, not knowing what to say. He stands placing his hands which are warm and comforting on my arm. I feel a tingling sensation and my breathing becomes heavy as a heat spreads through my body. My eyes are closed and when I open them, my wounds are healed. It felt as if he mended the pieces of my broken soul, as well as my flesh. "Now tell me what happened?" he says as we sit on the floor together. I tell him that I hurt myself falling and he says "Falling would not leave your heart stricken with fear." I do not know how to respond and say "I have to leave." and I prepare to walk out, but not before I sense him calling me. "Lilly, I will wait until you are ready to come to me. I need to rest. I can not leave this place as I am not strong enough." he says, with a hint of sadness. I turn around and say "Do not worry, I will be back." I head back to my room and lay on my bed feeling restless. I hear my father stirring around in the other room, I jump for the door and quickly lock it. I can not have him near me tonight. I finally close my eyes dreaming of being in Jaran's embrace again.

The morning starts like any other morning, cooking breakfast and daydreaming of Jaran. I searched my dress for the herbal packet.

"Looking for this, maybe?" I turned around to see my father standing there with the packet of herbs in his hand. My stunned look must have said it all. "I was wondering why I was sleeping so much after my meals. To my surprise, I found this in the hallway by the entrance to your bedchamber." he walks over to me and shakes the packet in my face. With a wicked smirk on his face he says "It seems I have not been giving you enough fatherly attention." Before I could react, he moved behind me and wrapped his arm around my throat. I can barely breathe as I think: Is he finally going to kill me? I am dragged into his room and he grabs some rope nearby and hogties me. Now I can only see his feet, as I am laying on my stomach. He tears my dress violently off of my body. "A little pleasure before some much deserved pain, my sneaky little bitch!" he mocked, lording over my fear. Like so many so many moments before, there would be no use to struggle or scream. When I know he has finished all I can do is think of Jaran. The crack of the whip brings me back to reality. No. This time, I refuse to allow him to hear me cry and I press my lips firmly against the floor. My body jerks from the whip slicing through my back. The blood drips down towards my face from the occasional lash striking my head. Between the pain all I can hear are his insults and I whimper into the floor thinking that it will end soon. Please Gods, let it end soon.

I wake up noticing my hands and feet are untied again my body aches. I cover my mouth to muffle my scream as I manage to sit up. Darkness covers the room I crawl to the door. The TRUE monster is nowhere I can see him. Placing my hands on the wall, I struggle to pull myself to my feet. I stumble outside heading towards the barn. Jaran stares at me as I continue to hold myself up, until I lose my balance, and before I fall to the floor I am in his arms. His head touches my forehead and again, the warmth spreads through my body. His lips touch mine and I hear him say "Show me." and all at once images of what that monster did to me appear. I see myself laying there, tied up like some animal. Jaran sees every moment, even the first slap after my mother died. The endless blood and tears that I have shed are on display. Never before have I felt so... NAKED. I feel myself shaking in his arms. He lets me go and the images end. "Go to your room and rest." I sit up from his arms and obediently walk back to the house. Am I dreaming? I feel like I am in a cloud, as I come into my room and fall asleep as soon as my head hits the pillow.

Later, it was more of the same. Another meal with my father, as per the usual. My head feels like it is in a haze. I can not seem to concentrate, and soon my father breaks the silence. "I've noticed you have been frequently going to the barn. Are you fucking stealing supplies from me?!" he accuses as he slams his hand on the table jolting me from the fog of my thoughts. I am startled by these accusations "Trying to get enough silver to leave me alone, eh? You will never leave me, because only I can marry you off, and I will never give you away! You are mine alone! FOREVER!!!" Before I answer him, he grabs me and pushes me to the floor. I can not take another beating, but I do not have enough strength to run. If I did, where would I go and what about Jaran? For the first time in my life I say to him "What did I ever do to you to make you hate me so much to do all these cruel things to me? What have I ever done what was so wrong?" In a brief moment of clarity, he sobers up. "I don't hate you, you are all I have left." He sits quietly and contemplates and then says "I know that I can do this one more time. Just this one last dark, ugly thing. You are of age. I can have a child with you, and things will be like they used to be." I look at him horrified at the thought of what he is suggesting, and I respond. "No! No!" screaming as he reaches for me wildly. I accidentally swipe and scratch his face. Suddenly a wave of rage illuminates his face and he slaps me. "So I am going to have to beat you into submission..." he said as he grabs his horse whip. I braced myself, closing my eyes, holding my breath, and awaiting the first lash.

I hear a growl and the horse whip hitting the floor. When I open my eyes wide, I see Jaran holding my father by the neck. He struggles to breathe, trying to pry Jaran's hands from his throat. Jaran looks at me. "Lilly are you well? I heard and smelled your fear." His eyes are blackened like coal, like when we first met. "Yes" is all I can say in a whisper, as my father glares at me. "WHAT!? YOU KNOW THIS CREATURE!?! YOU BROUGHT THIS ABOMINATION IN MY HOME!!? I SHOULD HAVE FUCKING KILLED YOU!" he screams out these words. I can not speak as I watch in awe, what happens next.

Jaran touches my father's chest as his mouth opens. He sucks from my father's mouth, but not quite in a kiss. As if Jaran had taken his soul, my father twitches and his eyes roll back exposing the whites. Just as quickly as it begins it is over, and Jaran drops his body on the floor as I faint from the shock.

CHAPTER 2

I awaken in my room and Jaran is stroking my hair as I am lying in his arms.. "Lilly..." I hear him saying. This is all I hear him saying. All I can do is feel lost in his emerald eyes. "Lilly?" he repeats, making my name sound like a song. "I'm sorry I couldn't stop myself." he says, with a child-like look of remorse. I recall the events of the past few hours, when Jaran killed my father. "He's dead isn't he?" I ask. "Yes", he replies, gently touching my face. "Surely you must believe me to be evil and wicked now..." Jaran retorts shamefully. I'm not sure if that was a question or statement. "I have never hated anyone, not even my father after everything he has ever done to me. I can not hate him now and I do not hate you." I reply. Tears rolled down my face. I place my arms around his neck, and squeeze him tight, and I realize that I am in love with a demon.

I am still in Jaran's arms as the sun rises, and his wings are wrapped around me like a cocoon. Maybe I am dreaming, but if this is so, I hope that I never wake up. I place a kiss on his forehead feeling refreshed. I get up to walk into my father's bedchamber, where I discover my father's body is nowhere to be found. Was that a dream? No, I could not dream something so horrific, as I remember my father's twisted face aware that the end was coming near. I wrap my arms around my body and breathe a sigh of relief that the nightmare is over.

I prepare myself breakfast. As I hungrily devour each bite savoring it and smiling, I begin my chores humming as the sun shines on this beautiful new day. Even the animals appear in a lighter mood as I spread the feed into their pen. I wonder, am I truly happy that I am free of him? I go into the barn realizing that we are running low on supplies. "I do not understand why you have to leave and head into town?" Jaran asks, and I can hear the tension in his voice. "Jaran," I lovingly touch his face "I am a human, and there are things that I need to sustain myself." Jaran grabs my hands pleading with me "It is not safe. The Hunters are still within the town looking for me. I smell more Hunters arriving. I can't risk you being killed because of me." He squeezes my hand and I press my forehead to his, our breath becoming one air. "I will be cautious and return to you." I say, as our lips touch.

The trip to town is the only time I have been on my own. Dread feels my body as I descend the hill of my estate, getting closer to the town. I see many cloaks with flaming swords, more than the last time I visited with my father. "You there, girl!" I turn around as a Hunter stalks towards me. He seems to tower over me, brandishing a longsword near his waist. Intimidated, I remain still. "I want to ask you some questions, have you seen anything suspicious?" the red-faced Hunter asks. Flustered I quickly stammered out "No, nothing at all, sir!". The Hunter glances me over and narrows his eyes. "I have seen you before when you were with your father. Always looking around. Where is your father?" Searching the area for my father he steps closer, "He is home ill, I have come here on my own." The longer I am standing in his presence I increasingly become more uncomfortable. From behind me I hear a townswoman,

"Oh my you poor child, someone go fetch Healer Vincent!" The woman places her head over my shoulder comforting me as we walk away from the Hunter. The Hunter appears to be angry and turns the other way.

My relief is soon replaced with more panic as Healer Vincent Goodwind rushes towards me with Old Man Nesbit following behind him. Healer Vincent embraces me; he is wearing his custom robes as I notice that he is adorned with many jewels. In his hand, he carries his silk bag that contains his herbs and potions. His face shows wisdom and warm concern for me. Over his shoulder I notice Old Man Nesbit smiling at me with contempt, a toothless grin on his weathered, sunken face. He rubs his tattered rags and scraps of leather with his boney fingers. From his hands to his sleeve of his arm are a fascinating yet repulsive web of varicose veins. His skin is a rice paper sheet that barely disguises the sparse amount of flesh remaining on his withered old bones. His hair is a dark, garish, ratty mop that comes together to a point in the form of a ponytail. His breath was truly putrid, as was the view of his many coarse, gray hairs sprouting from his ears and nose in bushels. "It seems we will have to go see about Mr. St Peter, Healer Vincent" Old Man Nesbit speaks to him with a delusional sense of authority. I shake the thoughts of his eyes glaring at my body, like a dog studies a side of beef. "My dear Lilly, you should have come to me sooner," Healer Vincent says, giving me an assuring look. "We will come in the morning to visit your father." I can only nod in agreement.

I return home as quickly as I can, placing the supplies on the table. I feel like I can hardly breathe, I close my eyes and suddenly I hear. "Lilly? Lilly, what is wrong?" I turned around to see Jaran standing there, with a look of concern on his winsome face. I run to him, and in his arms I begin to sob heavily, as he holds me tightly. I begin to realize that maybe I spend too much energy crying.Thankfully, I've come to learn that in times of trouble, Jaran is my rock. For the remainder of the night, we talk about what will happen in the morning. Jaran reassures me that everything would be alright. I believe him, as in his arms is where I always feel the most secure. Before the sun rises, Jaran awakens me. "Lilly, I want to show you something." he says to me. He reaches for me, and we are standing face to face. As if he were made of clay, Jaran changes (or 'shifts' as he calls it) into the image of my father. I place my hands over my mouth in shock. "Lilly it is okay, it's me." his lips move to form the words, and my eyes widen as it is not my father's voice, but Jaran's. I realize that it is Jaran's hands I am holding, and not my father's. I look out the window and see in the distance Healer Vincent's horse drawn wagon approaching the house from down the hillside road.

Instantly reading my thoughts, Jaran says "Go meet them outside, and whatever happens know that I will return to you.There is no time to explain further, now hurry!" Without any other questions, I rush out of the house to meet Healer Vincent. His wagon pulls up and before seeing him, I also smell the lingering stench of Old Man Nesbit. I again ignore his perpetual gaze, and approach Healer Vincent with a weak, unconvincing smile on my face. He places his hand over my hand with an encouraging look as we enter the house. To my horror, we walked into a terrifying sight. There, at the hase of my stairway, lies my father's body on the floor, broken and misshapen. A pool of blood was forming around the crown of his head. I fall to my knees, sobbing relentlessly, yet again. I can't believe that this is happening, as my hands are covering my face. Healer Vincent and Old Man Nesbit walk over to his body as they lean over him. I hear Old Man Nesbit say "The poor bastard is dead, and from the smell of it, he took one to many drinks." Between the blur of my tears I see Healer Vincent nodding his head solemnly. "We will have to give him a final resting place next to his wife." he said in hushed tones. Looking over at me, my hands covering my mouth as tears continue to fall from my face, Healer Vincent kneels before me, cradling me in his arms like a new born baby as I shake uncontrollably from the loss.

It does not take them long to wrap his body in white linen. Old Man Nesbit dug the grave, mumbling curses under his breath as he worked. "You never...deserved... your wife... it all should have been mine!" one could hear over the whisper of the wind. His finger coiled around the wooden grip of the shovel like the skeleton of a snake, if one could imagine such a thing. With each plunge of the spade into the soil, Old Man Nesbit's joints snapped and popped, sounding like dried twigs underfoot. Healer Vincent stands next to me bracing me as if I would break if he were to let go. Old Man Nesbit places the body into the grave, steps away, and nods towards Healer Vincent in disgust and exhaustion. I hear Healer Vincent sigh as he begins to say a prayer. "As the sun rises and set so has the sun set on our brother Thomas St Peter. As we mourn his passing, we can only hope he finds peace in the hereafter." Old Man Nesbit could be heard snickering with his spinderly hand covering his wicked, toothless mouth. I want to smack that smile from his face, such a disgusting human being he is. "Ahem..." Healer Vincent continues. "Ashes to ashes, dust to dust" and he throws a handful of dirt and ash into the grave. I weakly do the same, watching as the earth slips between my fingers. I scowl as Old Man Nesbit kicks some dirt into the grave spitefully, and I chuckle to myself when Aidos, Goddess of modesty, respect, and humility, causes him to lose his footing, almost joining my father in the grave.

I'm breathing heavily as Healer Vincent walks me back into the house. Over my shoulder, I see Old Man Nesbit filling the grave he glances up at me licking his pruned lips, sending a chill throughout my body. I am sitting at the dining room table, this all seems so unreal to me. Somehow, Jaran is dead. This is the first time that I connected the thought of death to Jaran's name. Why is this happening? I smell the rot of Old Man Nesbit as he slithers toward me. "You know my dear child, before his 'untimely' demise, I spoke at length to your father about how it would be such a shame if he was unable to marry you off. By the Old Laws it would be his duty to marry you as a second wife and sire a child." he said with insidious glee. I can not believe what I am hearing, and horrified, I realize the sick idea was planted by this monster! I feel myself begin to retch, as I watch as a sinister smile curl on the lips of Old Man Nesbit. He places his clammy, skeletal hand on my shoulder, and leans forward over me.

I shiver with discomfort as he continues "Now that your father has passed, that responsibility falls to the elder patriarch of the village." and suddenly, as if the thought had just occurred to him, with a twisted smile he says "Of course, that would be me..." he says with no attempt to disguise his perversion. As he continues to smile, I notice his teeth are rotted beyond repair, and as he continues to lean over me, panting heavily, one wiggles itself loose and falls on my shoulder. I quietly retch again, as my throat balloons with vomit, refusing to be rude I swallow it back down. I am now obviously visibly shaken by the disturbing mental image.

Healer Vincent entered the room, much to my relief. "Nesbit, this is not the time for such talk. Lilly has just lost her father, and I am sure she will be able to find a suitable man of her own age." Healer Vincent says. Puffing out his chest, Old Man Nesbit responds "I am only thinking of the welfare of this poor child! The rules-" "-That were put in place before I was even born." Healer Vincent intrudes. "She needs a man to take care of her, and why NOT me?" Old Man Nesbit offered in rebuttal. Healer Vincent crosses his arms over his chest. "I am sure Lilly appreciates your 'concern', but again this is not the time, nor the place." As he looks at me his eyes are filled with such warmth like a real father should look at his daughter. "Lilly we are going to take our leave now. Will you be alright by yourself?" Healer Vance asks as he kneels in front of me. With tears in my eyes, I nod. "If there is anything that you need, you know where to find me." he concludes. "I as well..." Old Man Nesbit adds, visibly frustrated.

I hear in the distance the wagon pulling away from my home. I am finally alone in this empty house. After some time I prepare a meal as I sit down at the table, when I suddenly realize that I have no appetite. By candlelight, I sit near the tombstone where Jaran lies. "He's not dead!" I shake my head, closing my eyes, willing it to not be real. I open my eyes, staring at the tombstone, sitting on the earth, caressing it, which gives me some comfort. In the distance I hear the howling of a wolf. I stand to return back inside the house when I suddenly hear and feel a rumbling from the ground. I look over at the grave as a hand shoots up out of the earth. My heart is beating so loudly in my chest, I could faint. This is clearly not a dream. Out of the earth bursted Jaran, and like a fairy tale, he stands before me once more. His face is covered with dirt as his wings stretch out from his back. He smiles at me, I try not to blink, because I fear that if I do, he will disappear. In my mind, I hear the soothing tenor of his voice saying "Uh, Hello." I happily ran into his arms, holding onto him for dear life.

I decide to bathe him first, cleansing his face as he smiles, and I am once again in awe that he is sitting in front of me. I resume washing him clean, wiping towards his stomach. He begins to moan at the touch of the warm water. His eyes are piercing through me, watching each movement that I make. I finish washing his clawed hands, wings, and tail, which I realize are sensitive to my touch as I hear low growls from him. Once I have washed his claws I realize that he has fallen asleep. I crawl next to him joining him in the tub in a duly deserved rest for the both of us. The following night, we opt to lay in the bed, his fingers entwined with mine, it all feels so natural "Lilly?" he says, breaking my train of thought. I nudge my head towards him. "What does it mean to 'marry you off'? The one human mentioned this, the unpleasant one. Does it mean that you will leave me?" There is a sad pleading look in Jaran's eye as he asks. "No, marrying someone off means when a man is given a woman's hand in marriage. They can be together and start a family." I explained. I notice that he is deep in thought and responds "This is similar to having a mate to bear offspring with, yes?" his face lights up when I nod in agreement. He sits up looking deep into my eyes "Will you be my mate?" he asks, searching my face for an answer as I hold his hands. "Yes!" I practically leap into his arms without any hesitation in my mind, only hope for the love we share with each other.

Jaran's mouth finds my own as I open to him. I am breathless as he kisses down the nape of my neck. I feel the same heat from before spread throughout my body. This must be how love truly feels. He begins to undress me, touching each part of my body until he reaches my core which is trembling, yet already wet for him. Never have I felt this craving in my womb before. Jaran retracted his claws, sliding a finger in me carefully, massaging the deepest, softest parts of my inner self. As I arch my back, he began to use his smallest finger to manipulate the crux of my modesty in ways that never even occurred to me.I feel so high, I could almost touch the heavens! Jaran continues to have his way with me, until I reach my climax with a yell that threatens to shake the foundation of our home! Jaran proceeds to then stroke his fingers through my hair while he kisses my stomach gently. All I can do is grab the sheets moaning his name, he moans as well, and I see his manhood. It is so much bigger than my father's OH MY GOD!!! I begin to panic. How could I think about him at this moment? I cover my eyes in shame, yet Jaran senses my thoughts and says, "It is okay." I can only respond "I'm so sorry..." as he kisses my hands and places them on his manhood, which feels stronger than oak, while I guide him into my entrance. The smooth crown of his throbbing sword, fills my deepest reaches and strikes true. We become one as he deeply kisses me. I lick at his skin while he goes deeper! Is there no end to the miracles my lover can perform? Jaran lifts me on top of him, sliding himself ever deeper into my hungry, thirst quenching well. I am unsure how to move, but he guides my hips. I nibble on his horns while massaging his wings, I hear him moan. The moaning continues on both ends, as I begin to gyrate my hips, feeling him deeper inside of me, in a steady rhythm. "Lilly, yes please just like that, we are mated..." Jaran gasps as he wraps his wings around my drenched body that is saturated with a mixture of his and my own sweat. I could have never imagined feeling this way as we remained in this position, falling asleep in each other's arms, after surrendering to the depths of passion and electricity between us.

We wake up together, and like an orgasmic ritual, we make love each night. Jaran decided to shift into a human form in order for us to better communicate with each other. Jaran's human form was as handsome as his demon form, with the same black hair and green eyes. I laughed realizing that he was naked and that he would definitely need some human clothing. I found some of my father's old clothing which he used to wear when my mother was alive. Jaran looks at himself over in the looking glass. "I'm not sure that I can get used to wearing such clothing. Did I say that correctly?" he asked, tilting his head to the side in contemplation. Smiling, I reply "Yes you did." as he holds me, and I notice that his scent has changed as well. "We can adjust and learn from this together, we have plenty of time." I added. I look up and smile at him as he leans down to kiss my nose. "First things first, you need a human name..." I said, thinking to myself. "A human name has never occurred to me to have. I would be honored if you would give me a name, Lilly." I look him over carefully. He appears excited as I circle him and think of what to say. "Hello, Mister Calvin Smith!" I bow to him and he delightfully cups my face to kiss me.

Our daily routine starts with us having a meal together. It is the first time Jaran is introduced to eating food from a plate using a knife, spoon, and fork. I giggle as he uses his fork to eat his bread and a knife to stir tea. "Okay, I am obviously doing something wrong." he sulks before he winks at me and laughs. "My kind eats from a being's life force or essence. It can be from animals or humans." he continues. "It is another kind of gift that sustains my kind, which is why we can live longer than most humans. We age differently, but we are not immortal." I hang on to his every word, but then he remains quiet for some time which I become concerned by, and finally, he looks at me with a forlorn expression. "I must confess to you that I have fed off of you when we first met and became close. When I killed your father, I fed from him as well." he lowers his head in shame after saying this. "You must hate me now because you know what I truly am... A wicked being." I walk to him, and lift his chin, smiling. "Calvin, I love you more than you will ever know." I say as I kiss him and say "If you need to feed I will gladly be your sustenance." I climb into his lap as he smiles and holds me tightly. "So, let me show you what this fork is used for!" I say, and he laughs as we continue with our breakfast.

I take Jaran outside and show him how to feed the animals on the farm. The animals appear to be nervous around him, and I laugh as he falls into the pig pen. "You have to be patient with them. They are trying to get used to you as well, my love." Wiping the mud off of his face he pouts before saying "They started it." I am laughing hysterically as he grabs and pulls me down in the mud as well! Next, I show him how to tend the land, which consists of planting and harvesting. He seems to catch on quickly, and I offer to show him books on the subject, as well as other topics. He is so eager to learn more, which I am happy to cultivate.

It is a full moon tonight, and a shadow emerges from the bushes. Old Man Nesbit licks his lips as he approaches the St. Peter property. Since the day of her father's death, all he can think about is Lilly and her ripened body. He palms his stiff pecker in his trousers, fantasizing about imbibing upon her nectars. Tonight will be the night he gets what he deserves. "FUCKING THOMAS!" he curses to himself "I offered him one hundred silver pieces for his daughter and then some, but that GODDAMN DRUNKEN BASTARD turns me down!!! Greedy ASSHOLE, wanting her all to himself." He spits and smirks. "However, that will all change soon, very soon." He peers into a window hoping to see his lovely Lilly, his eyes, almost bulging out of his head when he sees instead a young man standing in the room reading a book.

"WHAT THE HELL??!" without a thought, he abruptly storms into the house. The young man does not appear to be taken by surprise and calmly closes the book he was reading. Snarling and breathing heavily, the old codger points an arthritic finger at the young man. "WHO ARE YOU AND WHY THE HELL ARE YOU IN MY HOME?!!" Old Man Nesbit asks, narrowing his eyes. A puzzled look appears on his face as he responds "Your home sir? This is the home of my betrothed, Lilly St Peter. I have no idea who you are either, but I do know this is definitely not your home." A chill goes down Old Man Nesbit's spine causing him to stand erect so he can be at eye level with the young 'intruder'. "Where is Lilly?" he demands, sneering with a slight smile. The young 'intruder' calls out "Lilly my love, we have a guest!" and defyingly stares into Nesbit's gray, bloodshot eyes. Rage fills his crooked body, hearing him calling her HIS LOVE. Elsewhere, I am brushing my hair, smiling at my reflection in the looking glass. Our home is filled with laughter and joy. I could not imagine my life without Jaran, 'or do I mean Calvin?' as I giggle. I hear Calvin call me "Lilly my love, we have a guest." fear creeps in my heart as I dash into the room. To my horror there stands Old Man Nesbit with Calvin. My eyes go back to Calvin, who appears to be amused. Old Man Nesbit looks as if he will explode at any moment, as his face is as red as a beet.

I compose myself as much as I possibly can while Old Man Nesbit narrows his eyes at me. "Lilly my dear, this man says he is your betrothed? Who is he, and where on earth did he come from?" he huffs out the questions. Slowly. I walk over to Calvin placing my arm into his. "Old Man Nesbit, may I introduce my betrothed, Calvin Smith, a son of a long time friend of my father. He heard the sad news of my father's passing and came calling to offer his condolences. We are very much in love, and will be married soon." I said this with a broad smile on my face. Old Man Nesbit's jaw is gapped open in pure shock. At first I thought he may have died due to his paleness in his face, honestly his passing would be of great relief to me. "It is a pleasure to meet you, Mister Nipplebits!" as Calvin reaches out his hand to him to shake. 'Nipplebits' leers at Calvin in disgust, and takes a step back. "I will be bringing Mayor Crowley and Healer Vincent with me as this Calvin Smith needs to be questioned by the higher authorities and myself!" he yells, staggering out of the house. "We will look forward to your next visit, Mister Knucklebutt!!" Calvin laughs and I join in as we head to the bedroom to retire for the night.

The wagon was speeding along the hillside trail, threatening to tilt and crash several times after they left town. Healer Vincent notices this as Old Man Nesbit whips the horse harder and faster. "Nesbit! Nesbit! For goodness sakes!! There is no need to be in such a hurry! If what you say is true the couple will still be there. I would like to see them in one piece, which will be quite difficult to acheive on a dead horse!" Healer Vincent says, contemplating turning the riding crop on Nesbit himself. Nesbit seems not to hear him, or maybe he is completely ignoring him which would not be the first time. He observes Mayor Crowley who is holding his jolly stomach and hat in a panic, looking as though he may bounce off the wagon at any moment. He screams as he feels the wagon jump over an uneven bump on the road. Healer Vincent only hopes Lilly is safe. From what Nesbit told him and the Mayor, this young stranger could be dangerous. He could not bear the thought of Lilly getting hurt after losing all of the family she has ever known. Vincent said a quiet prayer that they should make it there alive at the rate they are going, He hoped to keep down my breakfast.

The wagon approaches the St Peter house. Lilly and I notice, and she grasps my hand. "Listen carefully, my love. I have another gift, a special talent you may say, when I touch the skin of a being, I can compel them to do anything I request." Lilly considers what I am saying, and nods awaiting to hear more. "It was the reason why I reached out to that old pervert under the guise of a friendly handshake to prevent this from happening. Now, it seems that I know what I will have to do. Whatever happens, just trust that everything will be alright my mate, my love." I plant a kiss on her luscious, cherry lips. I will have to reward her for continuing to be so patient with me. I proceed to walk outside to meet our upcoming 'guests'.

Finally, we have come to a halt. Nesbit pulls the reins of the horses. Mayor Crowley vomits near the side of the wagon, as I say a prayer under my breath, thanking God I am still alive. I adjust my glasses to see a young man rubbing the horses with a smile on his face. "Welcome, gentlemen, my name is Calvin Smith. Lilly and I were expecting you!" I hear Nesbit grunt.

"Yes, this is the bastard that I told you about" Nesbit squawks as he steps forward. "Healer Vincent and Mayor Crowley, I presume?" the polite young man says, as he shakes our hands and I feel a sense of familiarity. "And Mister Noodlebelch, it's a pleasure to see you again, ha ha!" patting him on his back. "It's Mister NESBIT!!! It is not hard to remember or pronounce, you imbecile!!!" Nesbit grumbly replies. With a hearty laugh he firmly takes Nesbit's hand, and apologies for any percieved disrespect. This may have been the first time that I ever saw Nesbit genuinely smile since when he was last with his beloved departed wife, bless her soul. We all head into the home, where I see Lilly, she appears to be so happy, it looks as if she is glowing. We embrace in a hug, and she bows to the other two men beside me, and begins to offer us an enormous feast of food and drink.

Engaged in so many topics, Mayor Crowley asks the question that is on all of our minds. "So you two are betrothed to be wed, when is the date?" he asks with a chicken thigh in his hand and taking a big gulp of his drink. I held my breath looking at Nesbit, fearing he would create a very unpleasant scene. To my surprise, he smiled awaiting the answer as well from the couple. The couple seem to look at each other for a moment in surprise. Lilly says "Well we haven't decided on a date as of yet." We all jump as Mayor Crowley slams his hand on the table and shouts; "Let's get you two married right now!"

I was taken aback and surprised by Mayor Crowley's outburst. I was just so thrilled to be Calvin's bride to be, even though I was already Jaran's mate. Searching everyone else's faces, they all appeared to be happily in agreement. This gift Jaran possesses is very potent. I noticed even Old Man Nesbit beaming with positivity compared to his typical, brooding, morbid self. I am wearing my mother's wedding dress. I remember her showing and promising me that the dress would be a gift when I was wed. A tear slides down my face at the memory of her, when I hear behind me "You look so beautiful Lilly." I turned to see Healer Vincent, smiling so proudly. "I hope you will give me the honor of allowing me to give you away. I know I am not your father, but I feel that he would want this for you." I am not sure of what my father would have wanted, his soul was truly twisted towards the end. All I want is Calvin, nothing else matters at this moment as I place my hand in his as he takes me to my future husband.

It is a small ceremony with only the five of us. Healer Vincent walks me to Calvin who is wearing a simple shirt and trousers. He looks uncomfortable, adjusting the shirt frequently, but winks at me. Mayor Crowley stands in the middle while Old Man Nesbit strings a sweet melody on a viola, which was one of my father's instruments. He would lovingly play it for my mother and I at nights after our family meals. This day is full of fond and beautiful memories of my parents. Healer Vincent places my hand in Calvin's hand. I hear Mayor Crowley start to speak but his words are drowned out by another voice. "Does this make you happy?" I hear Jaran speaking to me in my head. I continue to smile and nod in a secret reply. "I know how much you were looking forward to this moment. You dreamt of it, and I wanted to make it a reality for you, for us." More tears flow down my face, as Mayor Crowley says "You may now kiss the bride."

Mayor Crowley, Healer Vincent, and Old Man Nesbit take their leave, and head back into town. I felt a sweet sorrow to see them leave, it was almost as if we were a family. Calvin grabs me into his arms. "Was it what you expected, my flower?" I giggle and kiss his lips knowing that I will answer him soon enough. He gently places me on the bed and slowly undresses me. He senses that I want to see every part of his body, which is even more beautiful in his human form. Standing in all his glory. I crawled to him, placing his massive, swollen cock in my mouth, using my tongue to lick his shaft from the base to the tip. I worship his body, as I know he will do the same to me. He slowly caresses my face, I hear him moaning as I take it all in feeling it go well beyond the back of my throat. Breathing through my nose, his breathing increasing with each moment of my head. I know what is coming when his sweet juices spray into my mouth. I swallow every drop and glance up at his green eyes which are now replaced with the lustful, all encompassing black. I know this moment, I growl at him as desire fills the room.

He shifts into his true form, his crimson skin appears brighter as he pounces upon me, and his tail wraps around my neck. I feel the wetness building underneath me like an ocean wave, as his claws reach for me, digging into my skin. I moan in pleasure as he bears his fangs, smirking at me. He loves this as much as I do. I grab him on the bed as he easily allows me to take control. He could easily over power me and we both know it, I straddle him as he removes my dress with his tail, all while he looks at me so lovingly. I motion my hips grinding his pulsating serpent deep within my center, groaning I lick one horn while stroking the other. Jaran suckles at my firm nippled breasts, as we both arrive at our trembling, explosive, orgasmic climax together, and I collapse on his chest.

I hear him growling as I peer up at him, as he hungrily stares at me. The lust in his eyes still felt in the air. He lifts me, and I realize we are on the ceiling. He chuckles seductively, and I know I should be scared, but this side of him makes my body crave for him more.

Suddenly, I feel his fangs sink into my shoulder, and I feel the need to scream. However, my body is flushed with an intense sensation that drives me to hold onto him tighter. I rake my nails into his back as he throws his head back and roars in pleasure. I close my eyes as we land back on the bed, he then turns me around on my knees. I am frozen as I remember my father focusing me in the same position so many times, I suddenly start to shake with fear. "Trust me." I turn around and see Jaran's face. I lean back to kiss him while he guides me from behind. I've never felt him so deep inside of me. I feel a pressure swelling inside of my womb! He is dominating my body, yet I swear, each moment is euphoric! He grinds into me faster and faster as I scream to every God in the pantheon. Each wave sends me higher as I scream for more. I'm not sure how long it lasts, but when he erupts deep within me and removes himself, I release water from myself, as though Jaran had busted open the floodgates of my body! Then, he surprised me further, and lowered his head, lapping up my release. As we pass out on the bed, Jaran shifts back into his human form, tracing his fingers on the mark he has left on my body. Before sleep captures me I hear him say "Now you are truly mine" as I smile in his arms. I belong to him truly, body and soul.

The next day, I awake with the feeling of giddiness, after returning Mayor Crowley and Healer Vincent back to their homes. I haven't felt this way since before the passing of my lovely Marianne as I succumbed to slumber. Amidst all the joy and happiness at the wedding, there was one unnoticed. Far behind the other guests lurked a lone sneering figure, with a forced smile that partially looked painful. Arthur Nesbit thought to himself "What a truly beautiful ceremony, why it almost reminds me of what my late wife and I shared. This is a marriage that should last forever, or at the very least til death do they part. Truly a shame about her father though, such a waste of a perfectly good burial spot. Perhaps I'll do them a favor and rob his grave and cremate his body. So that when they pass they can be buried next to each other. Of course, I'll be relieving him of the golden family heirloom ring he is wearing. After all, labor must be paid for." When I finally awake, I stretch out of my bed and smack my lips. Damn the sun, always blinding me. I stumble to close the window shutters, as my stomach growls. Some nice steamed gruel sounds good for breakfast. I have to make sure my humours do not cause me to have an irritable bowel movement. Later today, I think I shall go to the launderers where I frequently use the service without paying. Why should I pay? Blasted fools need to know how important of a person I am.

My thoughts lead me to what I should do before visiting Healer Vincent. Damn fool will have me running errands all over town with him. Hurt my fucking back, which he says he treated long ago. Why does it still hurt then? Huh? Fucking charlattan. I lay back on the bed after breakfast, my stomach full and I start to pleasure myself. Closing my eyes I think of my sweet Lilly, and how I wish I could have been between her legs. I sneer, thinking yes, yes she would have been screaming my name if it was not for that fucking asshole Calvin Smith. I open my eyes and sit up in the bed rubbing my face, "Calvin Smith" I mumble to myself. Last night felt unnatural. I actually shook that fucker's hand, and joked with him. I hate him for taking my Lilly away from me. There is a knock on my door, and it gets louder with each step I take towards it. "Hold the fuck on!" I yell at the person on the other side of the door. "It is too early for this shit!!" As I open the door, two large men enter my home. "We are inspecting all the houses for the demon that is still at large." the taller one says.

I notice the cloak with a flaming sword insignia. Fuck, these are Hunters! Fuck! I step aside, and realize they are dragging a hooded woman by a chain around her neck. She looks very young, as my eyes are directly focused on her supple bosom. What a tasty thing she is, making my mouth water. one of the Hunters takes notice of me staring at the woman. "Hey old man, haven't you ever seen a witch before?" They both chuckle as I shake my head. "This is a witch?" I ask them. "What do you need a witch for?" glancing at her as her eyes turn white. "It makes it easier to track this demon's energy." The witch looks at me saying words I cannot comprehend. The Hunters stand back, and draw their swords. "You are coming with us, old man." The portly one says. "What??!! What??! What do you mean I'm not a demon!!" I yell and stammer. They drag me out of my home and into a black carriage, all I can think, is awww fuck..

I woke up to a sensation of flying and a painful sensation in my stomach area. When my eyes open I realize that I am soaring across our bedroom! I hit the wall with a sudden thud and before I can hit the floor, my husband is beside me. "Don't move my love." he places his hand over my stomach, and like magic, the sensation has stopped. I look up at him with a feeling of deep concern.

"The baby is resting now..." Jaran says plainly, as he helps me up to my feet. We walk into the other room where he helps me sit at the table placing a warm cup of tea in my hands. "I am with a child?" I ask, as I take a sip of my tea. I am trying to remain calm. I wouldn't want the baby to wake up and toss me around again. Calvin smiles at me warmly. "Yes my love, you are carrying our child." and kisses me as I feel a stir within me. I pull away cautiously. "There is alot I have to tell you about my kind, myself, and our baby now." he says. With that, I remain seated and think to myself it's going to be a long day.

CHAPTER 3

Knowing that I am a demon is not the same as truly knowing what I am. The type of demon that I am is called an incubus. The counterpart, or female of my race is called a succubus. We are an old, primordial race of creatures. It was said that my kind was born from the darkest corners of existence. Whether or not that is true, my first memory is of holding my twin brother's hand. To understand my kind, it starts with the mating between an incubus and succubus. If the incubus has a strong scent gland he can attract his true mate, a mate he will spend his entire life bonded to until death. This was how it came to be with my father and mother, him being a strong Alpha or leader among our kind, could have had any mate of his choosing. His skin was the color of blood with black hair and black eyes. All incubi have the same characteristics of having a tail, horns, and wings, but may have a different skin color altogether. My father was called Rharrel, and he was far greater than any other incubus. He gained much respect, notoriety, and loyalty from the brood of our kind. My mother, on the other hand, was of midnight complexion, with blonde hair and blue eyes. Her name was Oriness, and I despised her before I could open my eyes.

After mating, a succubus will lay five eggs in a nest where she will guard them against other predators, even those in the brood. The incubus will store enough life essence for himself and his mate who feed any excess energy to their offspring. Oriness only laid four eggs with my father. To their surprise, during the hatching, my brother and I were born from one egg. It was the first time I sensed pride from my father, something I always carried with me ever since that day. My brother was of onyx complexion, like my mother and I, garnet of an apple. Like my father, we both shared the same black hair and green eyes. He gave me the name Jaran, and my brother Dynlyx, as he held us high in his arms he smiled at Oriness, hoping she would share in his joy.

"They are bad omens." she said, and turned away from him, and tended to the other offspring.

Legend has it that twin brothers of an incubus will bring the end of days to their kind. It was like a fairy tale that succubi mothers told their offspring before rest, maybe to scare them into behaving or to keep the story alive. My father however, did not believe in such things. He placed us in the nest. I reached for him as Dynlyx was still resting. He tasselled my small patch of hair, and smiled. He arose and bellowed at his mate; it was a command that she could not ignore. Gradually, she slowly gathered toward him, head bowed. He wrapped his tail around the base of her tail sharply yanking it. Oriness shrilly falls into submission, panting at him willing to do anything for her mate.

ASuccubus' true purpose in life is to mate, and bear offspring. survival was only important if you had that will to do so. Once a succubus has found her mate and he accepts her, her only drive is to serve him at all costs. Oriness was possessive of her mate Rnarrel, battling other non- mated females that advanced towards him without her permission, but her jealousy was most aggressive towards her very offspring, especially my brother and I. She would snarl at my siblings and I if we even looked in my father's direction. My brother and I often cowered in fear of her wrath., I frequently would need to step in front of her defying her with a growl of my own. Oriness raised her clawed hand to strike me. "Enough!" my father roared, as she froze in place, lowering her hand and narrowed her eyes at me. "Prepare the offspring for our leave to Destiny Peak" he commanded. As he departed, he gave me a glance with a wry smile on his face. I sensed sadness in that moment in my father's heart.

My siblings and I proceeded towards a cliff. There were other succubi mothers with their offspring there as well. Above us, incubi circled us, howling at their mates below. I easily located my father among them. I held Dynlyx's hand reassuring him as he gave me a hesitant look. Oriness clutched one of my siblings walking towards the edge of the cliff, in a swift motion she hurdled the offspring over the cliff. I heard the wails from my sibling as she fell to her death. A heartless smile spread across her face, as she continued the same method with my other remaining siblings, I closed my eyes, hearing their final cries as my heart raced in my ears. Dynlyx squeezed my hand tighter as we were the last of the offspring. She collected us in her arms and said; "Your deaths would give me so much pleasure, I can have more offspring with my strong mate." she whispered closely in my ears. Dynlyx whimpered, holding onto me as I wrapped my arms around him. I peered into her eyes as they flashed black with bloodlust. She hissed, and hurled us over the cliff. I heard my brother's plaintive wailing, as my instinct kicked in and my wings spread open to take flight. Dynlyx observed this action, and before we were about to reach the bottom, his wings opened up as well. We glided towards our father who was thunderingly howling with joy. Below, I saw Oriness sneering at me before returning back to the nest. That day, I met my first enemy and she bore the face of my mother. I swore on that day I would get stronger for myself and my brother.

My father taught my brother and I to hunt prey. We learned to feed off of creatures' life essence either to the brink of death, or we can leave the prey half alive. This way, we could continue to feed on it during an extended period of time, depending on the size of the prey. I became very skilled in tracking and hunting my prey, improving on my skills more with each attempt. Dynlyx was much slower and feebled by comparison. My father noticed this, but placed his hand on his head lovingly. My father was just pleased to spend time with his surviving offspring. Between hunting and flying, he would chase us through the forest easily pursuing us. How I cherished those moments with him and my twin. I dreaded the thought of heading back to the nest to Oriness. She would always greet my father giddlefully wrapping her arms around his neck and feeding from him happily. I sometimes longed for her to be as loving to us as she was to him. She glared at us instead as I always realized that would never be. Dynlyx and I slept near each other and to keep him safe from her, but I knew it gave me comfort too. "Jaran" he'd say in my mind. This was a skill our father recently taught us. "Why does mother hate us so?"

My brother longed for her love as well, so my response was not an easy one, but I knew he would understand and accept it. "It is her way. Remember what father taught us about our kind evolving and devolving." he curled closer to me to make sure he heard every word I spoke in his mind. I smiled and continued. "To evolve means to understand and advance beyond our kind's basic instincts and natural limitations. This gives us the strength to become powerful Alphas, and to attract a suitable mate." My thoughts trail off and Dynlyx nudges me. I smile at him and ponder the thought of a mate, which was not appealing to me. "Jaran, what is it?" his eyes searched for an answer. "It is nothing Dynlyx" I remarked as I continued. "Devolving is the opposite, we become like our ancestors having only the basic nature of mating and killing. There is no coming back from that once we are branded evil demons and become hunted because we no longer are concerned with being cautious. Hunters will end our lives if we are too careless." I explained. He shudders at the thought of Hunters. Father said we should not fear them, although our kind must always be wary of their presence. I placed my hand over his shoulder. "Then there is that fine line, where our kind does not evolve or devolve, and there is not even a word for it."

I stared at Dynlyx, who had a solemn look on his face. "Jaran, I think I am like the word that not does not exist. I can not evolve or devolve, but I walk the 'fine line'." he said, as he smiled weakly. I shook my head as he held his thoughts. "I am not as good as a hunter. I am slower even in flight. I will never find a mate to love me." he breathed heavily. "I should not be alive." he said. I sat up and grabbed him in my arms. His body was smaller than mine as I pressed my forehead to his. "I exist because you exist. Without you, there is no me. You are my other half, so we can exist together as one, my brother. I will always be there for you." I noticed he had fallen asleep, possibly exhausted from our conversation. I glanced over to see Oriness mating with my father. I thought how I detested her as she scorned us for just breathing. I succumbed to rest knowing it would be a bleak one.

"Jaran, where are you?" Dynlyx called out to me through our mindlink. I was stalking our prey as he approached. "Get down, or it will catch your scent." I said as I grabbed him, pulling him to the ground near me. He looked wide eyed to see a large oxen five times the size of him. I smirked as we were much older, which meant we needed bigger prey to feed from. "I'm not sure if we can take it down, Jaran."

he said doubtfully. I sighed, as we had hunted and practiced together on how to tackle down prey. I needed him to be more confident in the hunt and against other predators, especially our mother. Oriness sneakily taunted Dynlyx reminding him that he was 'an inferior incubus', 'frightened weakling', and that he 'would never be an Alpha'. These words resonated in his very being from wake to rest. At times, he would leave the nest without me. I would frantly search for him, only to return, finding him back safe at our nest. He did not look at me as I confronted him. "Dynlyx, you will come with me to the forest in the morning." It was more of a command than a question. He nodded, going to rest for the night. My father gave me a small smile, as Oriness stared at me in shock.

"Dynlyx, we will do as we have practiced with every other prey before." I said, as I continued to stare at the prey that resumed grazing. "It is not like the other prey, Jaran." as Dynlyx continued his reluctance, my anger built up as my eyes flashed with bloodlust. He trembled at this sight. Normally, I never lose my temper with him, so this was a rare moment. I realized that I may have taken it a bit too far, and I noticed the fear in his eyes. Calming myself down, I apologized to my brother who kept his head bowed. I reminded myself to be patient with him, as I was the eldest of the two. "Yes, you are right, he is not like the other prey, but just like before, we will take him down by working together!" I said, doing my best to encourage my brother. He looked up at me with a hopeful smile.

I began to roundabout towards the back of the oxen to take my prey by surprise. I pounced on it quickly, using my claws to dig into its legs to stop it from running. I hated to attempt it, but my brother was correct. This prey was much stronger than I thought. All that meant was that its life essence would be more than enough to satisfy our hunger. I heard Dynlyx screeching above me, as I held down the oxen that resumed to struggle against me. Suddenly, Dynlyx landed on the oxen's neck. With his tail he drilled into its neck. It buckled and he dug his claws into its hide so as not to be thrown off. I felt the beast breathing slowly. Dynlyx triumphantly roared as we began to feed. "Did you see how I was able to take it down?" Dynlyx was on a high from the kill leaping around me. I was proud of my brother. "Yes, but next time do not take so long to strike." I warned. He frowned at me. "Well I thought you could have handled it and like you always say." Dynlyx erupted in childish frustration. "Be precise with your blow." I nodded in agreement, laughing as he joined me in laughter, echoing through the skies above the trees.

We were heading back to the nest, when a scent caught my attention. I smelled honey and pine in the air. I raised my hand to halt my brother. He seemed puzzled, and in the far distance, he saw the same sight as I. "Wait here." I warned my brother, trying not to sound demanding. He nodded as he understood what was about to happen. I cautiously approached, finding myself face to face with a succubus who bowed her head to me. She shrieked "MATE!" and lowered her head to me again. She was golden complexioned with hair like the color of the sky. Her eyes were the same as her skin. I noticed her eyes when she glanced up at me, waiting for my reaction. I had always dreaded this moment. I did not expect it to happen this soon. She presented herself to me standing with her wings outstretched, awaiting my embrace. She shrieks again. "Mate, I am Lilnara and I am yours." she introduced herself, stepping closer to me. My heart raced as I was consumed by her scent in my nostrils. My member responded to her aura. The closer she came, the more my bloodlust rose. I closed my eyes. "NO! NO Mate!" I bellowed in protest at her as she cowered back, lowering her head again. I knew what I had just done as I felt it in my chest. I had just rejected my mate. Lilnara hollered in pain, hissing at me as tears streamed down her beautiful face. She raced away, leaping to take flight, still hollering in the distance. I am not sure how long I stood there watching or waiting for her to return. Her scent no longer lingered in the air, as I felt Dynlyx's hand on my back.

"Why Jaran? She was your mate..." I faced him as he was pleading with me for an answer. I placed my hand on his head and I revealed to him my reasons for my horrible actions.

One day, I was searching for my father on my own, while my brother was ill, resting at the nest. I would not normally have left him behind with Oriness, but for the first time, she showed concern for his well being. Maybe she had hoped to see his death with her own eyes. If he had died by her hand, I wanted my father to know the danger, and severely punish Oriness for her actions. I had no choice, but to leave him and search for my father. I soon found him in the woods overlooking Destiny Peak, where the next generation of succubi were killing their offspring. This vile act was a twisted tradition performed by so many of our ancestors before them, while their mates circled above witnessing it all. My father watched on, and on his face were tears. He had never allowed us to see him cry before and I wondered why he wept. "Father?" he sharply turned to me, surprised.

"Jaran, what are you doing here?" he asked. I expected him to be upset with me, but instead, he laughed heartily. "If you tracked me all the way here from the nest, you will be a wonderful Alpha one day! I am so proud of you, my son." he said, with a warm smile. My emotions were a mix of joy and fear, as I explained what was happening to Dynlyx. Him being ill, as well as my mistrust of his mate. After he considered this, he touched my face. "Do not worry, my son." A feeling spread through my body, this is what you know as compelling. He had only told my brother and I of this power. It was so strong that I did not have the will to break it. "Your mother has given me an oath on her life to never harm you or your brother, especially after you both survived the Culling at Destiny Peak." father explained. In his eyes, I believed him, as I felt the compelling ease from my body. He pulled me close as we watched the tragic events that occurred at Destiny Peak. I finally mustered the courage to ask him "Father, why were you crying?" He looked down at me and explained, with sad words. "Jaran, what we are witnessing is what all succubi; our destined mates, have done since the beginning of time. I cry, my son, because it will never end. The mate whom you will someday love with all that you are will kill your offspring, and in a way, kill you."

This revelation shocked me to my core. I never wanted a mate if this would be the cost. I was determined that it would end with me. Many of my kind had to mourn the loss of their siblings, as my brother and I did, as my father did before me. On that day that was the oath I made in his name, as I continued to watch with my father, and we cried together. When I finished my tale, I removed my hand from Dynlyx's face, and noticed the tears in his eyes. "Why did you never tell me this before?" he asked, his voice choked with betrayal.

"I couldn't have you bear the burden alongside me, brother." I said, sighing in response to him. "Father is a proud Alpha, and it appears I am as well." Dynlyx embraced me. "You chose to reject her, knowing the pain could have killed her and you both. You truly will make a strong alpha." he said as he bowed to me. "I accept you as not only my brother and companion, but as my Alpha. I will follow you to Hell and back." I was thankful for his words, as we flew back to our nest with a stronger bond as brothers.

"We will be heading to the winter nesting grounds." my father blared at the Brood. All the incubi and succubi clamor in response, as they looked forward to new prey to hunt. The prey in the winter nesting grounds was said to be always plentiful. It was where a new kind of prey could be found for my brother and I, called humans. One night, my father spoke to us about them. "They carry so much delicious life essence, especially in their lovely females..." he laughed. Oriness snorted to his comment. "They are more trouble than they're worth, and they bear Hunters." she retorted with a raspy hiss. My father gave her an ignoring look, to which she whimpered and shied away. We were younglings when he told us about humans, and this would be the first experience for Dynlyx and I to learn first hand. "Are you looking forward to seeing a human for the first time, Jaran?" My brother glided next to me twirling in the air, mid flight, with excitement. Seeing him so hopeful made me feel hopeful to experience this new kind of prey.

A succubus and incubus broke past us, slightly startling us. It was Lilnara, and what appeared to be her new mate as they glided, holding hands and tails intertwined. She turned to hiss at me. I was unaffected, as our bond was severed. Instead, I unleashed a growl that sent her and her mate further away from us. I could have easily crushed them both. Seeing me clearly upset, Dynlyx attempted to distract me and resumed his topic on humans. "I hope the females ARE tastier than the males. Male life essence on animals tastes like deer shit." he said. I laughed fiercely being thankful that I had him nearby.

When we finally reached the winter nesting grounds my father commanded us all to rest before hunting. A pale complexioned incubus with scarlet hair and black eyes boasted. "It has been a long trip, we need food now!"

I had never seen my father attack anything else other than prey, but with one swoop of his hand he grabbed the insolent incubus by the throat. He dangled him off the ground, shrieking could be heard all around us. "Quiet, I said!" father roared, as everyone trembled at his voice. "This was not a request young one..." his eyes filled with blood lust. "I'd rather not waste my energy spilling your blood and making your female mateless. Do as you are told, and know your place or there will not BE a next time." The incubus whimpered in his hand, understanding my father's true presence. Satisfied, father set him down, and the incubus crawled away in defeat. Oriness seductively walked over to my father and began to purr in his arms. They would mate before hunting. Because my brother and I were unmated, we no longer needed to nest with our parents. I was thankful for this as my brother and I could now speak freely without having to mindlink. "How many humans should we feed on?" my brother asked, sounding excited at the thought. "We should rest first and then talk about hunting later." I said. Dynlyx pouted with his arms crossed over his chest. "Well, will we at least take down them as we always do?" I yawned in reply, to which he huffed and I snickered. "Yes." I relented, as I let slumber wash over me, also secretly looking forward to our new prey, humans.

Dynlyx and I left the nesting before the Brood arose, taking flight towards the scent that was unfamiliar to us. It must have been humans I thought, as we positioned ourselves in some nearby bushes. A female left a dwelling. She was obviously a female as she had a similar body to a succubus, only without the wings, tail, and horns. She smelled delicious as I breathed in her scent. My brother swatted me with his tail. In our mindlink he said "It's a human and it is a female. Do we strike now?" he asked. The female gathered something from the earth, and raised it to her face. I admired her smile, until again Dynlyx gave me another swat of his tail. I growled in response. Finally, I said "We corner the female, you come from behind and I will be in the front." "Right" he affirmed sternly. "Then I will strike her in the neck." I sighed. "We may not have to, as she is our first female and we should savor the taste." I explained to him. He gave me a determined expression. "I will follow your lead brother." He moved to advance towards her from the rear. He never mastered the art of timing, but he compensated in enthusiasm. Without waiting for my signal, he growled, baring his fangs at the human. The hapless female screamed, and ran straight into my arms.

The female was frozen with fear. "She was faster than I thought!" Dynlyx exclaimed as he smelled the female's hair. "I didn't think it would be THIS easy to catch a human, Jaran. What should we do with her?" he asked. I compelled the female not to scream and placed her in a hypnotic state. Groggily, she fell into my arms.

"We will take her to the forest to feed on her essence away from other humans." I was thinking about Hunters. I did not want to say anything to Dynlyx about this so as not to cause him panic. We flew to an isolated spot. I placed the female near a grassy patch. "Should you wake her?" Dynlyx asked. I decided I would, as my eyes flashed with blood lust. His eyes flashed the shade of midnight with blood lust as well. The female awakened as we were about to pounce on her, the scent of her fear was so enticing. I touched her skin, which was soft. Her breasts were heaving as I felt aroused. Dynlyx's tail struck her in the neck which broke me from my trance. The female fell into my arms yet again.

"I'm sorry Jaran I... I...I just thought it was the right time. You said not to take so long. Please don't be upset." Dynlyx said, the blood lust lingered in his eyes. The female was still barely alive, and I smiled at him. "It was the right time." I said, as we began to feed on the female until her heart stopped. We left her in the field, it seemed as if she was smiling as we flew back to the nest. My brother and I successfully hunted humans. Dynlyx obviously enjoyed it much more than I. We were heading back to the nest, this was the last day as it was time to return back to the summer nesting grounds. I'd had my fill of humans, they were not a challenge for me. Humans were weak and beneath me. Dynlyx sensed my distaste. "Jaran you do not seem satisfied." I appreciated his concern. "I am ready to leave this place, is all." I stated as I smelled a familiar scent. In the distance, I saw Oriness who appeared to be wounded as we stalked towards her.

"Mother! Mother!" Dynlyx called out to her. Oriness had deep cuts in her body from her stomach down to her legs. She breathed heavily and with wide eyes she shrieked

"H-Hunters!" My brother and I both growled with shallow breaths as she told us the Hunters had discovered the nesting grounds while she and my father had hunted together. They were ambushed by Hunters and she became injured because of the attack. As the Alpha, my father left to protect the Brood as he had felt them screaming for him. My brother yelled in anger. I saw the bloodlust in his eyes. Suddenly he flew to the nest before I could stop him. Oriness grabbed me and compelled me to stay by her side. Even though she was wounded, her compelling was stronger than I expected. I could not free myself, and I turned to face the nesting, the Hunters, and the Brood are fighting. All I could see was swords, and claws clashing.

There was so much smoke that I could only see shadows of wings that sliced through the air. The Hunters had set fire to our nesting grounds! I felt the cries of the newborn offspring. I still couldn't move. "Let me go!" I screamed at Oriness "I can't. I need you to heal me with your life essence." I was disgusted as even then she thought only of herself. I turned my attention back to the nest. I saw my brother in attack mode, surrounded by Hunters. "Set me free! I have to save Dynlyx!" she laughed wickly. "He is and always will be weak. His death is inevitable, you are the future of or kind." I was enraged as I heard my father, who risked all to protect my brother. They were soon surrounded by more Hunters. I knelt next to Oriness opening her mouth and reluctantly started to feed her. Her wounds instantly began to heal from my life essence. I felt a sharp pain in my chest. Oriness screamed in pain as well, something had happened. We both flew to our demolished nesting ground and the scene was desolated with so many bodies of incubi, succbi, and Hunters. They all laid sprawled everywhere dead, the stench of blood overwhelmed all of my senses.

My thoughts were focused on finding my father and brother. When I headed for where my father was, I soon found him, dead. Oriness wailed for her lost mate. It became deafening in my mind. When she ceased, I realized more Hunters came near us. As quickly as she was by my side, she tore through them easily, shrieking in blood. I moved my father's slumped body to reveal my beloved brother beneath him. Even after everything, knowing that he was not strong enough, my father gave his life. The Alpha in me mourned my father as the brother in me grieved for my twin. I was overcome with sorrow, which was quickly replaced with rage. "Alpha!" Oriness cried. My bloodlust radiated through my body. She lowered her head as blood smeared on her face.

"This is no time to grieve, for death awaits our enemies. Our Brood demands revenge!" she shouted as I laid my brother next to my father. Roaring, I summoned all the remaining Brood that had survived, as we spilled the blood of the Hunters that had desecrated our nesting grounds.

We left the remaining bodies of the incubi and succubi for the predators to devour to become suitable prey in time. As we returned to the summer nest grounds, the Brood bowed to me in unison declaring me their Alpha. It is a role that I was groomed for, and one I never truly wanted. I attempted to avoid Oriness as much as I could, however it was my duty to take care of her, a decision that was also not mine. One of my new roles consisted of me deciding where our new hunting grounds would be. I chose for the summer nest to be our only hunting ground. It was not safe to migrate anywhere else as the Brood were few in numbers following the attack. My days were filled with rage, killing more than feeding, while the emptiness consumed me. Oriness approached me submissively each night. Wearied, I was obligated to feed her. Since our arrival, she has remained weak from the battle. Afterwards, sleep was no comfort. I realized I was lost without my father and brother. I lashed out at anyone who dared challenge my authority. Until one day, I thought to myself; Was I devolving? The thought thumped in my head as I bawled with discontent, breathing heavily. I noticed Oriness was fixated on me as with a bowed head she crawled towards me.

"My Alpha, please let me comfort you." she said as she nudged my arm. My eyes flashed with blood lust as my hand swiped across her face and sent her flying across the room. "Just like you comforted my brother and I?" I growled. I grabbed her face and dug my claws into her skin as the blood dripped from her nose. Oriness had a wicked smirk on her face. "Unlike your weak brother Dynlyx, your potential is endless." I grabbed her throat and growled. "Don't you EVER speak his name in your foul mouth!" Her body dangled in my hand. I could have crushed her, and I would have had the right to do so. Instead of struggling against me, Oriness wrapped her arms around my neck and her hips and full thighs around my waist. She slid her body onto my hardened member as I groaned and grinded my teeth. My hand remained on her throat as she appeared to be enjoying the pressure. She continued to straddle me shrieking with each climax. I grunted as I released my seed into her howling in intense pleasure involuntarily.

Oriness sank her fangs into my neck. "Hmmm..." I heard myself saying. Why was I enjoying this with her?? I felt myself grab her by her wings, as I pulled her off of me, and placed her on her knees. I shoved my member in her mouth, which she happily accepted as I grabbed her head, filling her mouth with my seed. She licked her lips as she turned over and lifted her tail presenting her female entrance. "Claim me, my Alpha." With unknown instinct, I thrusted my member deep within her, as I yanked at her tail. What was happening to me?

"Jaran my son!" my father called out to me as I had finished catching a prey. "Dynlyx is in the river cleaning himself off and attempting to catch a fish!" We sat and watched as one hit him across the face and he leapt to capture it, hissing at his failure. "You and your brother are precious to me." he said as we sat at the riverbank. "That is why I must tell you about something that occurs with every Alpha in a very dark moment of our kind. I tell you this because you are destined to be an Alpha." I was saddened as I looked over at my brother, who I knew could never bear the burden.

"The moment is called the Airsing; It is when you lose all control of your being. It will bring you to the darkest depths of our kinds basic instincts. If you do not have the will to come back from the abyss you will kill anyone around you and yourself." I was stunned that such a thing could possibly happen. Sensing my anxiety he placed me in his arms playfully. "However, you have nothing to worry my son" as I laughed in his arms. "Your will is strong enough to find the light."

As I pulled out of her body I forcefully grasped her. I whispered in her ear "I'm not done with you yet." She was panting as I rubbed the entrance of her rear end. I smelled her heat as my finger pushed through her opening. I shoved her down to the ground as she gasped for more. My thick member slammed into her. I clawed at her hips as I sank my fangs into her back. Oriness cried in pleasure, I went as deep as my body would allow me. I was lost in the darkness with each breath that I took.

The light, I remember as I climaxed again, leaving Oriness purring in front of me. The bloodlust left my body as I stood, she smiled at me lapping at my feet. I backed away as she gave a puzzled look. "My Mate?" she asked. I glared with a disgusted look on my face. "I am neither your mate, nor your son, you vile female." The hatred and resentment emanated in waves from my aura as I turned around to walk away from her. I left the nest as the sun rose, taking flight. In the distance, I heard the Brood bawling for me to return. I ignored their pleas, I may not have known my place in this world, but it was not as their Alpha. I was filled with hope that someday I would find where I belonged.

Some time had passed, and I was feeding from a male boar, when I caught the scent of four Hunters who suddenly surrounded me. I was slashed across the stomach and chest. "WE FINALLY FOUND YOU, DEMON! THIS IS FOR OUR BROTHERS YOU SLAYED!" one Hunter shouted as he attempted to strike me again. I was able to catch his arm before the swipe of the swords sliced into me again. I ripped his arm off as he screamed in pain. "FUCKING BASTARD, MY ARM!" He fell to the ground as I was able to rip into another Hunter's chest and took out his heart in my hand. I was badly wounded and I attempted to flee. "FOLLOW HIM! HE MUST NOT ESCAPE!" I heard them as I dashed through the forest on all fours. My wings had been slashed by the sword and I couldn't take the chance of flying not until I could get further away. When I knew there was enough distance between the Hunters and I, I leaped into flight. My vision became blurry, there had been too much blood loss. I crashed into what appeared to be a field. I was not sure if I would die here. Before I passed out, I smelled the sweet scent of vanilla and wildflowers.

CHAPTER 4

Upon completion of my tale to my mate Lilly, I have become unsure of her reaction. I have prepared her meal, which consists of raw meat, which she has started to crave. She does not look up from her plate, as she rips and tears through her meat with a savagery that even I could not emulate. Our child has begun to feed from her life essence, which is a natural part of the reproductive cycle for my species. I left early one morning, to travel into town to purchase fresh meat and supplies. It was my first time entering the town as Calvin Smith, Lilly's husband. The humans in the town were kind to me, but if they knew I was an incubus, I know that I would surely be shunned and attacked. I still had to be mindful of the presence of Hunters. On this day however, I did not sense any danger in the town. I had to keep my guard up, as threats could be lurking anywhere at any moment. I am relieved that there are no Hunters, especially due to Lilly's condition. During my time in town, I saw Healer Vincent. He politely waved at me, approached and clasped my hand.

"Calvin Smith! It is so good to finally see you in town." he said with a smile, looking around. "Where is Lilly?" He asks with a concerned look on his face. "She is a little under the weather today." I respond, hoping not to see his unpleasant assistant.

"Well, I will just have to pay you two a visit..." the Healer pondered, giving me a pat on my back. "Healer Vincent, I noticed that Old Man Nesbit is not with you today?" he frowns at the mention of that archaic nuisance. "Well no, he isn't. For some blasted reason he was taken to the Hunter's Camp. The fool went and got himself into some kind of trouble, I assume." he said, scratching his head. "Fear not, I'm sure it is some misunderstanding. The man couldn't hurt a fly. They will get tired of his smell sooner than later, and bring him back post haste, I guarantee." We shared a laugh and I bid him farewell. I think to myself that Healer Vincent is a decent fellow, as I return back home.

"I want some more!" Lilly orders me. I smile, realizing that she is finally responding to me between bites of her food. She looks even more beautiful with trails of blood in the corners of her mouth. "My Love you must slow down, you don't want to make yourself sick" I urged as I wiped away the blood from my statuesque flower. She growls and my bloodlust flares. The meat gives her the extra nutrients to help her while she carries our child. I place a rack of lamb in front of her, Lilly gnaws, gnashes, and tears into the flesh of the lamb. Once she is satisfied, I explain to her our situation. "I am glad we have satisfied your hunger, but we must be cautious." She looks up at me and asks "Why? Why do we need to be cautious?" I sit across from her and begin to tell her the origin of the Hunters.

"I'm sure you have learned from our interactions that everything is not as it appears. Hunters appear to be human, but they have undergone a great change to aid them in their mission." Lilly hangs onto every word I speak. "I only know the legends that have been passed among my kind in hushed whispers. It is said that Hunters date back to the beginning of human civilization as you know it. The world was far more primitive and creatures not so different from my own race wandered the earth freely, and in far greater numbers. That said, even in those days, humanity feared us. Man has always been fascinated by what you call dark magic, and upon their discovery of that which bumps in the night, mankind has tirelessly sought to find ways to defend themselves. "It was the first Grand Magister, Ivan Duke III, who created the method of repurposing a demon's blood by consuming it. With this method, a human would obtain above human strength, stamina, and fortitude. Between that, and a special form of training, they ever so slightly tipped the scales in their favor." as I continued, the look on Lilly's face was one of astonishment.

"For you see, we are not the only threat to humans, but we largely prefer to be left alone. However, creatures such as witches, werewolves, and vampires, who are far more aggressive and do not share our seclusionistic ways also exist. So it was said that these humans were the first Hunters, yet there was a problem. While they did have enhanced physical attributes, their weapons could not bring down any of our kind. So once again, the Grand Magister, Ivan Duke III, came up with a solution. He began consecrating the wood where the Hunters made camp. Thereby blessing the wood and metals that were used to craft their weapons. This proved deadlier than anticipated.

Surely were it not for one simple fact, our kind would have been routed completely. There was one bit of misfortunate left in the form of the process of consuming a demon's cursed blood. These men, as penance for their prowess, were cursed with barren loins, never to sire an heir. The end of a lineage, the ultimate sacrifice for the power to combat what you know as 'the supernatural'. While there were female Hunters, they could only mate with non-Hunter males, and then could no longer hunt themselves. So if we struck the Hunters in a greater number, we could slowly wear them down, but the humans became tricky. Besides the blessed weapons, they created other tools. The enslaver collar, for example. It is common knowledge that witches live freely today among their covens, however many of our kind use our natural gifts to disguise ourselves as I do now. It is for this reason that they devised the enslaving collars. The idea was that they could use the witch's magic against their will to locate and destroy our kind. Far more than an imprisonment tool, this enslaving collar is charmed so that anyone who wears it must do the bidding of the one holding the connected chain. I can scarcely imagine a worse fate than to be robbed of your very freedom. For all their power, the witches have nothing that can resist these powerful charms. If Hunters have truly been focused on the town, 'tis but a matter of time before they bring their own enslaved witches to track us; and yes I do mean us." I clarify as I place my hand on her belly.

Lilly curls next to me in bed, with her arms wrapped around my neck. My hands are on her belly, the baby moves at my touch. Even stretched as it is from the rapid expansion of my progeny, Lilly's skin is soft and lovely. I never thought I would have an offspring of my own. The baby senses my pride giving a small kick. Lilly groans and buckles as I compel our child to calm itself and rest. There is much I must tell Lilly to prepare her for what is about to come.

Healer Vincent arrived to visit Lilly and was he not astounded at the sight of her in a state of expectancy. "Blessed be to God, you are with child!!" he exclaims as he gives Lilly a loving embrace, not unlike a father. "Well, I can tell you didn't wait terribly long after marriage to consummate!" he jokingly slaps my back and I return a hearty laugh. Lilly blushes at this comment. "So now, let me examine my patient, ot should I say patients" he says with a big smile that causes his eyes to squint shut. He sits Lilly on the couch and begins to look through a leather bag for his tools. I sense Lilly is nervous and I gently squeeze her hand for support and reassurance. Healer Voncent examines the size of her belly, listening for the movements of our child, and checking Lilly's feet for any swelling. This is all odd to me, but I assume this is how human healers treat other humans. He does seem to be a rather gifted physician. This child will be different from any human child, or even of my own kind. In fact, I suspect it may be something new entirely. Healer Vincent did not need to know this however. As he finishes his examination, he gives Lilly a hug farewell and speaks with me outside before departing.

"Calvin, Lilly seems very emotional. I do know this being her first child, that during this pregnancy her emotions would be high. However, as I examined her she cried one moment, and then giggled the next without reason." All I could do is nod at his concern, as it is true with her emotions, but this was a delicate situation. "Please administer some of these calming herbs of valerian and passion flowers. This should help with her fluctuating emotions. I will be back to visit in a few days." Healer Vincent says, then departs as I turn to head back into the house to my lovely paramour.

As I walk into the room, I sense the cup hurling towards my direction as it clashes against the wall. Lilly glares at me, seething with rage. "SO I'M EMOTIONAL⁉! IS THAT HOW YOU TRULY FEEL ABOUT ME NOW???!!!!" she continues to shout and searches for something else to hurl at me. I can not believe her sense of hearing has heightened so much as well. Healer Vincent and I were far away from the house during our conversation. I am amazed as I duck while a book misses my head and I walk towards her. I feel my bloodlust building as she growls at me, lifting herself off of the couch. To my surprise, she charges me. With surprising force, she strikes my chest as it jolts me back a little.

I cannot believe Calvin. I am so infuriated, and can not believe my husband thinks so little of me. Doesn't he love me anymore, or the child that grows in me? Without a thought, I am quickly facing him and his eye flashes black with bloodlust. I want to scream, but he hungrily rams his tongue in my mouth, as I melt in his arms. My little one wiggles in my belly happily. He notices this and smiles. Rubbing my now protruding belly, I have become so girthy that it is sometimes hard to walk while carrying this child inside of me. With my hands remaining around his neck, I realize that he has shifted into his true form. Jaran lifts me into his arms and heads to our bedroom, and without hesitation, we make love. Afterwards, I forget what I was angry about in the first place as I fall asleep on his chest.

I watch as Lilly ravages an entire turkey leg. I was able to dash some of the Healer's herbs on the meat. I have noticed that the herbs have helped soothe her temper as I rub my head remembering the last incident. She smiles up at me, "what?" I ask as she licks her lips. "Am I truly that disgusting now?" She takes another bite without waiting for my response. I kneel close to her, wiping her mouth with a handkerchief. "No, my love, you are as beautiful as the day I first laid eyes on you." She rolls her eyes chewing thoughtfully. I laugh as I stand. "I am going to feed the animals now." It was past breakfast, and I was sure they were looking forward to their meal as well. Before I could leave for the barn, I took a sip of water, since being in human form I require more sustenance than I realized. At first it was unpleasant, even annoying at times. I did however, love Lilly showering me with attention during our lessons. She will be a patient mother to our child. A far better mother than I had, I shake my head trying to forget that hateful creature.

I hear Lilly say "I'm coming with you." She has not left the house since we discovered she was with child, and her being thrown across the room. Lilly frowns with arms crossed resting on her belly "Well? Is there a problem for me leaving the house?" She is so sexy when she is on edge. "It is not that my love, I just want you both to be safe. I don't know what I would do if anything happened to you." she huffs in frustration, blowing a strand of her hair away from her face. "I am not a child Calvin, I am only carrying one, so don't treat me like a child. Healer Vincent did not say I could not go outside ever in life." I am still watching her carefully, these mood swings can lead to more trouble, and so I have to pick my words wisely.

Lilly embraces me with a hand on my face, gently stroking it "Also, my love, the herbs that you have been sneaking in my food have been helping me. Let me come with you. I miss the fresh air, which I desperately need." she sweetly says to me. I stare at Lilly in awe, realizing that my mate is using compel on me. It is very strong as I am unable to free myself. I feel my head nodding and she removes her hand, I let out a slight gasp, as no human has ever been known to compel our kind before. I can not deny that our child is and will be very powerful. I am filled with the same pride as my father once had for me. I extend my hand to my amazing mate as we head to the barn together.

It was such a beautiful day, the sun was shining so brightly, and the birds were singing. I was gleefully holding Calvin's hand. I hum a joyful melody skipping, with each moment stopping to twirl. I'm so happy he agreed to let me feed the animals with him. I would never confess to him, but I become so lonely when he is not near. At times, I talk to the baby for company. My bundle of joy responds to me with little kicks here and there. As we approach the barn, the animals begin yelping, whimpering, and cowering away from me. I try to reach out to them, but their cries grow louder and louder. I am saddened and hurt. I can't breathe as Calvin is holding my body. I feel myself trembling with my eyes closed. My ears are hurting from the sound. Deep within me, I let out a threatening roar. I see the fear in the eyes of the animals that I have always loved since I was a child, that no longer recognized me. "I will wait here until you are done." I decide as I kiss Clavin and make my way towards the field to pick some flowers. When I am alone, I walk towards my mother's grave. I haven't spent much time here. I still miss her, but I'm not alone anymore. I know she would be happy for me and love Calvin/Jaran and our baby. I place the fresh flowers on her grave. Before he approaches, I pick up on Calvin's scent. All I can do is smile, feeling thankful for my new family.

Before a succubus lays her eggs, the incubus will rub her feet to reduce the tension and ease her pain. This also promotes cell repair and growth in their mate. It's an important ritual that I wanted to share with Lilly after we finished our meal. I laid her on the bed, and began to caress her feet. Instantly she responds to my touch, and relaxes as I continue the ritual. I need to connect with this child, and this is the best means for me to do so. Lilly falls into a deep slumber. I mindink with the child, knowing that the child will only be able to communicate through emotions for now. The child is a female, something I could only know because of my unique abilities. Pleased by this discovery, I contain my howl of joy as to not wake Lilly. My daughter sends me feelings of love, excitement, and peaceful contentment for her mother and myself. I can sense her smiling and looking forward to her mother singing to her. I release our link, and kiss Lilly's belly. We lay together and I lean forward. Knowing the child will hear me, I whisper: "No matter what happens our spirits and love will always be a part of you... Always."

Healer Vincent comes for yet another visit to check up on Lilly and the baby. "Well" he says after examining Lilly. "I believe I know what sex this child will be..." Lilly looks forward to the news. "Congratulations! It will be a baby girl!" Lilly squeals in excitement, hugging me. I am truly impressed that Healer Vincent was able to discern the sex of our child. He truly is an amazing physician. "Congratulations to the both of you. I look forward to bringing the little one into this world." He turns to look into his bag. Lilly and I silently glance at each other, sensing the same uncertainty, wondering how Healer Vincent would handle helping to bring a human/succubus into the world. Certain other thoughts come to mind, because in fact Healer Vincent is truly a man of status and means, and perhaps there was a time in his youth that he wanted more. So I deigned to break the silence. "Healer Vincent, have you ever heard of a Grand Magister?" He suddenly stiffens in his posture, and a look of alarm plagues his face.

"Where have you heard of that term?" he asks as I nervously question myself wondering if I said something wrong, possibly exposing myself. "Well we have heard tales of such a title among the villagers and healers." I said. I noticed as his look became thoughtful, his posture softened. "Some things are better left unknown. I had been offered that position at one time, and while it is a title that brings great prestige, the cost is too great. I had to decline that offer, some of the work that would have been required of me I would have found entirely too unsavory, to say the least. Besides I'm quite happy with the life I have made for myself here. I have the love and respect of the people, I live comfortably, and this village is my family, what more could I need?" he explained in an overlong exposition. He stands up to prepare to leave and smiles at us. Even after the grim topic, he displays a cheerful disposition. "Now my dear, get plenty of rest and take the herbs that I have given you." he said. Lilly pouts, as she does not enjoy them on her meat, but she nods with a smile in agreement.

As I am on my way back home in town, a sense of dread washes over me with the thought of the Grand Magister. Not wanting to shed any light to the unseemly and unholy deeds that they have done in such an organization. Riding into town I push those thoughts behind me. The past needs to remain in the past. Calvin, Lilly, and their child are the future. "Hello Healer Vincent!" I wave as I see I was greeted by the Local Baker. I stop to see how her back is holding up after my treatment. She gracefully gives me a fresh loaf of bread as a simple token of gratitude. I enter my home as I see my wife Candance holding our newborn son, Eugene. He was born soon after I started visiting the Smiths. "Hello dear, welcome home!" my beautiful wife greeted me, as she looked up from nursing the baby, who greedily suckles from his mother's breast. I kissed Candace and our son's forehead. Yes, I made the right decision for me and for my family's life. I do not live with any regrets as I sit in my favorite chair, feeling hopeful and blessed for another day.

I look over at my scrolls, studying the new supplies that arrived the other day. I placed a few flasks in my bag, preparing for another visit to the Smiths before the upcoming birth of their daughter. "William my boy, I need you to come here!" A young, lanky, energetic boy with straggly, shoulder length blond hair enters the study. He approached me several days ago about becoming my apprentice, since Nesbit had not returned from the Hunter's Camp. I could only assume the worst had happened, or some unforeseen calamity. William beamed a bright, optimistic smile at me during our first meeting. He explained that he needed the wages to care for his ailing mother, who I was treating at the time. I knew he was a hard worker from the smears of dirt on his hands and face, but that spirit and work ethic is what I admired about this lad. "Yes, Healer Vincent?" William hurried to heed my call, attentiveness glistened in his eyes as I perused through my bag. "We are heading out to visit one of my patients, Lilly Smith. She is expecting her first child with her husband. It is of the utmost importance for you to assist me, a pair of strong young arms and a firm back to aid me." I say, feeling my age. William nods with youthful vigor and ethustaisam.

William brings the wagon around and I climb in, clutching my bag close to my body. We rode into town at a brisk pace. I noticed the clouds parting while streaming sunlight broke through. It has rained a lot the past few days. I feel the painful, arthritic stiffness in my hands as I start to rub them together. "It sure is going to be a beautiful day eh, Healer Vincent?" William asked, breaking the silence. "Hmm? Why, yes. Most certainly, William." I respond as I see Penelope waving as we approach her. "Good afternoon, Healer Vincent!" she says as we pull up to her and William beckons our steed to stop. Penelope is the Local Baker's daughter. She is a fetching young lady, and William seems quite enamoured with her. "Hello, William." She smiles widely. It is obvious that she also has feelings for young William, but is too shy to tell him. "Hello, Penelope! Looking as marvelous today as ever!" William replied, tipping his cap as she blushed, swooning from the compliment. Oh, to be young again, I think to myself with a chuckle. "Penelope, I have something for you to give to your mother for the delicious bread she gave me earlier..." I dig in my jacket pocket and hand her a gold coin.

Her eyes widened. "Healer Vincent, this is too much for just a loaf of bread!" I laugh heartily. "Well it was some exquisitely good bread that my family and I enjoyed!" she giggles at such a comment, which causes William to join in the laughter. "Now, tell your mother I will be coming to visit her soon for a checkup!" I say, and she nods before leaving and smiling widely at us (mostly to William I assume). The people of the town have fallen on hard times of late, especially with the Hunters arriving and throwing their weight all over the place.

They were here to help us, not to abuse their authority, which they did far too often. "Let us proceed onward William..." my mood seems diminished for thinking about them. William must have noticed this, as we continued our trip in silence.

I hear Healer Vincent's wagon approaching the house, I am harvesting corn from the field. Lilly is taking her afternoon nap. She has been more easily fatigued lately due to the baby. I go and greet Healer Vicent as he pulls up to the house. I also notice a young man with him as he waves at me. "Hello Calvin, always a pleasure to see you." Healer Vincent says as I dust my hands off to help him down from his wagon. "It is always a pleasure to see you as well, Healer Vincent." I always look forward to seeing him, and now think of him as a family friend. I observed the young man who also climbed down from the wagon carefully, as despite the good Healer's character, his taste in company has proven to be less than ideal. "Well, where are my manners? Calvin, I would like to introduce you to my new apprentice William." I grasp his hand and shake it, as per the human custom, sensing his nervousness. "Nice to meet you, Mr. Smith, Sir." he said, with kind eyes. I know he will not be one to cause trouble. With that thought I ask Healer Vincent; "What about Mister Nesbit?" curious about where the cranky old pervert man is. "Oh dear he still hasn't been seen since the Hunters took him unfortunately. I'll have to continue my work without him." he replies as we all work towards the house. "I see I do hope he is well." I lie.

I settle my curistority, being peaked with the thought of Hunters and what their next actions could be. We enter the room where Lilly is resting, who of course hears us and is now fully awake. Healer Vincent introduces William to Lilly. I notice he blushes when she compliments him that he is a handsome young man. Healer Vincent jokingly says, "Well, I'm not chopped liver over here, you know." I too enjoy his humor most of all and it always brings a joyous laughter to Lilly's beautiful face. As with his other visits, he asks her about any changes in her eating habits, sudden pains, exercise regularity, as well as how much rest she is getting. Healer Vincent has his apprentice scribe her answers on a scroll and parchment. "Well, I believe I will give you a good bill of health." he smiles while standing up. "With how the baby's growth has been developing, I would say that you will be delivering your child within two moon's passing(two months). I will return around that time." William swiftly jots this information down. Healer Vincent gently holds Lilly's hand. "I remember helping your mother bring you into the world. I am so honored to be doing the same for you." tearfully, Lilly thanks him and says her farewells. Healer Vincent and William board the wagon and return back to town.

Later, it is a quiet night as Lilly lies in my arms while I stroke her hair and belly. Our child is growing more and more with each rising and setting of the sun. I have noticed her cravings and mood fluctuations have increased as well. Therefore, it is time for me to tell her about the Purge. "Lilly, this child will be unlike any child that has ever existed." She looks at me with so much love, as I continue. "You have experienced two of the three symptoms of carrying a succubus child. The craving of red meat and the shifting moods, but there is one more. A third element, which you have not yet encountered. It is one far more horrifying, and yet it is an obstacle that we must overcome." I say, squeezing her hand ever so slightly. "I pray you have the strength to withstand it, for it is the very reason my kind has never mated with your own before."

After Calvin discussed with me in detail what was to come, I attempted to rest because I was feeling tired and out of sorts, which was a state of being I was quickly growing accustomed to. He forewarned me that this final stage would be sudden, brutal and excruciatingly painful. My mind was puzzled by what the nature of this stage could be. Amidst my heavy thinking I gradually felt my eyelids grow heavy as I was carried into the merciful bliss of slumber, and then… IT BEGAN.

I felt a sudden burst of pain envelop my womb. My eyes darted open, and my body convulsed uncontrollably. I let out a roar from the deepest part of the bowel of my soul. It sounded far less human than I'd care to admit. Calvin rushed to the bedroom door, shifted into his true form, but he would not dare take another step further. Slowly it felt as if every drop of blood stored within my body was replaced with liquid fire and it seared me to my very soul.

Jaran took a deep breath and linked with me. "What you are experiencing now is the Purge. You are a human female and were never made to be a suitable vessel to bear a demon child. So because you have a child of our kind within your womb, your body is making a transition in preparation for the precious being you carry. You will no longer be a human nor will you be one of my kind, but like our child, you will be something entirely new. Other incubi in the past have attempted to do as we have done, but the human females were weak, and the puge simply destroyed their bodies. I only hope you are strong enough to survive it. If not, I fear our mating has doomed both you and our child, for if you fail, the child's life is forfeit as well. I am forbidden to interfere, I can only watch." he finishes his thought, as a single tear rolls down his cheek. I notice my fingernails readily sprouting longer out of my hands until one by one they completely fall off. They are soon replaced by similar looking fingernails that are black with sharpened points at the tips. A throbbing pain lingers in the front of my mouth as my top teeth grow longer until they fall out as well, replaced by lengthy black fangs.

I feel muscle groups flexing and contracting that I never noticed before. I glance at my husband through squinted eyes and clenched teeth, and notice Jaran's expression transforming into one of sheer awe. These small blue lights start pulling themselves away from my body and begin swirling in the air above me. I am at the point where I am in so much pain, that to give word to the confusion that I feel would be impossible. Something pokes my flesh from the inside of my back which, like the rest of my body, looks as though it had been in a torrential downpour of blood. At first, I feel a mere annoyance, but the fire inside of me soon intensifies. It pushed harder and harder until it culminated in one violent thrust I felt in my back, as large feathered wings sprouted from my back beneath the shoulders. Flames spay from my mouth which are blue, matching those swirling lights above my head. My feet grow larger and change to match my hands, complete with matching talons, when all of the sudden my body collapses on the floor, and my transformation is complete.

Jaran rushes to my side "are you alright my Love?" as I look at my hand, I notice our clawed hands are entwined as I ask him; "Do I look different now?" He tips my head by my chin. "You are truly the most beautiful creature that I have ever seen." but my jaw drops at the realization that we have spoken words without mindlinking with each

56

other. Suddenly the blue light comes together lowering itself before us in the shape of a young woman's body. It grew features until I realized that I was looking at myself. She ran her fingers through my hair. With a sad expression, she said "Never again, goodbye, Lilly..." With that she reached her arms into the air, and disappeared into the night sky. I glanced at Jaran. "Was that-?" he interrupted "Yes, that was the last vestiges of your humanity, taken shape as a soul-self. Come what may in the future, you may never return to this life. In choosing me, you have abandoned this part of yourself for all eternity. Have you any regrets, my Love?" he asks. I smile, and take him in my arms with the new strength I did not have before and say. "Regrets? None at all."

A black carriage slowly heads towards the village of Blood Oak, coming to a halt in front of the local inn. Five shadowy figures emerge from the carriage. One speaks with an eerily familiar voice. "Welcome to my town, the village of Blood Oak." pulling back a hood to reveal the face of Old Man Nesbit. "Tis a quaint little town," says a male voice, his cloak adorned with a flaming sword. "Aye, but do they have any places to eat?" says a female with a similar cloak. "I care not as long as there is death to be dealt" as he trips and stumbles from the carriage, losing his hood as he lands face first in horse shit.

There is a rattle of a chain that can be heard as the fifth figure is jerked into position. "Have a care. I bruise easily, and you wouldn't want to harm your magical source or would you?" To which the other female replies "Hold your tongue or lose it, bitch." "Come now," Nesbit speaks "surely we must all work together..." as the female Hunter resumes glaring at the Witch, who is dragged by the chain.

"There is a tavern a short walk from here where we can fill our bellies and quench our thirsts, if you will follow me." Nesbit says directing them to the local tavern. They walk a short distance until the witch stops suddenly as her eyes change to white and begin to glow. "Evelyn? What seems to be the matter?" Nesbit asked. She lowers her hood revealing a beautiful, porcelain looking face, and says: "we are on the right track. A very short time ago... someone in this village has been through The Purge."

CHAPTER 5

After we return from the tavern, the five of us are in the room at the inn together. Two of the Hunters are strategizing their next moves. The female is called Hunter Allison McClary. She is the leader of this group, and the man next to her is her second in command, Bryan Longsword. They seem very close as they continue to talk together. The third Hunter is uh... well damn, I don't know his fucking name! How am I supposed to remember every damn person I come across? Whatever his name is he is a fucking oaf, sitting there snoring in his chair. Hunter Bryan kicks him and he jolts awake looking around the room. Then, there is the lovely Evelyn the witch, whom I know is here against her will. I would love to feel in between her legs. She notices my lustful looks at her and twists her lips in disgust.

"I don't think she likes you..." Hunter Oaf chuckles idiotically, walking toward Evelyn roughly adjusting her chains around her hands and neck. I huff in frustration. How in the hell did I end up with these fucking characters? The Hunters absconded with me back to their camp, where I was interrogated. "Arthur Nesbit, where is the demon?" one large Hunter approaches me. "Who are the strongest people in your village? What is your male population? Have there been any new villagers as of late?" I am so frightened and tired that I have no strength to answer when the torture starts. They began by first slapping me across the face with such force that I lost consciousness several times between strikes. Eventually, I am put into a dank cell 'until further notice' I hear, given gruel which I have to crawl to in order to eat. Dumb bastards, if they only knew this is my favorite type of food! 'Tis more of a treat than a punishment to me.

There are Hunters that come near my cell, throwing water on me in an attempt to have me cleaned. "Ugh he fucking sinks! It would be better to kill him than to deal with this horrible stench!" a Hunter shouts. "True," another Hunter says "but we have our orders. I could be performing real work, rather than being stuck in this low shit duty. Would be a crying shame if the old bastard had an 'accident' while trying to escape." He pulls out his sword from his shealth and my last thoughts as I lie there was that I was going to finally meet my maker. Suddenly, I heard a female voice. "Stand down Hunter, that won't be necessary. Get him cleaned, dressed, and in my office as soon as possible." The Hunter grunts and puts away his sword as he responds; "Whatever you say". I smile a weak smile thinking I have been saved by an angel.

I come to the office to realize that I'm actually standing in front of the fucking devil. With red hair, a scar that runs the length of her face, and all at once giving an image of a damaged beauty. She had a firefly look in her eyes like a wild mare, eager to be tamed. I smirked, "What the fuck are you smiling about, cur?" she sternly says as I'm a little taken aback at her language. I feel my arousal growing, I place my hands over my trousers to conceal it. I lower my head briefly, "You are here because we know you have been in contact with the demon that we have been searching for for sometime now. I'm sure you don't know who it is, but it makes no difference. You are only our guide. You will do this by either choice or by force. Do you understand this?" She asks, then slams her hand on her desk to make sure I am paying attention. "Yes… yes.." I stammer my words out. "Good." she smiles as I notice an evil glisten in her eyes. "We will leave in the morning." she dictates. My mind is drifting, losing focus as my hands are communicating with one another. If I'm being forced into servitude, maybe I can find a way to wet my wick in the process.

Back in the room, I can not help but watch the bewitching beauty, Evelyn. She is sleeping in the corner of the room. If I could only touch her soft skin, as I lick my lips imagining lapping at her pink inner lips while she moans in my ear. Oh, how it would feel to caress her supple body, feeling her heat comfort me, as I explore her inner cavern. Yes, such a tasty delight it would be, like moments in heaven, I suppose.

Then I hear the devil shatter my dream. "Nesbit, you fucking pervert. Maybe you should be more focused on the mission objective, and not the bosom of a fucking witch. Or maybe I should chop your cock off to help you concentrate on the present task." she sneers. I shake my head, sobering myself, and ask myself what have I done to deserve this kind of treatment.

I do not know who I desire to slay more, the pervert old man, the incompetent Hunter that I was saddled with, or the filthy witch whore that continues to gaze upon me. Narrowing my eyes, my mind illuminates with fantasies of the fucking Witch, of gouging her eyes out as she fills my ears with the orchestrated cacophony of her blood curdling screams. She seems to always be watching me, as if she knows more about me than I do myself. I hear Bryan whisper "I know my love, all in due time…" as he brushes his hand against mine. Feeling his warm breath against my ear and neck gives me a gentle throbbing sensation within my loins, and my breathing becomes labored. Byran has always seemed to know my inner thoughts as I glance at him lovingly. Oh, Byran, my darling, I shudder to think where I would be, or who I would be without you.

I never knew my parents. My Aunt Gloria raised me and loved me more than I could have asked for. I never asked about my parents. I just always figured as long as I had Aunt Gloria, she was all I needed. We lived in a small cottage outside the village of Thornbush, a quiet town which I loved to visit. I was a happy child, and grew into a happy young woman. My favorite place to go was behind our cottage where there was a beautiful field of wild white roses. I could have lived among the roses forever. I found peace as I smelled their lovely fragrance. "Allison!" I could hear Aunt Gloria calling me. "Supper is ready!" Even though I wanted to stay in the field, my stomach grumbled at the thought of Aunt Gloria's delicious culinary masterpieces. I rushed into the house where Aunt Gloria waits with open arms. Her hair alway smelled like fresh rain. I remember thinking how I always wanted to hold onto this memory. While we are having supper, Aunt Gloria says "You know Allison, tonight is a full moon." I look up from my plate with a keen interest. "There is a legend that says during the moonlight, among the white roses the moonlight causes them to glow. No one knows why this happens." With a surprised look on my face, I realize she is talking about my white roses. "Aunt Gloria, may I please be excused to go to the field? I just have to see it for myself. Please, please!" I excitedly beg, almost jumping out of my seat! Aunt Gloria laughs "Of course you can my dear. Your smile lights up my world!" Tears fill her brown eyes. I dive into her arms. "Thank you Aunt Gloria, I love you so much."

As I leave the house, I peer to see the moon high in the night sky. I dash towards the field where my beloved roses await. I stood near the edge of the field. As my face lights up, I find the legend to be true. The roses almost give off a mythical radiance, while I gently brush my fingers on their lustrous petals. I'm filled with so much jubilance as I twirl around giggling. Then from the shadows I hear a growling coming from the forest, threatening to shatter the fragile vitreousness of my mirth. I tremble, feeling my bottom lip quiver with fear, as three large wolves emerge. I am paralyzed with horror, even as my mind begs my legs to flee. My eyes widen at their size, while they take steps ever closer to me. I watch as the brown and red wolves stand on their hind legs and sniff the air quickly, darting towards the cottage while shifting their forms into something almost... humanoid. Is this what they called a werewolf? My only thought is of Aunt Gloria. Before I can move a step I see the remaining black werewolf growling angrily and stalking towards me. Feeling more scared I hear my own heartbeat racing in my ears. Within a hair's breadth of an instant, he is on top of me, pinning me to the ground baring his enormous, drool saturated fangs. He begins to sniff my face, licking me with his elongated tongue.

I involuntarily taste his slobber in my mouth, making me want to vomit, but feeling scared, I swallow the bile. Just as quickly, he rips my clothes and underwear into shreds and begins to sniff, and then lap and lick at my body hungrily. I can smell the blood on his fur. My blood will soon become a part of his collage, I think sadly as I stare at the moon. That is when I feel it, ripping and forcing its way into my body. This wolf was eagerly thrusting his erected member into my nether regions. "NO!" I scream, "PLEASE NO!" attempting to push him off of my body to no avail. Noticing my struggle he slashes at my body, and then my face, opening a long wound upon it. I can not struggle much longer while he pushes himself frivolously and violently. I gazed into his eyes. He appeared to be almost smiling, knowing that he has now stolen my virginity. In the distance, I hear a scream emanating from the cottage. Turning my face, I see in the distance, it is Aunt Gloria. I want to call out to her, but my own blood chokes me, preventing me from making a sound.

In my horror, I watch as the two wolves gash and claw at my aunt's body, as chunks of her lay at their paws. Eventually, there are no more sounds from her. They continue to consume my beloved Aunt. I weep, yet I am filled with so much rage as this beast continues to pant on top of me, violating my modesty to no end. More and more with each moment, as his eyes are closed, I think of my beautiful white roses, their petals glowing, yet smeared with my blood. Then I notice the thorns on each rose's stem. With my last remaining strength, I grab the rose and stab it into the beast's gaping mouth. The wolf opens his eyes as wide as the moon that called him, and jaws closed as he swallows the rose whole, then lifts himself from my body. The wolf violently jerks its body on the ground and spasms before finally letting out a deafening howl. The wolf's body thuds as it collapses to the ground, and is no longer moving. Mercifully, it is dead. I smile, I killed a werewolf, and now I am about to die too.

In the darkness I hear voices. "Will you look at this shite, damn werewolves always leaving a fucking mess. Looks like they had a 'breakfast of champions' over here. Damned fur fuckers..." Laughter can be heard from several other male voices. "Well what the bloody hell do we have here guv?" I feel this man is standing over me. "Poor dear, seems like the werewolf assaulted her in a most unnatural way."

"So it appears..." another male's voice leans closer to me, as I feel him rub his finger on my thigh. "She was but a virgin too, couldn't be more than 15–" he stops. "Holy fucking hell!" he shouts "By jove, she is still alive! Brothers, come over here, quickly!" There are more steps approaching me. "She is still alive," the same man says "and it looks like she took out a fucking wolf! I'll be damned, it only has a whole tuft of wolfsbane inside its mouth!" A new male voice speaks; "Sadly, with how the beast has left her, with the Wolf's cursed seed tainting her womb, she will never be able to bear children."

Stepping away from me, I can barely open my eyes, as a man walks towards the dead wolf. "Guess I'd best get to work on this fucking shite before a Necromancer brings it back, then we'll have more trouble on our hands." he says as he takes a wood axe, and starts chopping the beast into small, gory pieces. "Why in the hell can't those blasted assholes bring something back that is pleasant, like a fucking whore with big tits?" The other men laugh at him.

"Because they bring back the dead you fucking idiot, guess you want corpse rot on your cock!" the man with the axe yells. I can't believe these men are talking plainly about such a matter. My Aunt Gloria is dead and I might as well be dead myself. The man chopping the beast huffs into irritation as the other two laugh at him. I cough up some blood and bile, hoping to speak to the man who looks at me with a genuine smile. He wraps his cloak around me, securing me in his arms. "It is okay little one, save your strength, you're in the care of the Hunters now." Hunters? What kind of Hunters are they? My puzzled mind ponders, as I slip back into all enveloping darkness.

I wake up startled with a man standing over me, attending to my wounds. Noticing that I've awakened, he says; "Well hello miss! I'm so glad to see you finally awake, I was worried there for a while. You have been asleep for three days." My head hurts as I try to lift it. My throat is so dry I can barely speak, only offering moans and groans from my lips. He places a cup of water to my lips, "Slowly dear..." he says, tipping the cup. I greedily drank, almost choking, but taking big gulps in my mouth. "I am Healer Paul." he says and sits the cup down while another man enters the room. "Healer Paul, how is our guest doing?" This man wears the same cloak as the other men that found me, with black hair, piercing blue eyes, and a solid build. "She is doing well, Hunter Darren. Her wounds have miraculously healed. This one has a fighter's spirit." he says, smiling at me. "So I have been told" the man says, standing in front of where I lay.

"Tell me your name?" he asks me. I stare at him and reply. "Allison... Allison McClary..." my voice sounds so different now that it shocks me as I speak. "Well Allison McClairy, welcome to the Hunter's Camp." Hunter's Camp? I attempt to sit up, feeling unsteady as the Healer notices this. "Whoa there," looking at Hunter Darren. "I believe she still needs a little more rest, she has not yet regained all of her strength." Hunter Darren nods and leaves the room. I hear some muttering outside, as I fall back to sleep. In my mind, I still have so many questions.

I am awakened to the disruptive sound of shouts outside. I find myself alone in the room. I attempt to lift myself off of the bed. I succeed, and my body feels so stiff, but with considerable effort, I am thankfully able to walk. The sunlight blinds me as I lift the tent opening, a group of men and women appear to be swinging swords at each other. I am so confused about what is happening. I feel a hand on my shoulder as I turn around, and I see Hunter Darren, "Hello again Allison, looks like you're feeling much better. That's good!" Glancing at my body from head to toe, he frowns as he looks behind me. I turn to see it is the Hunter who had chopped the wolf.

He is wistfully snoring in a chair. In my mind, I wondered what kind of dreams a man who's seen the manner of things he's seen would have. "You fucking asshole!" Hunter Darren yells, and kicks the chair out from under him, causing the slumbering brute to tumble to the ground. The others have stopped, and are now observing the commotion.

"You were ordered to guard her, not fucking take a nap, Sleeping Beauty!" The Hunter shies away, looking embarrassed. "I'm sorry, Darren." he rubs his head and Hunter Darren reaches his hand out to help him up. "What am I ever going to do with you? Hmmm okay, no harm, no foul." he smiled, patting him on the back. I notice he has a nice smile. "Why don't you go check on the armory provisions, eh?" He turned to the group of men and women, and raising his voice he said; "Everyone else, get back to training!" He turns back to me; "Sorry about all that distraction. Why don't we go chat in my office?"

We walked together a short distance to what appears to be a larger tent than the one I was resting in.

Hunter Darren sits across from me at the head of a long table, which separates us. I am a little nervous being alone with him. He had served me a drink of what I taste as wine which burns down my throat, and I begin to choke a little. He smiles,; "I'm sorry, maybe I should have told you what that was. I thought you would need it to help you relax. Allison, I know all of this can be very scary for you, so let me explain what we Hunters are." It takes me a while for it to sink in about Hunters being the protectors of humanity and fighters against evils such as vampires, werewolves, and witches. All matter of supernatural creatures to be exact, to which apparently there are multitudes. Hunter Darren is patient with me when I ask how I survived the werewolf attack. He gives me a stern gaze before saying; "We know that if attacked by a wolf, you are either turned into a werewolf or die." He clears his throat before continuing "Their weaknesses are silver, beheading, and/or wolfsbane, which you used to kill the wolf that attacked you. How did you survive such a vicious attack? It must have been God's will, my child, which leads me to my next question..."

He rises from his seat and comes closer to me, and I examine his handsome features with my eyes and listen to his next words. "Do you want to be a Hunter Allison?" he asks, and without hesitation I respond "Yes." He continues to describe to me what is called a Joining Ceremony, where the brothers and sisters will vote to see if I am worthy to be a Hunter. "We are a brotherhood, and all of us are equal. Male or female. Good or bad. We all reap the same rewards." Before leaving the tent I ask "Are there many female Hunters?" He chuckles; "I'm afraid women are not coming by the droves to become Hunters, but those who have chosen the path are the equal to any man here, and just like the men, they have earned their title through the ranks with hard work."

I am pleased with his answer, and look forward to the meeting. As I enter my tent, I see a full length looking glass. I walk towards it, and I see the reflection of a woman who will someday become the strongest Hunter.

I am standing, looking at my reflection. That was ten cycles (years) ago, and here I still stand, unbroken. I remember drinking the blood of my first kill, that rapist bastard werewolf. He stole my innocence, and I took his life in exchange. Bryan says we need magic supplies. I step near Nesbit, and slap him far harder than necessary. "Wake up, old fool!" He jolts out of his sleep, and falls to the floor like a heap of garbage. I give him the scribe of what is needed, and send him on his way. "Hurry up and gather these supplies, and don't have us waiting long." He nods his head in response. Soon, very soon the Hunt will begin. The thought excites my body. I touch the hilt of my sword, to eviscerate those wretched creatures, and spill their blood gives me so much pleasure.

"I SWEAR SHE IS THE FUCKING SPAWN OF THE DEVIL!!!" I swear. She is always threatening and insulting me all the time. I rush to the supply store in the dark of the night, holding my cloak close to my face. I can not afford anyone seeing me with these fucking Hunters. Rumors would fly like a moth towards a flame. The shop is still open, and I begin gathering the herbs on the list: mistletoe, yellow evening primrose, fuzzy weed, and porosela. I am amazed that I can find half of this shite, finding the last two ingredients of a rose compass and a lantern. I know its best not to ask fucking questions or that she devil will likely cut out my damn tongue. I pay for the supplies and swiftly return back to the inn, as fear guides my feet expediently back into the room.

"Ok Witch, it's time to do your job!" Hunter Allison yells and jabs at my chest. I wake back to this nightmare that never seems to end, yet ironically, the only time I feel free is in my dreams. She yanks at the chain that is attached to the collar around my neck, I don't dare give her the satisfaction that she is causing me intense pain. The old bastard has returned with the supplies. I stroke each item, blessing them while infusing my power to my aid. The old bastard gasps at what he is witnessing. The Hunters, on the other hand, stand stone faced and unimpressed. "It is done." I say. "We need to cast the location spell in the middle of the town in order for it to be effective, and locate the target." I say nonchalantly. Hunter Allison says stoically; "You had better find this demon, witch!" narrowing her eyes at me. I feel her unnerving hate pulsing towards me. I nod, and sit back in the corner, not needing to be guided like an animal. Hunter Allison sends the other Hunters and the old bastard to ensure that the middle of the town square is clear for the ritual. When we are alone I look up at her standing there with her back towards me. "Hunter Allison, is it true that you can not conceive a child?" On impulse, she drew her sword, and in one fluid motion, pressed the point of the blade against my neck, as I felt a few droplets of blood begin to trickle to my collarbone.

"Be mindful witch, your gift may have its uses, but not so much use that I can't end you at any moment that I choose!!" she grits the words between her clenched teeth. "What if I could restore what you have lost?" I asked with a modestly thin smile. She slowly lowers her sword, signifying some interest in what I am saying. "Even if you can do what you say, the one I love cannot give me a child." her tone is much softer now, almost in a whisper. "I can restore him as well, in exchange for two requests." I hold up my fingers "One, when we have captured the demon, I am not to be in its presence." and holding up my second finger; "Two, you grant my freedom." I observe her deep in her thoughts, closing her eyes. I feel myself doing the same as well. Our breathing in sync with one another. Hunter Allison finally speaks; "Yes witch." I smile at her. It is the first smile I have given anyone since my enslavement. "Excellent, and then we all will get our 'happily ever after'."

Hunter Allison dragged me along, drawing closer to the town square. I walk confidently, with a new sense of freedom drawing nearer, almost as if I can taste it. The townspeople are standing around the edge of the town square, resembling cattle waiting for the slaughter. They avoid my gaze, but cannot overlook what is about to happen. I stand at the center, and begin to cast the spell of detection. My power builds within me as I am levitated from the ground. An image materializes in my mind, and I am lowered to my feet. The Spell has ended, and I know where the demon is and I point the party in the right direction.

The Witch has finally fucking found that bastard demon, and he was Calvin! No, not fucking Calvin, that's not even its real name! He was with my Lilly, MY Lilly! I can not contain my rage. "The demon is with Lilly. She married a demon! She has brought unholiness into our town!" I shout, trembling. I hear the other townspeople yelling; "SHE IS WITH CHILD! SHE IS CARRYING THE DEMON'S CHILD!" More and more shout in disbelief, fear, and hatred, until a mob begins to gather. Suddenly I am dragged from behind. "YOU FUCKING FOOL, OUR JOB IS NOT DONE!" Hunter Bryan shouts, while throwing me into the black carriage. I land on the floor, looking up at the Hunters and the witch.

The Hunter Oaf taps the carriage as the driver heads toward the location of the demon. "I'm not sure what you were thinking, Nesbit (first time she has ever said my fucking name), but we are Hunters. We find and kill our target first, and then clean up any leftover mess,"

Hunter Allison leans close to me. "and you will see this through to the end, or it will be YOUR end." I feel as if I will shit myself, but instead I just breathe a sigh of relief. I look over at the witch who sits calmly. How can she be so fucking calm at a time like this?

I am holding Lilly in my arms. I have come to the realization that since her transformation, I have never felt closer to her. Hearing her lovely voice in this new form is music to my ears. She purrs in my arms as I rub her back, our hands entwined and resting on her belly. Our child will be born soon. I look forward to completing our family. I am consumed with bloodlust, as I can sense that the Hunters have found me, and are approaching quickly. Lilly senses the danger as well, and hisses. "My Love," I say, tilting her head towards me by the chin. "there is something I must show you before it is too late." I reveal to her a map that I had kept in a safe place, and explain that there is a cave east from here. "You and our child shall meet me there in three days time. Once our daughter is born we will start our lives over somewhere new, in an insular community, where they will not find us." There are no more words spoken between us, as Lilly knows that I must leave her and our unborn child. I could not risk putting them in danger, I refused. With that, I leave my mate knowing she has the will needed to survive carrying our precious little one. My wings open and I leap into flight, shrieking in the night sky, heading towards the west knowing that the Hunters will follow.

I feel the demon changing direction. "He is moving, head west." I say, trusting my instincts. The Hunter shouts to the driver; "Head West!" I feel the carriage shift to the exact course of the demon's movement.

I was young when I started feeling my powers growing within me. My parents and I were part of the Scalded Raven Coven. How they loved to show their prized trophy child around. The High Priestess Ava showed interest in me as well, as I had so much potential to one day benefit the coven. She trained me personally, taking me away from my parents at an early age. I chose to abandon my family, as now I had a goal to be the next High Priestess, and would not let anyone stand in my way. I became ignorant and reckless, practicing necromancy, and magics forbidden to the coven, but I didn't care. I was reckless, and I needed the knowledge and power. Certainly, it was power I did have. That is when I came across a Blood Wraith, a demon with large wings, claws, and bloody red bones and scales for a body. It's fangs and tongue were designed to funnel the blood of its victims. They are unnaturally gifted in the manipulation of darkness, and the dark arts of possession. I thought I could tame the beast, but it was intelligent, and capable of speaking to humans. I became its slave as it attacked me, draining my blood and leaving me a drop of blood to live. By this method, I was ensorcelled, and completely under its control. If it wasn't for the forbidden ritual of possession and control I performed, I would never have the chance to be free of the demon. I would have considered enslaving it myself, but chose instead to destroy it.

I had ascended, meaning that I had reached my highest power or so I wanted the coven to believe. The current High Priestess must bestow her power to the next High Priestess of her choosing. I knew that it only made sense that it would be me. My new fame of position brought envy and jealousy from my sisters in the coven. It did not matter, so long as they would follow my rule without objection. While I slept I smiled, looking forward to my Ascending Ceremony. When suddenly I felt something around my neck, and a burlap sack was placed over my head. I felt myself being dragged off in the night. I could hear my sisters scream; "IT IS HUNTERS! THEY ARE RAIDING US! EVERYONE FLEE!" Hunters have always raided coven settlements and enslaved witches, but they had never hunted us as it was far simpler to abuse our power. I never thought that this fate would befall me, a powerful witch, lowered to the stature of a slave. It was then that I realized that I had made the mistake of reaching too close to the sun.

"So you have her. I have done what you asked." I heard a female voice that sounded eerily familiar. The bag was removed from my head, revealing my sister witch, Naga. She had betrayed me! The Hunter placed ten pieces of silver within her hands, as she smiled greedily. I screamed in anger; "WHY SISTER?!!" as the tears begin to stream down my face. I attempted to use my power, but I quickly learned that the slave collar cancelled my magic. Naga smiled at me with an evil smirk. "It was all too easy, but to put it simply, it was done to teach you humility," she said. "You should be thanking me, how the mighty have fallen!" with those last words, and the ensuing laughter I felt echoing in my skull, I was taken away from my coven, my home, and my goals.

I am jolted awake in the carriage. The demon is close, and appears to be weakening, enabling us to track it quickly. We are in the dark forest on holy ground, near a town south from us. I am chained to the holy ground, where I am unable to move. Hunter Allison is keeping her word to keep me absent from the battle. The Hunters are tracking the demon on their own, and for some reason have dragged that useless old man along. I'm not sure why, but he is not my concern. I look up and see the full moon. I know this moon is called the Hunter's moon. A fitting name for a fitting end I think as I wait.

They are going deeper in these damn woods, why in the hell did they bring me? What am I going to kill the demon with? I know they are using me for fucking bait. My God, is this how my humble life ends!?? I don't deserve to die like this, as my knees tremble together in fear, and then we stop. The Hunters spread out, then suddenly the demon emerges, hissing at the Hunters. My God, it is huge! This was Calvin? The hunters surround it in a circular formation, striking it with their blessed swords. I run and hide to keep a safe distance, peeking at the action from behind a tree. The demon dodges the blow of the Hunter Oaf, and burrows his claws deep into his chest, with the final blow coming from the demon's horns being driven into the Hunter's belly, then forcefully tears his horns free, disemboweling the buffoon. As he falls to the ground dead, I hear "Slag!!!" It is from Hunter Allison who sheds veritable oceans of tears. So that was his name, I think to myself. She rushes towards the demon in rage, and the demon is close to ending her life as well, but Hunter Bryan pushes her out of the way. I believe he was struck, but swings his shortsword at the beast knocking it back with one blow. Falling to one knee, Hunter Allison races to his aid. "Nevermind me, put the chains on the damn creature, Allison." She nods and locks the chains on the demon's arms, legs and tail. I slowly come out of my hiding spot. I can't believe they captured it, as the demon comes unglued. It struggles to move, is unable to, and growls at me. "I know you understand me, demon. I want you to know something before you meet your end. You will lose your precious Lilly tonight. I will make sure of it!" I say as he hisses at me with pitch black eyes. Hunter Allison swings her sword over her head, landing the final blow on the demon's neck. The demon's head rolls onto the ground, yet it appears to still be alive. I notice a tear appears to be seen on its face. I met the teardrop with a phlegm loaded spit! Dancing alone, I cackled in victory. I had defeated the demon!

It is finally over, as Hunter Allsion is walking towards me while holding up Hunter Bryan. The old fool appears to be alive as well. The third Hunter must be dead for sure, as he is nowhere in sight. Besides, none could survive disembowelment, I assume. Good riddance as he was the one who captured me those six moons ago. Hunter Allison places Hunter Bryann on the grassy knoll of the Holy ground, telling the old fool to stay with him. I smile. "It is done," she says. "I grant your freedom after you restore my womb and his seed's fertility." She points to Hunter Bryan. ``I casted a restoration spell which leaves me slightly weakened. "It is complete." She frees me from the chains and collar. "I hope our paths never cross again." I say to her as I turn around, heading to the nearby town.

I know it probably wasn't a wise decision to free the witch, but she kept her promise. Now Bryan and I can be together and start a family. Walking away from being Hunters is a life I had never dared to consider before today. I approach Bryan and Nesbit smiling, but no such smile appears across Bryan's face as he shows me a gaping wound. The demon injured him while he was trying to save me. Damn you Bryan, you were always trying to save me.

"Come on Allison, we can't be late for training!" Bryan grabbed my hands as we ran toward the training grounds. "I'm not going to let you get in trouble with me again, go ahead of me..." I said, even though I enjoyed his warm hand in mine and the attention he gave me. "Shut up, we are in this together, brotherhood, sisterhood, and all that fluffy shit!" I laughed and he smiled. "Look who finally made it, late as usual..." a female trainee Hunter said. I didn't bother remembering her name or that of the snarky bitch that was always with her. "Maybe she isn't worthy after all to be a Hunter. Glad I didn't vote for her, just another disappointment," the bitch behind her laughed at the trainee Hunter's comment. "You know, if you weren't my fucking Hunter sister, I would cut your tits off and stuff them in your mouth, right?" Bryan calmly says, leaving their mouths agape as we walked to our assigned line. At that moment I realized that I loved him, and I wanted to spend the rest of my life with him, no matter what. That night we made love, and he told me I was beautiful. I called him a liar, knowing that I was scarred and half a woman. "If I had just balls with no cock, would you still love me?" he asked, meeting my eyes with his own crystal blues. I nodded. "So this scar on your face and the curse upon your womb does not make you less of a woman to me. I love and respect you, I would follow you anywhere to Hell and back. If I could, I'd steal the stars from the sky just to lay them at your feet." he said, gently tracing my scar with his fingertips. I kissed him under the full moon declaring to be his forever.

Thus, Bryan dies in my arms. I knew he had no other family, as the Longswords disowned him for fighting with a short sword, breaking the code of their clan. They are all dead now, slaughtered by the Silver Wolves. Fuck them! I was the only family he needed and wanted, as I cradled him in my arms, sobbing. I think, what about my 'happily ever after'? Nesbit places his hand on my shoulder. "I'm sorry, Allison." I look at him. With a somber tone, I say; "Go back where you came from. Forget what you have seen, and never cross my path again." He ran off in the night. I placed Bryan's body in the carriage, and instructed the driver to take him back to the Hunter's Camp to ensure that he is given an honorable burial. He rides off. Without any words left, there is still one more job I have to finish.

I can't believe I am free! I marvelled at myself as I purchased some supplies before heading somewhere, anywhere but here. I leave the store and start out of town. The night air is crisp, and feels good on my skin. "That must feel nice." I hear someone say. It is Hunter Allison. I haven't regained my powers fully, so protecting myself is not an option at this time. I shouldn't be concerned, as she did just grant me my freedom. "I mean the freedom and happiness to know that anything is still possible." she continues to say. Why is she speaking to me like this? Coming closer to me, I suddenly see the moonlight reflecting from her steel. Before I can flee, I feel the sharpened blade enter my stomach, my eyes asking 'why?' as blood spurts from my mouth. "I deserved my happily ever after in the end, remember?" Allison wickedly laughs as I can only hear her laughter on the wind as I bleed out and die at her feet. Allison turns away and departs in the darkness of the night, no longer a Hunter now becoming a wanderer. The last thing I hear as the world darkens is a tear choked voice saying; "and they all lived happily ever after..."

A mob gatherers in the town square of Blood Oak, planning to storm the home of the demon and Lilly. My thoughts are racing as I enter my home and I grab the flask from my bag. My wife looks at me frantically, as she holds our son in her arms who is sleeping peacefully. I tell her whatever happens that she must keep herself and our child safe. I didn't have much time to explain anything else, as I kissed them both, hoping that I am not too late. My wife cries silently, but nods her head that she understands. I grab a horse and head quickly out of town before the mob. I arrive not a moment too soon.

When I enter the home, I call out; "Lilly, are you here?! Please answer me!" A creature steps out of the shadows with wings, white feathers, claws, and a full belly with a child. "Lilly, is that you?" I ask. She nods and then I hear her voice in my head. "Yes, Healer Vincent." "Oh thank God," I say as I rush over to hug her. "and is the baby well too?" She nods again. "There is a mob coming. Take this flask, and flee from this place. I won't let them hurt either of you." Lilly begins to cry tears that seem never ending. "You are helping us, even though you know what I am, what we are?" she continues to sob. "My dear child, I do not care if Calvin is a demon or what you have become. I saw the love that you two have for each other and this child. I have and always will care for you both always, know this in your heart. You both are MY family as well." We embraced each other for what may be the very last time. "Now go, I will try to buy you enough time and remember to drink from the flask during childbirth. It will ease the pain. Always remember, I love you, child." I kiss her forehead, finding that now I too, am sobbing, and head toward the approaching mob.

"MY GOOD PEOPLE OF BLOOD OAK, PLEASE HEAR ME, I BEG OF YOU! PLEASE HEAR ME! LAY DOWN YOUR PITCHFORKS AND TORCHES. THIS IS NOT THE WAY!" I shout as the mob halts briefly. The perspiration filled my brow as my pleas were completely and utterly ignored by the angry mob. They are out for blood tonight and only blood would satiate their thirst. Still I will not relent. "YOU WILL BECOME THE THING YOU FEAR

THE MOST. REMEMBER THAT YOU ARE ALL GOOD MEN AND WOMEN. YOU ALL KNOW ME. I ONLY WISH TO SPEAK GOOD OF LILLY AND HER CHILD, WHO ARE NOT EVIL!" I only hope my pleas have not fallen on deaf ears. "YOU FUCKING TRAITOR VINCENT," I hear, as a rock is being thrown at me striking me on the head. "THAT BITCH MUST HAVE TURNED YOU! WHEN WE DONE WITH THEM, LET'S KILL HIM TOO!" Everyone shouts in agreement, as I am placed in chains and hauled back into town. I turn to see the mob setting the house on fire. I can only pray Lilly and the baby fled as far as they could. I sit back in despair, unsure of my fate, but knowing I made the right decision.

I have gotten as far from the house as my legs could take me, taking leaps with my wings that I am still adjusting to. I am thankful that Healer Vincent bought me some time. I gathered what I felt I needed, placing the flask in a bag. Holding my swollen belly I lean against a tree for support. I see in the distance, a glowing flame and in my shock I realize what it is. THEY HAVE BURNED DOWN MY HOME! I fall to my knees, shrieking in pain, as I feel a sharp pain in my heart. I think of Jaran. I know he will meet us at the assigned destination, then we can create our new home. The baby kicks in agreement and I smile. As long as we are together, that is all that matters. I have to survive at any means necessary. I spread my wings, covering my face while wrapping my baby for protection, as I take a leap into flight toward our new future.

CHAPTER 6

I t took me three long days to get back to Blood Oak. I stole a horse I had discovered while observing two lovers in the throes of passion and carnality in the nearby strawberry fields, much to my delight. I was relieved to be away from the Godforsaken woman whom I thought was going to kill me. Riding deeper into town I spotted several villagers who immediately recognized me. "OLD MAN NESBIT!" someone shouted. "OLD MAN NESBIT'S BACK! SOMEONE FETCH MAYOR CROWLEY!" A crowd started forming around me as Mayor Crowley made his way through the crowd. "Nesbit...Nesbit" he appears dogged and out of breath. "What has happened? Where are the Hunters? Is the demon dead?" All eyes are on me, anticipating my answer. "LOOK WHAT I HAVE DONE FOR MY PEOPLE! THAT FOUL BEAST HAS FALLEN BY MY HAND, AND MY HANDS ARE PAINTED IN HIS BLOOD AS PROOF OF MY HEROISM. BEHOLD, I HAVE KILLED THE DEMON!" I announced, as I raised my hands covered in blood that illuminated my glory. Truth be told, I had picked up the demon's head but dropped it once I saw its eyes still blinking. Fucking bastard scared the shite out of me.

The villagers cheered for me. "HE SAVED OUR TOWN, OLD MAN NESBIT IS A HERO!" They believed me, I think to myself with relief as the Mayor hushes the crowd. "On this day I declare Old Man Nesbit to be the new Healer of our town of Blood Oak!" a smug feeling arose in my body. I say to everyone "NO, MAYOR CROWLEY. TODAY I WILL NO LONGER BE KNOWN AS OLD MAN NESBIT, BUT RATHER AS HEALER ARTHUR NESBIT!!!" The villagers continue to cheer for me. Things are about to change for the better for me, about fucking time...

With my newfound authority, I am placed in the Mayor's estate temporarily, until I can get suitable accommodations for my own home. I am weary after my trip, as I am shown to my quarters in the guest house by this fetching, young house girl. Her command of the King's English is limited, suggesting her to be a primitive native of some lesser country. Still, even Godless heathens have their uses. As I study the girl's wide hips, long legs, and ample breasts, I decide she may as well be of use TONIGHT... The bed looks so inviting, as if she could do anything more than menial tasks for me, at least for now... I snicker as I close the door behind her.

It is now evening. The house girl leaves my room, crying as I lay in the comfy bed gleefully smiling and satisfied with yet another challenge met and conquered. I could definitely get used to living like this. What annoyed me however was having to cover the house girl's mouth in order to deep stroke in her creamy valley. It was also necessary to stop her incessant babble and lies, claiming that her copper skinned ancestors founded Blood Oak, and that my 'kind' appropriated the land through acts of barbarity. Pure poppycock it was, I tell you. It was, however, worth it when I finally reached my relief. She should have been honored to give herself to me, the selfish bitch. I am still in my thoughts, when I hear a knock at the door. Perhaps she thought better of her station and learning her place, came back for seconds. I smile, but it quickly fades into disappointment, as a portly house boy enters to inform me that the Mayor has returned, and that dinner is being served.

I enter the dining hall to a plentiful bombardment of food. GREAT ODIN'S BEARD!! I don't remember ever seeing this much of a spread before in my life. I see Mayor Crowley, he slapped his bear paw hard on my back, laughing and greeting me with a welcome, all the while with gravy and giblets running down his chin. This gluttonous fat fucker has been eating and living like a king! We proceed to be served our decadent meal, and he begins to explain to me the events that have occurred since my departure. I nearly choke on my food as he tells me that the mob burned down the home of the demon, Lilly and child being presumed dead, and Vincent Goodwind being hauled away to prison in chains, awaiting judgement.

Good fortune is smiling down on me! I am looking forward to visiting Vincent soon. The news of Lilly however, brings me a slight ping of sadness. I desired her so obsessively, as she was all I wanted. Ah well, at least that spawn child of hers is dead. Thank God. So there is a silver lining in the end, after all. I take my leave to retire to bed, as I have so many plans to work through my mind as I am embraced by sweet dreams.

It has been several days since I have been remanded in a cell. My only thoughts are of my wife and son. I hope and pray that they are well and safe. The chains are heavy on my wrist, as I attempt to lift the fork to feed myself the gruel that was given to me. After several tries, and carving deep cuts into my wrists, I decide to get on all fours and eat with my mouth. "Well well well, how the tables have turned..." I look up, hearing a familiar voice, as a lone figure steps out from the shadows. I see Nesbit. "Nesbit?" I whisper, adjusting my eyes, squirting as my glasses were taken away when I was taken. "Correction, it's Healer Arthur Nesbit now!" he smirks, wearing the white and red robes of a Healer. his skeletal fingers adorned with rings, and his lips turned up in disgust. I sigh; "What do you want, Nesbit?" he slams his hands against the cell bars startling me with the sudden act. "Mind your manners, Vincent. You shall address me as Healer Arthur Nesbit, or maybe I should visit your lovely wife. I'm sure SHE would know how to address me properly, on her knees!" The thought of him touching Candace brings my blood to a boil, but I will not give him the satisfaction of seeing my anger.

"What is it you want, Healer Arthur Nesbit?" a smile creeps across his sunken face. "Oh just to visit a dear friend who has found himself fallen on hard times." with a fake, insincere tone. Before I can retort, two guards quickly approach my cell, as Nesbit stands aside. "Vincent Goodwind, the Local Baker is terribly ill. She needs your healing tonics. Might you still have any with you?" None were discovered in your office, but it was confirmed to be one of the regular personal effects you are known to keep in your supplies." the guard stares at me intently. All I could do was lower my head and sigh. "YOU GODDAMN BASTARD, YOU GAVE IT TO THAT DEMON BITCH!!" I hear Nesbit spouting curses, as I close my eyes tightly, fighting back my tears. How could I have known that this was going to happen?

The guards gasp, not believing it all could be true. "HE'S A TRAITOR TO NOT ONLY THIS TOWN, BUT ALL OF

HUMANITY!!! HE MIGHT AS WELL HAD KILLED THE LOCAL BAKER WITH HIS BARE HANDS!" Nesbit continues to shout. They all leave swifty to report to the Mayor. Most likely I am to face punishment for my 'crimes'. I cry when I am alone, as my heart is heavy for my family, the local baker, and her daughter, Penelope. I am unsure of how much time passes, when a guard drops a bowl of gruel in my cell. "Eat up, you bastard traitor." he says to me. "The local baker is dead because of you, and your punishment is to be decided tomorrow. The charges are of treachery and murder." He leaves, and I hear the familiar slam of the dungeon door as I await my fate.

It was raining when my mother died. I remember thinking that God was crying with joy, welcoming her home into His arms. My tears lined my cheek as they fell from my eyes, and I found that I could not leave my home after she was placed in the ground. I wrapped her in her favorite blanket to keep her warm. I feared that she would need it in case her body caught a touch of the coldness. This gave me so much more sadness. I sit in the chair holding myself from falling apart gazing at the fireplace. William enters my sitting room with more wood to feed the flames. He started visiting me after my mother passed, helping me around the house, and even in the Bakery without me asking. His kindness has been a comfort.

I am so lost in my grief, but still, I manage to smile as he feeds me, saying that I need my strength.

My handsome William, how I have loved you, but never spoken from my heart. Now it is too broken into pieces for me to possibly present it to you. How can you love me now? "Healer Vincent's trial is tomorrow, and I am going to attend. He needs to see that there are still some sane people who believe in his innocence." he explains to me, smiling and running his fingers through my blonde hair. "I'll be back to check up on you after, Penelope." he gives me a gentle hug, and leaves. I draw my attention back to the flames of the fire. Healer Vincent; I think to myself, he must feel lost as well. I start to cry now for Healer Vincent.

The trial starts with the entire town in attendance, minus those who would prefer to tend to their own businesses. Mayor Crowley gives a formal speech, as he will hand down the sentence with a guilty or not guilty verdict to be established. Healer Vincent is escorted into the room. He looks so frail, as his clothes dangle on his body. The chains dangle, clanging together from his wrists. I hold onto my anger at this injustice being committed to a man I continue to admire. Mayor Crowley reads the charges against Healer Vincent and asks him how he pleads. He can barely lift his head. When he speaks, he answers "not guilty." and the room erupts with angry shouts, and insults. I am relieved that he has not given up hope, and I decide that I can't give up on him, either. Mayor Crowley bangs his gravel to silence from the room, that's when the so-called new 'Healer' addresses the crowd.

"Dear Villagers of Blood Oak, it is clear that Vincent Goodwind has conspired with demons bringing despair to our peaceful village, incurring the wrath of the Hunters." Disapproving sounds can be heard from the townspeople. "Even I, myself a simple man, was captured and the reason is because of this man." Nesbit says, pointing at Healer Vincent. "Mayor, I speak for not only myself, but also the noble people of Blood Oak. I demand swift justice!" He walks away taking a seat. I have just realized that a snake has spit poisonous venom into the soul of this village.

Mayor Crowley passes his decision "Vincent Goodwind, I, the Mayor of Blood Oak hereby sentence you to be hung by the gallows until your natural death. This execution will be carried out in three days." I hear a cry in the crowd as I see Healer's Vincent's wife running out of the room in tears. Healer Vincent looks up at the Mayor, accepting his fate as he is taken back to his cell. He glances at me with a small smile on his face. No, I think to myself, it can't end this way. I can't let this injustice happen. I have to save Healer Vincent.

Three days, I think. I would have sentenced him to death at that very moment. The quicker that sanctimonious shit is out of my proverbial hair, the better. I lean back in my easy chair with my hands finger-folded behind my head. The Mayor continues graciously to allow me to stay in his mansion after the trial. I will be considering where my new home will be in the meanwhile. This is the life I have always wanted, ever since my dear sweet Marianne departed from my life. She died from a mysterious illness. I had not the money to get her proper treatments, instead I had to rely on the meager resources of that fucking bastard, Vincent, who failed miserably to heal her. Oh, how much I've always despised him because of this, and his considerable natural damn talent as well. I clench my fists lamenting what I have lost. I suffered for a long time, but not anymore. I lick my lips at the thought of Vincent's death. I think I will go visit his grieving wife, Candace. Just the thought of her large breasts just begging to be suckled by me, is sweet enough to give me rotten teeth(if I still had any). Those child bearing hips waiting for me to grind in between them. Yes, I may have to pay her a visit, and then I think about that lovely Baker's daughter. Penelope, I believe her name is. Her mother was ugly as a horse's arse, but that daughter of hers with her supple rear, and pink suckable lips! Oh, what I could do with them! I could definitely put them to good use. Hee hee, I would love to pull those pigtails while pumping her hard from behind.

With my eyes closed, I start stroking my manhood. I hear the door creak open, and to my surprise, it is my sweet house girl. I discovered that her name is Alice Redwing. "Oh! I'm sorry Healer, I was just coming in to clean the office." she lowered her head. "Come in girl," I say with a stern, authoritative voice; "I want you to come here." She obeys, and walks over reluctantly. I didn't really look at her face at first, but she has curly black hair with hazelnut eyes, and her lips were pressed together but were full and sultry. Truly, she was something to desire. I stood up and placed my hands upon her shoulders. Her body is trembling as I touch it. I forcefully grab her by the back of her neck and bend her over the desk. She gasps, but with my free hand I place a finger to her lips, shushing her. "No screaming this time, my little Redwing bird..." I whisper as I lift her dress. I drilled myself into her as she muffled her screams into the decorative pillow I keep on the desk. I grab her hips digging my yellowing nails into them, and with my final thrust, I fill her with a generous portion of my liquid. I then grab her by her hair while I yell; "Now clean this off!" as I shove my semi erect cock into her sweet mouth.

I hear William returning as I am sitting in the chair holding myself. When I see him, he smiles. "Penelope..." he places his hands on my shoulders. "My God, you're freezing! I have to put more wood in the fire!" He then wraps me in a blanket. Kneeling in front of me, he says "Penelope, there is something that I have to do. I'm not sure if or when

I shall return. I need you to look after yourself, if the worst should happen..." He closes his eyes for a second. "I should have told you this the first time I felt it, but the whens and whys of it never aligned for us, so hear my words. I love you Penelope, and I'm going to come back for you, if possible." He kisses me on the lips. William leaves, and in that moment, I hear myself call out to him. "I love you too!" as I touched my lips. This was my very first kiss, and I am breathless.

The guards normally leave their post for infrequent breaks. I have been counting the time ever since the day of the trial, planning to free Healer Vincent, and today is the last day before his execution. I have to act fast now to get those keys. Pretending to be drunk, I bump into the guard, carefully swiping the cell key. I rushed to the prison. "Healer Vincent!" I whisper loudly as he lifts his head. "William? What are you-" I lift my hand and open his cell, with a finger raised to my lips. "There is no time to explain." I say as I unlock his cuff and lift him up, bracing his body against mine. We make our way to the wagon, which is located in the back of the prison. I place him in the back covering him with a blanket. Things had gone remarkably well, but before I could board and grab the reins, I heard; "Stop right there!!!" We are surrounded by guards, and I see Old Man Nesbit with his wicked smile. They grab Healer Vincent from the back of the wagon. I am placed in shackles and dragged to the town square. I'm sorry, Healer Vincent, I didn't make it in time. My last thoughts are of Penelope, my sweet Penelope. I'm so sorry, my love.

I was able to will myself from the chair and walk out of the house, feeling as if I am in a daze waking from a dream. I see villagers heading towards the town square. I don't know what awaits me, the first thing I see is the Sentinel of Blood Oak. He is a large man with broad shoulders, and a musculature built that might have been designed by Hephaestus himself, and sculpted by Michelangelo. He carries a great axe that is rusted with the blood of others that have met their ends on the edge of his gargantuan blade. The very sight of him is enough to send chills up my spine. Rumor has it that he was abandoned here as an infant, and was actually raised by Healer Vincent himself. That is when I see William, laying on a bench, his head on a chop block. No... He sees me, and for a moment we were locked in place, as if we were the only ones around, suspended in time. In a flash, I see phantom futures. I see lives we could have lived, our wedding night, our children, a boy for him, and a girl for me, and then, our golden years after a beautiful life together. I feel the tears well in my tear ducts, as time resumes, and I remember where we are. His lips move, saying; "I love you, Penelope. Be Strong." Then the blade swoops and strikes him, as I observe something so sick, so sad, so infinitely profound as the moment between when the love of my life existed, and when he did not. His head makes a collision with the dirt, staining the grass with blood that may never wash away. I hear myself screaming, drowning out the gasps and applause from the crowd. I fell to my knees. I have lost the love of my life, and with him, all my optimism for tomorrow. As I finally pull myself up to my feet, I head back to my home, not knowing what I shall do next.

With a heavy weight in my heart, I watch as the life of my young apprentice is snuffed out. I'm hurt, not angry. Hurt that this village I have tended and worked, not unlike a farmer on his field, has yielded such rotten fruit. Truly I see the time fast approaching that I must reap what I have sown. I mutter a silent prayer for poor William and poor, young, heartbroken Penelope. There will be suffering for a time. With a gruff voice I hear the gentleman known only as Sentinel, who only I know his true name, who turns his attention to me. "Vincent, formerly known as Healer Vincent, for conspiring with demons and their kind in the village of Blood Oak, You have been sentenced to hang until the end of your natural life. Have you anything to say on your behalf before your sentence is carried out?" the Sentinel asked with a pang of sadness and guilt.

Around the wooden elongated podium, the villagers have gathered, rich and poor, young and old. I hear the muffled tears, sobbing and weepings for me. Small children burying their faces in the bosoms of their mothers, who do not understand the events taking place, yet somehow can partake in the sense of dread I feel. The Sentinel places my head gently in the hanging noose, and tightens it ever so slightly. In the distance I see Mayor Crowley hanging his head in shame. He is but a pawn in these events, while the true culprit is somewhere skulking in the shadows. Most likely cackling with eerie delight at the death and mayhem he has deliberately caused. Yet, for all his wickedness, my deepest regret is that I was unable to save his precious Marianne. She was a noble soul, and Arthur was a good man for a time until he lost her. Mishandled grief can do powerful things when not given its due.

I step up to the central podium for what will be my final address to this village. In the distance I see Candace, my dear, sweet Candace. You have given my life more joy and purpose than any one man had any right to hope for. I only wish we had more time. With a chill in the air, I clear my throat as I feel the cloaked Spectre of Death slowly approaching the village square.

"People of Blood Oak, you all know me. Many of you I have hand delivered into this world. In many ways, I am not unlike the father of this village. I have-" I stopped as I felt myself choking back a heavy sob. Unable to dam the water that has long over welled in my eyes, streams of tears flow endlessly down my face. "I have loved all of you like my own children. Though I first came here as a youth at ten cycles, already I was well versed in the healing arts. Using my gifts to benefit the people of this land I called home." I locked eyes with the Mayor, who is now sobbing as powerfully as I am. "But you never forget your first baby, and I hope that wherever my soul travels to after I have departed, that you will not forget me, because I love all of you... so very much." My eyes leave the Mayor for just a moment, to turn to my focus on the Sentinel. So young, so strong, forced to carry out all the most unmentionable tasks that no one else in the village would dare to do. I feel for you truly, Alan, for the darkness that weighs on your own soul must be heavy, and soon...

"Soon..." I say, then turn to glance back at Mayor Crowley once more, only he is not there. Instead Nesbit stands there, leering at me with a wretched scowl upon his face. "That will be quite enough out of you, Goodwind. Justice must be served, and it is time for you to die. Fear not, for the demons and co-conspirators that loved you so very much will all be plentiful to greet you, in your reunion in HELL!!!" With that Nesbit pointed to the Sentinel and gave him the slightest of nods. I look in Alan's eyes and see an ocean trapped within them, threatening to flood his headgear at any moment. His eyes meet with mine as he whispers the last words that I will ever hear. He grasps the handle for the mechanism of the trap door of the podium. With a heavy sigh, he says "I'm so sorry... Daddy." and pulls the lever.

In a flash they see a suddenly jolting neck break, along with an audible snap. my soul drags out of my flesh and lands on the soil below. Next to me is the reaper itself, a tall, robed, hooded, skeletal figure. "Am I to go to Hell now? I am ready." Death shakes its head and with a low, softened, almost female voice says; "Vincent Goodwind, you have lived your life in service of others, not for material gains, but simply for the sake of good." With that, Death grabbed my hand, and the scythe and black robe vanished, revealing a beautiful, white winged, long brown haired angel. It lifted me into its arms, and we flew. I will miss my family here, but now it is time to begin my journey into eternity.

I stood in horror as my husband's body hung from the taut noose. It felt like a nightmare, one that I could not wake from. I returned back to our home where our son still peacefully slept. He was protected from the barbaric reality that his father would no longer be able to kiss him on the forehead every day. The tears stream down my face in multiple tracks that threaten to form rivers. Oh Vincent, how can I live without you...?

It was a bright sunny day as I walked back from the school house with my books in my hands, looking forward to another day. I saw Mayor Steven with a man whom I had never seen before. He had black hair and smiling grey eyes. I allowed myself a secret, silent chuckle when his glasses almost fell off of his nose. He wore a red and white robe, the official garment of a Healer. "Oh Candace," the Mayor waved at me. "This is the Fisherman's daughter, Candace Littlefield. She is one of our brightest young ladies here in the village of Blood Oak." I blush at his praise. "This is the new Healer, Vincent Goodwind. I'm showing him our fair town so he can acclimate himself." The Mayor pats Healer Vincent, who again, almost loses his glasses off his face. I can't help but giggle. "Well thank you Mayor Stevens, and it is nice to meet you Miss Littlefield..." he bows at me, flashing me with such a smile that it made my heart flutter.

It was after eight moons of courtship before Healer Vincent asked my father for my hand in marriage. I was overjoyed when my father agreed. Vincent became my other half, and I felt complete when our little Eugene was delivered into our lives. He became our miracle of love.

I continue to look down at Eugene, who is still resting, while my heart breaks. I wish Vincent was here and that is when I see a large kitchen knife on the table. I grab it, and quickly leave the house heading towards the town square. I scan the area and carefully approach my loving husband's body, still hanging. With the knife in my hand, I start cutting through the rope. I freeze when I sense a presence close to me. "Miss Goodwind, please drop the knife. I do not wish to satisfy my blade's thirst anymore today. As much as I am with a heavy heart, Daddy's body must remain in its current position." the Sentinel says. His enormous hand covers my trembling one handling the grip of the knife. "I must follow my orders at all costs. Your death would not give me pleasure, now please go home to your son, he still needs his mother." I dash quickly from his presence as I enter my house. Eugene has awoken. He cries as I hold him close to my chest, sharing in his tears.

I visited Candace and her baby son Eugene bringing them a loaf of bread each day since Healer Vincent and William's death. We found comfort in each other during our grief. Eugene always looks forward to seeing me, reaching out his chubby fingers at me. There is always a sense of joy when I see him as well. Candace finally asked me to live with them as she enjoys my company as much as Eugene does. I suggest that Candace become the new Local Baker as she makes much better bread than I. Candace agrees as it gives her a sense of purpose helping the town similarly to how her husband did. This new family seems to quickly settle into their new roles and eventually grief is replaced with a new love.

Vincent Goodwind's body hangs at the gallows for five days after his execution, with a sign nearby saying: 'THIS IS THE FATE OF ALL TRAITORS.' On the sixth day, the Mayor orders for the body to be thrown in an unmarked grave. He seemed morose as he made the request. However, it was strongly advised by Healer Nesbit. William's elderly mother approached the Mayor. "Mayor please, I beg you, may I give my boy William a proper burial?" The Mayor's body tenses at the memory of Vincent's last words before his death. Looking at this woman, he just nods without a word. He hangs his head and silently returns to his office.

The Sentinel has always been a quiet man keeping his own counsel, as his work gives him only stress which he could never share with another. At one time he had so much pride in his work, and the sense of justice he gave to his town. Since the death of Vincent Goodwind, the guilt eating at his soul each day and night, he decided he'd had all he could take. He watched his last sunset, and the next morning, his body was found swinging from the namesake tree of the village, the blood oak. Hammered to the tree was a sign that read only; 'MY RESIGNATION'. The great axe theSentinel once used was found a couple yards away, planted in the earth like a tree. None dared disturb it.

Two figures are seen barely visible in the moonlight, illuminated only by the reflecting incandescence. They began digging into the earth until they found the treasure they were searching for. They load it onto a small wagon and return from whence they came. Penelope, Candace, and Eugene stand in front of a freshly dug grave with a marker that reads; "Vincent Goodwind: Husband, Father, and Beloved Healer of the Village ". The women hold each other's hands and smile. Vincent had made a coffin for both he and Candace long ago, to ensure they would be buried together. This was his final gift. Eugene holds a bundle of wildflowers in his little hands, understanding that here lies his father's body. He misses him terribly, and places the flowers on his grave. Both of the women reach for his hands which Eugene glady takes. Walking back into the home for supper, they are thankful for the family plot they have established.

As the clouds loom over Blood Oak, I am overseeing a grand new undertaking. Too many of the men in this village have fallen, and we must not be afraid to be bold, to usher in a new era of splendor. The era... of Arthur. Long have I waited to see my enemies crumble at my feet. Those unduly blessed with what rightfully should have been mine. What, you may ask, do I deserve? Everything! I deserve it all. I deserve all the respect and adulation that was given to that pompous, self righteous, insufferable twit, Vincent Goodwind. Even the St. Peter's family were shamefully unaware of my greatness. Why, Lilly had the audacity to cringe at the mere thought of me granting her the honor of receiving my seed to bear my progeny. That shameful demon slut should have thrown her nakedness at the feet of one such as I.

No matter, this injustice has been rectified, even as we speak. The few men who are left in this cesspool of a town, are hard at work crafting what will hopefully be a palace. Yes, a palace, one that will come close to matching my new regality! The townsfolk weep for Goodwind. Blah! Let them cry!! He's gone, and at long last, everything that once was his shall forever be mine. I do mean EVERYTHING. His widow shall be mine as well. Will I marry her? Perhaps, if she manages to provide me with a suitable heir, then perhaps I shall grant her the slightest taste of my decadence. Of course the Goodwind boy will have to be shipped off to the poorest orphanage I can find, or left in the bloody streets to fucking starve.

It truly is a shame about Lilly, you know. Better if she had learned her place, and served her betters, but a fate more deserved befell on her. It matters not, during my travels with the mongrel Hunters, I have seen all manner of unnatural beasts. A body was not found in the fire so it is possible that she is still alive somewhere with that unholy spawn. However, any number of the scores of wolves, boars, or bobcats could make a swift meal of that pregnant whore by now. Well, youth is wasted on the young, and the young Penelope still has so much to offer within those child bearing hips. Ha ha ha, her nectar is likely far too sweet to have been saved for that boy, William. What she needs is to be molded by a man…

My estate was finally complete, as I took my first steps into my new mansion. I have built my legacy on the burning ashes of that bastard demon's property, as I smile to myself. If Lilly is somehow alive and is a good girl, maybe I will let her reside with me. If she is a good girl, that is. There is a downside to this new fucking position, waking up so damned early. How I still hate the mornings! I will have to speak to Mayor Crowley about switching to nightly duties, and shorter time spent in town, that is, if I can find that fat bastard. I prefer to be in my warm bed close to my new beloved.

"No Healer Arthur, Please, Please Stop!" Yes, this new house girl is a fighter. I struggle to hold her arms down and position myself to spread her legs. "Now, now, do what you are told, or it will hurt far worse." I stretch to reach the opening of my trousers. "I'd rather die!" she screams, loosens her arm from my grasp and smacks me across the face. My fury ignites. "YOU FUCKING BITCH! HOW DARE YOU RAISE YOUR FILTHY HANDS TO ME!" I yell, rubbing my face. "YOU SHOULD BE HONORED TO GIVE YOURSELF TO ME! KISSING MY FEET AND BEGGING FOR MY ATTENTION!" my cock has become flaccid. With her hand over her mouth, she giggles. Anger flares in my body. I grab her by her hair, her giggles now replaced with screams. I proceed to throw her out of my front door! she lays there with skinned knees, crying. "IF I EVER SEE YOU AGAIN, I WILL CUT YOUR WRETCHED TONGUE OUT, YOU CUNT!"

I slam the door behind me, adjusting my trousers while I walk towards the wine cellar to pour myself a strong drink. Fucking Whore! Damn women don't know of the blessing to be with a noble man such as myself. I calm my nerves by taking a swallow of my drink, as I look out the window, overlooking the grave of Gwendolyn St. Peter.

During my time with that asshole fraud Vincent, I learned much about herbs. He showed me the healing and restorative properties of them, and their many uses. Now this was boring shite to me, but there was one lesson that stood out. It was a preservative potion. With the proper blend of myrrh, cinnamon, and anise herb, a rotting body can be restored. I lean over and caress the body of my new beloved Gwendolyn. She may not be as lovely as when she was alive, but she is mine. I will preserve her body for as long as my desire requires. I smile before I begin yet another session of our love making.

CHAPTER 7

I feel as though I have been flying forever. My stomach starts to grumble. I begin to feel my swollen belly as it appears the baby is hungry as well. I land on a nearby tree, pulling the cloth from underneath my nose. I find myself leaping from tree branch to tree branch gracefully, until I see further off in the distance, a wild boar grazing in the field. It marvels me how much my sight has improved since my transformation. I have never hunted an animal before, I do wish Jaran had taught me before we had separated. How I miss him, yet the pain in my stomach jolts me back to the present moment. How hard can this be? I just have to be faster than the boar. As I spread my wings, I approached from above as I dove towards my prey. My instincts kick in as my toes on my enlarged feet spread and extract pointed talons, which I sink deeply into its supple flesh. I violently thrash and tear away the flesh of the wild beast, gnashing away at the uncooked, tusken swine. It had stopped moving, and I stood back to witness my first kill. I hungrily continued to devour the meat, savoring the flavorful blood with each bite I had taken. I recall back when I was human, I felt disgusted by craving meat raw and bloodied, but now I am truly a new being, as it clearly no longer bothers me.

I look up from my meal. With my keen eyesight, I spot a pair of men in a wagon riding up along the dirt road that is near the field I am now located in. At this distance I would not make it back to the trees in time and I would easily be spotted if I took flight. I can not afford the Hunters finding us, so I must remain hidden. I crouch down in the field next to my kill, which is little more than bones now. The grass is tall enough to shield my presence. "You will never guess who killed a demon." I hear the driver saying. "Who would that be? Only a Hunter can perform such works." the passenger replies. "Well listen up you fool! Do you remember Old Man Nesbit from Blood Oak?" the passenger only nods. "He killed a demon. In fact, he killed the very one what was plaguing their town, he did. I hear he is the new Healer too, though that bit of scuttlebutt is a wee bit suspect, what with him having no formal medical training and all. A shame to hear about Vincent Goodwind though..." The wagon continues down the road as I hear their voices in the distance.

My heart is racing in my chest. Jaran, slain? I feel my bloodlust rising as I smash my taloned hand on the carcass of the wild boar, its bones becoming dust with the earth. All I can do is howl in my loss of my mate and remember the stabbing pain I felt in my chest on the night I was fleeing Blood Oak. It didn't dawn on me that the feeling was because our mate bond was severed. I feel for the mark he gave me when we first mated. I frantically searched for it. The mark is gone. Jaran is gone.

The cold breeze caresses my face as I sob for my beloved mate. Then the cold realization comes to me, as I remember what the man had said about Healer Vincent. He gave his life for us, I thought to myself as I touched my belly. I howl again in deeper agnony. What am I going to do now? I've lost my home, my dear friend, and the love of my life. I hear the ocean waves, and contemplate allowing them to wash my baby and I away to a new home where none may recognize us. I fly towards a cliff bracing the edge, peering over the crash of the waves at the bottom, are broken spikes below. I remember Jaran's story of the Peak of Destiny, maybe this is my fate to join my mate into the unknown. I take a few steps closer to the edge and I close my eyes.

All I know is that I cannot tolerate being alone again. I take another step closer. "No, Mommy..." I open my eyes, fall to my knees, and hold onto my belly. After all I have endured, this is my mindlink with my daughter, at last. "Live, Mommy..." she says to me, as tears stream down my face. "I love Mommy..." I am so happy... she must have been learning speech through Jaran and I since developing within me. I will, little one. For you, I will live on. I stand and take flight, heading east to the cave that Jaran spoke of. It will have to be our new home for now.

I located the secluded cave only because of Jaran's scent. He must have known this day would come, where we could no longer reside in Blood Oak. I unload what I had carried when I fled, which was not much, but I knew the sparse belongings I selected would give me much needed comfort in the days to come. The hunger soon washes over me, remembering that the boar was merely a snack. I will have to hunt for bigger prey if I am to survive. At first I was reluctant to kill, but realizing that this new strength was inside of me made it easier for me to hunt. It's almost funny how much I have always relied on others to have my needs met. It's only now that I have someone whose needs I must meet, that I'm finally learning to stand on my own two feet. I guess I'm stronger than I ever realized. There seems to be plenty of wild deer in the forest, as I stalk the biggest one. It is fast, but I'm much faster and stronger, taking it down with ease. I love this feeling! The thrill of the kill is truly exhilarating, and I start to look forward to it each day. The hunger reminds me that I am alive, which keeps me motivated. As my daughter's birth fast approaches, I need to feed more to ensure she and I are both healthy. I do not know what will happen after she is born.

The nights in the cave are cold, even as I wrap myself in my blanket. I can still smell Jaran's lingering scent. He who once loved my body within this blanket. Even through the coldness I smiled, our love making at that time had increased tenfold mostly because of my newfound urges. Then I remember something from the time of my Purge, the blue flames that came from within my body. I close my eyes and concentrate on the thought of the blue flames. I open my mouth as I feel the flame forming from my throat and mouth. I finally open my eyes, they are right above me, dancing in the air in front of me. I use loose branches, grass, and straw to create a fire before me. I begin to become warmer and sense that inside, the baby is sleeping. I was hoping to speak to her through our mindlink, but her rest is more important. Thankfully with the blue light of the fire, I can see the cave more clearly.

With the interior of the cave now properly illuminated, it was easy to see why Jaran had chosen these meeting grounds to start our new lives. The inner walls of the cave stretched as high as the eye could fathom. With the glow of the blue flame, which looked almost sea green, I saw the entrance of the cave. It was like a gaping maw, with stalagmites forming a sort of row of teeth along the roof of the entrance. It looks a bit unsettling to be sure, but it functions as an excellent deterrent for any potential predators seeking shelter from the elements. A perfect place to keep my baby safe, at the very least I know that here I could protect her. Upon examination of the cavern floor I discovered a narrow sliver of broken stalagmite. If need be, this could easily be fashioned into a weapon.

I spread my wings and leap gracefully, swooping from the mouth of the cave into the open air. The feeling of freedom is so liberating! Suddenly, I happened upon something that made me come to a screeching halt. There, upon a large tree was a set of claw marks. four claws to be specific, vertically marking the tree in formation. I was learned in nature enough to know that this was a territorial mark. I haven't a clue what manner of beast it could be, but if it wanders to my cave looking for a fight, all it will find is death. Choosing to err on the side of caution, I drifted back into my gorgeous shelter to retire for the night.

When I was not hunting for prey, I was spending my time mindlinked with my daughter. It gave me comfort that she could understand and speak to me, if only briefly in spurts. She needed her rest more lately, due to her approaching birth. A string of sadness pulled at my heart.

"Mommy sad?" I know she can sense my emotions as well, so I am careful with my next thoughts. "No my precious one, Mommy is tired." I hear her saying; "I Love Mommy!" she giggles, and her voice is sweet and angelic. I hug my belly, sensing that she feels my love in return. I wrap us in the blanket and begin to hum a lullaby to her, the same song my mother used to sing to me. When I know she is fast asleep, I am able to relax, as I drift off to a deep slumber.

"My God, you're going to kill me, Lilly!" Jaran growls, licking the nape of my neck.

"Well, this is the most comfortable position for me." I reply as I lean back to kiss him deep on the lips. "You know that's not what I'm talking about." he sternly says, and I giggle as he swats my rear with his tail. "Ouch! Not so rough, my love!" We both end up laughing on the bed, embracing each other. I finally break the silence. "Between my increased appetite and mood swings, you being inside of me helps to calm me down. I always need you near." He strokes my hair as I yawn and stretch. "I've been thinking of a name for our daughter. What do you think of Angela?" He stares at me expressionless and silent, blocking me from his thoughts. "Jaran...?" He does not answer me. "Jaran!" I look at him with bloodlust and fangs bared. His face looks so calm, as he caresses my face. "Lilly, I do not think we should name her until she is born. A birth of this nature has never occurred in our kind." He sees the look of concern across my face. "I need to ensure that you both can survive. I don't want to lose either of you during the birth. I will be there. Since the baby will continue to feed from your life essence, you will be very weak and will likely die in the process, but..." he kisses my nose. "I won't let that happen." I press my lips together thinking, what if you are not there? I shake my head, refusing to speak those words into existence. Jaran places his arms around me, feeling my tears on his chest and rocking me to sleep. I had a beautiful night's sleep with just the three of us.

I awake from my dream hearing the pouring rain outside the cave. The wind has picked up as well, I smell it in the air. Flying in the rain is a challenge, which is why I normally avoid hunting during precipitation, remaining in the safety of the cave. However, my hunger was savagely racking my body with pain to the point of my head throbbing. I willed myself through the pain. My body ached with insatiable craving, as I took flight to search for my prey. I killed six deer viciously tearing through the forest. I was so teemed with meat I gorged myself in, that I could only waddle into the cave. For the first time since after Jaran's death, I laughed so much I cried, holding my sides, and I heard my daughter's laughter as well.

I shrieked when I felt a sudden spasm. A shooting pain from deep within was knocking my body to the ground of the cave. I was thankful as I had finished hunting for the day, but the pain I was experiencing, I was not anticipated. I keep reminding myself to not be scared. I have to be brave for the baby and Jaran. It's what he would have wanted. I braced against the wall of the cave, lowering myself as I felt one of my ribs shatter. I claw at the ground, crying. Over my sobbing, I hear another crack. My wings fully expand with another sudden painful jolt. My feathers begin to rapidly fall from my wings. I feel her claws pressed against the inside of my stomach. I sense that she is afraid, and she knows that she is hurting me. I breathe as calmly as I can. "Baby, it is okay. Push as hard as you can. You're almost here."

I wail and wail, until in one forceful tear, she bursts from my stomach. I pant heavily realizing my fangs have fallen out of my mouth. My hair is falling out as well. So, this is how it feels to die? I try to focus on her as much as I can. My breathing becomes shallow. She is so beautiful, with blue skin like the sky. What a miracle Jaran and I have created. Then there is nothing but light, and a soft hand and feminine voice beckons me. I am finally on my way home, but first a final word. A name.

"Angel..."

ACT 2...

CHAPTER 8

A somber shadow and gray clouds loom over the quiet little village of Blood Oak. The whistle of a strong wind can be heard twisting through the sleepy settlement. Intertwined with the howling of the late night winds, the creaking sound of agonized moans stretched as far as an ear could follow. Storm clouds could be seen on the horizon, a bad omen for the local farmers to be certain. The undertaker's home however, has decidedly different energy. For as all the people of Blood Oak are aware, the undertaker's business is dealing in death, and for him business has been very, VERY good. Outside of the undertaker's home can be seen a long grey tarp. Underneath that tarp was a collection of caskets of varying shapes and sizes. Yet despite the sounds and energy throughout the village, there was not a soul to be seen, at least not in the town square.

If one were to follow the trail leading from the square to the hills, where the wealthier inhabitants of Blood Oak reside, it is likely one could ascertain the epicenter of all the malaise and melancholy. In fact, it is at one of the Blood Oak residences, the home of Arthur Nesbit, Healer of Blood Oak, that a rather large crowd of citizens have gathered. At the front door of this newly established manor, atop the stairs leading to the entrance stood a lone, decrepit, warped, and deviant figure. This figure is none other than the Lord of the keep, Healer Arthur Nesbit, who is none too pleased at the moment; in fact, one could say he was absolutely inflamed.

"Begone from my doorway peons! I have naught to say for you and your ilk!" he declares, pointing a gnarled, withered claw back in the direction of the town square. One meek voice dared to break the hushed silence of the panicked mob. "Arthur, I really must insist you do SOMETHING about this plaque that has infected Blood Oak! It is your duty... !" Mayor Crowley pleaded. Indeed a plague had entrenched itself into the catacombs of the town, There had been tens upon tens of bodies discovered in a matter of weeks. In fact, the bodies were found to be practically skeletal, thought to be a result of the food shortage that came about once Nesbit had his estate built upon what was once the St. Peter farm. Alas, it has since proven to be an illness, a malady that threatens both the strong and weak alike. Disease cares not if you are rich or poor. Not even Mayor Crowley himself was immune, as his once morbid obese frame is now withered and emaciated.

Arthur scowled. "Bah! Perhaps had you bestowed these riches upon me sooner, I'd have been able to order the supplies to create the poultices needed to combat this dastardly illness. Now all we can do is wait until either the necessary supplies become available, or the Gods choose to be merciful. Now then, BEGONE!!" he said. As he prepared to turn his back on the deathly ill mob, one young woman stepped forward, clutching what appeared to be a pregnant belly. With a withered hand, she pointed at Arthur. "Perhaps we hung the wrong man!" she shouted, stirring up the group. Immediately, Arthur recognized her. "Lowly house girl! How DARE you?! Would you rather hang a righteous man, and blame him for your own folly?!! He was consorting with demons, and Vincent got what he deserved! Yes, now that I think of it, you DID love Healer Vincent, DIDN'T YOU?!!" Nesbit again pointed at all of the people. "I see this for what it truly is.. It is not a plague, but a CURSE!!! A curse of Divine Punishment upon all of you who wept for that evil charlatan. The Lord counted each tear shed for that shell of a man, and will take ten lives for each one. Now for the last time, BEGONE!! Trouble me no longer!! You all deserve your fate!! Hahaha." He laughed to himself as the people gasped in horror. "YOU MONSTER!!" Alice Redwing screamed. "What about our baby?! Does your own flesh and blood deserve this?" she asked, as a hushed gasp fell over the crowd. Arthur sneered and replied; "Rotten fruit from a rotten tree..." and closed his front door, abandoning the suffering people of Blood Oak.

The crowd disperses from the front of Healer's Nesbit's estate, muttering and cursing under their breaths. The house girl Alice is the last one still standing there looking up at the Healer's home, tears streaming down her young face as she holds her swollen belly. The day she discovered she was with child was the worst day of her life. She knew it was Healer Nesbit's child as he was the first and only man she had ever been with. She shuddered at the memory of how he violently stole her virtue, not giving one drop of concern to what he had done. Her father warned her many times that a suitable husband must know when to be loving, when to provide, and when to prove his worth as a true warrior. The Healer could do none of those things.

"Clean that up!" he said, with a look and tone of disgust. Alice had done what she was told. Once she was finished he proceeded to violate her again, as was his customary behavior. For most of the day, this was an endless cycle, until he passed out from exhaustion. April was so ashamed when Mayor Crowley discovered her condition. Believing that he would throw her out penniness, and with no family to speak of for help, she begged the Mayor to show mercy. To her surprise, instead he looked at her with a sad smile, and gave her new duties to be performed in his manor, that were less physically demanding. She would always be grateful for his kindness. On that day, she promised she would love her child unconditionally. As she now thinks of those thoughts, with a heavy heart she may not be able to keep that promise due to the arrival of the plague. Alice reached into her pocket satchel where she kept her needle and thread. She pulled out a small wooden totem of a bird. It was the Redwing falcon, the spiritual protector of her family. She said a silent prayer of protection. Her child would not survive very long in this cruel world, she feared.

Since leaving the cave, I flew as far as my wings could possibly take me before the hunger pangs set in my body. The prey in this land was much larger than what I was accustomed to, but I had gotten faster and larger myself. I am standing in front of my reflection, noticing the changes in my body. My horns, tail, and wings had gotten longer and these large mounds on my chest were new as well. I squeeze them, and my body gives a pleasurable sensation, reacting to my touch, and a wetness comes from between my legs. I can not help but smile, seeing that my fangs have gotten longer and sharper as well.

I found a new dwelling after one of my hunts. My prey was so frightened that it injured itself running headfirst against the dwelling areas. After finishing my meal, I proceeded to go inside. It was a small space. It felt familiar, so I decided on that day I would call this home. Besides the clothing on my body, which was beginning to tear when I had gotten bigger, there was my mother's ring and this strange clear vessel with a strange liquid inside of it. The liquid does not smell like blood. I am hesitant to taste it, as if it was on my mother's person, then it is very important. My mother, I heard her voice while I was within her. It is because of her that my thoughts are quicker. However I wish to know so much more.

I was flying, searching for a new prey to hunt, when I noticed a prey. As I landed, what I saw looked like me but it's flesh was pale and light colored. On its head was dark hair, and its eyes were the color of the fields where I hunted. I hissed, baring my fangs, preparing to attack. This strange prey did not react like my other prey. The prey held out what appeared to be clawless hands and moved its lips. I opened my mouth to attempt to mimic the sounds the prey made. I knew this to be speech from the time I had spent mindlinked to my parents. I therefore knew and recognized several words, although I was not yet comfortable trying to converse. The prey covered it's head and I saw blood pouring out of the openings of its face. I covered my mouth in shock. I caused a living being harm without touching or feeding from it. Something inside of my mind reached out to my prey, and then I heard it.

"Oh my Goddess, that was a painful shriek! I wonder if she knows that she can not speak?" This 'she' that he spoke of, was it me? The prey wipes the blood away from its face and I hear; "Hello." and I reply; "Hello." He has a shocked look upon his face. "I can hear you! Oh my Goddess! This is how your kind speaks to one another?" he continues to ramble on like this for a while. What a strange prey this is… I ponder to myself as I tilt my head back and forth, confused. After a while, I say; "my 'kind'? Your 'kind'?" He stops himself, and walks a little bit closer. "I'm sorry, let me introduce myself. My name is Jason of the Owl Talon Coven."

"Jason… Jason!!!" I awoke from my nap, "Did you hear the question I asked Jason?" the headmaster asks while tapping on his desk. I yawn. "I'm sorry, no sir." He narrows his eyes at me. "What is the combination spell for the transformation of the third degree of elements?" he asks with a smirk, assuming that I will not have the correct answer, and be swiftly punished. I roll my eyes and with my hands I conjure the correct binding element. To the surprise of my classmates and the frustration of my headmaster, who is so red, I think he could breathe fire at any moment. I yawn again as the bell signals the end of the school day. I am so advanced that sometimes I surprise myself. It may have looked as if I was being disrespectful, but I am a fifth generation Warlock, and the question was child's play to me.

Let me explain. In the Owl Talon Coven, you must adhere to strict rules, one such mandate being advancing the knowledge of the craft is forbidden, unless approved by the Council. I follow the doctrine more or less, but there are things in this world that I want to grasp with my mind. It is far too taxing to wait on boring approvals. My other studies keep me up late hence my exhaustion. However, I knew I would hear about my behavior in class sooner than later. I was in the library surrounded by towers of books, when a guard approached me. "Jason, your presence is requested by the Council." I peer up from my books, thinking this is not good. I stand up gingerly, to ensure not to knock over the books, and follow him to my unknown fate.

The Council consists of three OLD but wise men, all with white long beards, and very different demeanors. I have been in their presence twice. Once to congratulate me on my advancement of the craft, and the second time, to remind me of my rank(or lack thereof) in the hierarchy of the coven. I have a feeling that this third meeting will not end well. "Jason, it has come to our attention that you continue to disregard the rules of the school..." one of the Councilmen says while stroking his beard, as the other two nod in agreement. "I knew your father before he died, and you seem to be a bright young Warlock, with so much potential. Yet, you lack the discipline to follow or recognize authority. Due to this revelation, we, as the Council of the Owl Talon Coven expel you as a rogue. May you find your way through this life in another path."

A rogue is someone who is either casted out by their clan, coven, or pack by either a high authority, or given death of the said authority. Either way, you are cast down as a lesser being by everyone. I stand there feeling relieved. Honestly, I never felt that I truly belonged here, but it is where my ancestors established their roots and built our history. "You have my deepest apologies for any behavior if I have offended the Council, or this coven." I humbly bow to them, but before I am casted out as a rogue, I turn to face the Council once more. "I ask to keep the title, which has always remained a part of my father, and his father's father before him. "The Council looks towards each other using a mind link to communicate. I'm sure they are quickly coming to a decision. "We respected your father. He gave so much to this coven in ways you may never fully understand. We will grant your request. Take the title, and from this moment forward, you are branded a rogue. With that, I felt the mark of the claw on my neck dissipate, and I left the Owl Talon Coven

I was ensured that I would be able to bring all of my belongings. The best thing about being a warlock, is the power to conjure without all the mess of carrying anything. Now I needed to figure out where my new path would lead me. I headed west and settled near an unknown town and established suitable lodgings for myself. Knowledge is what I sought, and with my travels before I reached what would be my final destination which I carried within plenty. There were things I had to protect myself against, namely Hunters. This meant I had to hide my magical presence, and cast an illusion barrier spell. My nights were spent researching my new favorite topic, demons. They fascinated me. To know that such a being existed at one time. I just needed to know more about them. I was heading home from town, where I purchased some interesting reading material, as well as other supplies. That's when I felt a strong aura presence from above. I didn't look up, and continued to walk the road. That's when I saw her falling from the sky, landing so gracefully in the distance.

I couldn't breathe for a second, as she was so beautiful she took my breath away. No beauty did not do her justice as an adjective. Her blue skin was like the ocean, her hair was as red as the sweetest cherries, and her body was like nothing I had ever seen before. I could have ran, but I was too in awe of this breathtaking creature. I could only reach for her, listlessly wandering in the trail of her aura, until I found the prize that I sought. Face to face, "Hello." is all I could say. That is when she opened her mouth and a wailing shriek is the only thing I heard.

I instantly covered my ears, feeling the blood rushing from my nose. Suddenly, I hear a voice in my mind. "Hello." I heard her lovely voice for the first time. I am so excited beyond everything that has led me to this moment. Then I hear; "Your kind? My kind?" I introduce myself as she sniffs me. I assume this is to make sure I am safe.

It was a first step, and I was thankful she had not killed me. I persuaded her to follow me, which was a little difficult when she clawed my hand. So I reached out to her with my mind. "You come with me. Jason is a friend." I point to myself. "Friend, Jason." she replies. "Yes" and I reach again for her hand, this time she places her clawed hand in mine. My home is not far from where we are. Upon arriving, she enters my home in a state of alert. She seems to wander around, touching items, she seemed curious, and excited, as she squealed with excitement with each new object. It was a breath of fresh air to witness.

The first thing we do is sit on the floor, as she appears more comfortable this way. When I introduced her to a chair, she sat down feet first, and broke it into pieces. She seemed so sad and confused, attempting to put it back together. I reassured her that it was okay and with a snap of my fingers I fixed the chair. She looked at me in amazement. I am guessing I am the first human she has ever come across, which is a good thing. "I am Jason," I say, pointing to myself "and you are?" I point to her and she replies; "I am friend." I laugh and she laughs. It seems as if she does not have a name. Well, I will have to give her name as well. After some thought, I say in our mindlink; "I am Jason, and you are Angel." as I point to her. "You are Jason, and I am Angel." she finally says; "Yes yes..." and I instinctively hug her without thinking. She hugs me back. "Hungry, Jason." she says, and I pull back from her, but our faces are so close. "I can get you food." and I attempt to stand up, but before I can do so, she says; "No food, you food."

I barely had time to react to her words when Angel pulled me into a kiss. I have never been kissed before, but I suddenly realized what she was trying to do. She is feeding from my life force! With what strength that I could muster, I pull back and she gazes at me with those beautiful blue eyes. I grab an apple and say to her; "This is food. Jason is NOT food!" She lowers her head and quickly takes flight, leaving my home, and shattering my window in the process. A pity, that. I had just repaired that window myself after an incident involving a levitation spell and a serving of mutton. I call out to her, but she is already flying away. All I can do now is question, what have I done?

I almost killed Jason, he tasted so delicious! He was like nothing that I have ever eaten. Nothing has tasted this good. I could have killed him. When I entered his dwelling, there were so many items that felt and smelt different. It was overwhelming. I will soon return to him, but first I must hunt so I will not be so tempted to feed on Jason again. I found a deer grazing. This would be just the right kind of meal to satiate my hunger. I head back to retrieve my belongings and travel back to Jason's dwellings. I had decided once I 'mindlinked' as he called it, that I wanted to be and know everything about him and his kind. I felt so much from him and I am determined not to be alone anymore.

I stood outside waiting, hoping she would return. "Damn It!" I shout out loud. "Why did I have to frighten her away? What if I never see her again? STUPID!!!" I was getting frustrated. After a brief meal, I fell asleep wondering about my Angel. I woke to a starling sound from the other room. I instantly conjured a spear, prepared to defend myself from a wild beast. As soon as I entered the room, I dropped it. There was Angel standing in the room with a book in her hands. "Hello." she smiled, and I ran into her arms embracing her. "Angel!!! You came back!" I was so filled with mirth that I ALMOST forgot why she left in the first place. Almost. "Angel, before any more pleasantries, we must set some ground rules. You can feed on me, but please do not leave me again..." I was surprised when she said; "No Jason, you are not my food. I will find other food." Her command of speech and language had increased exponentially since when we first met. Angel was truly an amazing being.

From that night, I taught her any and everything that she displayed interest in. This consisted of nearly all of the thousands of books I had in my personal library. One book that I shared with Angel was actually a tome about demon subclasses, which was new to my library. Together, we studied until we reached the chapter on Incubi/Succubi. Angel viewed in shock as she saw an image of a succubus that appeared nearly identically to her. The book only gave a few details of these demons, due to their near extermination at the hands of Hunters. She remembered reading about Hunters and I could feel her bloodlust build, until I placed my hand on hers. I had a way of calming her, which she appreciated so much especially now.

"You are far more than just a succubus, Angel." I say, pulling out a scrying ball. "And how do you figure that?" she asks. She is more interested in what I will do with the mystic object. "I can show you better than tell you." I say, holding the ball near her body as essence filled the sphere. Within it our aura bursts forth as Angel looks on in amazement. The first aura was blue which was Angel's life essence from her succubus side. The second was yellow, I explained this was her life essence of a human. Angel appeared amazed at this discovery. The last was green, and I was puzzled by this aura as I had never experienced such a darkness of green aura.

"I have to ascertain what this means." removing the scrying ball from her body, I then frantically ran into my study. Angel walks to the entrance where more mounds of books lay spread across several shelves. She has never entered my study for feeling this is more of a place of personal privacy. I have already delved into my many books, conjuring more with a wave of a hand. Angel smiles knowing even speaking to me will not halt my research. She leaves me, closing the door, for she has studying to do on her own. Pulling up a comfy chair which has become her new favorite item in my home, she grabs a book and begins.

Once the craving took over, she knew she had to feed, stretching her body and she realized that she had maintained that same position since sunset. Checking on Jason, who is reading and mumbling to himself. She found he was absorbed in his books. Not wanting to disturb him, she left to hunt. Angel had promised Jason that she would not hunt humans, to keep the Hunters at bay, disguising their presence. She read about how Hunters were relentless, and if they could kill her kind, how could she defend against their attacks? For five days, Angel returned to the home and each day Jason remained in the study. It was not until Angel returned on the sixth day, she saw Jason entering the sitting room. He was fragile looking, and obviously had not eaten or slept.

Jason dragged his weakened body to Angel. "Angel..." his voice was hoarse and barely a whisper. "I've found the answer!" he uttered, holding out a scroll, as he walked towards her and suddenly fell into her arms. "Oh Jason" as she caressed his face. Before he can speak, Angel compels him to rest. Angel had read in one of the many books that this was a gift that her kind could wield. With the correct focus of thoughts, Angel carries Jason to his bed to rest. She heard him whisper; "My Angel..." which brings a smile to her face.

Jason awakens several days later. During his moments of rest Angel fed him from her own life essence to heal him, which she learned she could do from her readings. "Angel!" he almost leaps out of the bed, but stumbles instead. Angel appears in the entrance of his bedchamber after waking herself. "Jason I am happy you are well now." she mindlinks. After making breakfast, Jason explains what he discovered. Angel is also a descendant of the Harpy race which existed one thousand cycles ago. However, sadly their kind were completely exterminated by the Hunters. "Then how is it possible that I am part of such a race?" she asks as the curiosity slowly builds in her, as she attempts to remain calm. Jason continues to explain that he has not found the answer, but surely he will. Sternly Angel links to him. "You will not exceed your limit as you did before. You were almost at death's door. Promise!" she 'yells' with tears in her eyes. Jason stares at her, "Promise!!" she repeats, her voice booming in his head. "Yes Angel, I promise." Jason swears as he nods his head. He has never seen her this angry before, but he is thankful because it meant that she cared. He cared for her as well.

"There is something I need to show you..." she grabs his hand leading him into the room.

"I have learned a new gift that is called 'shifting'." Jason was impressed that her appetite for knowledge has grown since meeting him eight moons ago. Standing in the room, Angel closes her eyes and Jason can feel the change in the air of the room. Before his eyes, Angel's horns, tail and wings withdrew within her body. Her blue skin becomes a flush, cream color. Then her claws are replaced with fingers and toes. Jason is astonished, as Angel now appears to him as a human. She opens her eyes. He is lost in her beautiful blue eyes. "How do I look?" Such a question can not be simply answered. "My Goddess, you are speaking to me!" Jason is stunned. She giggles; "Yes, I realized I could do this as well, when I first shifted while you slept!" she smiles.

"I need you to tell me, do I have the body of a normal human female?" She walks slowly towards him, and begins to lift the dress from her body. Jason can only stare at this beautiful woman. She still has red hair and blue eyes, but her body was so voluptuous. He touches her shoulders, and back and is instantly drawn to her soft breasts. As he squeezes, she lets out a soft moan and Jason feels his arousal, but continues to examine her. Each part of her form from her rear to her toes as he touches, she reacts to each touch he gives her. "Jason?" she says in a seductress voice, "what about right here?" She opens her legs to expose her lovely mound. He brushes this most sensitive area and sees the wetness dripping from her entrance.

Instinctively he sticks two fingers within her, they slide effortlessly into her walls welcome embrace. She groans as he pushes further. He thrusts deeper in her with his other hand holding her hip, while he kisses her stomach. Jason feels her tremble and climax and withdraws his fingers, which are now drenching with her juices and light traces of blood. She stands up with lust in her eyes and a blush on her beautiful face, she breathes heavily. He lifts and cradles her in his arms, and walks toward the bedchamber. He has never been with a woman before. He takes off his clothes after he lays her on his bed. They kiss until both of them are breathless, she wraps her arms around his neck.

"Angel, this will be both of our first encounters..." he nervously says. "Are you sure you wish to go further?" "Yes!" she says in a husky, excited voice which builds his cock to full form. In one full thrust he penetrates her womanhood as they both scream in unison. This powerful moment rocks both of them to their cores. The ecstasy filled both of their bodies. After climaxing together they fell asleep and lie embraced in each other's arms. They no longer were lost, but found each other at the end of the same path, a path that moves ever onward.

CHAPTER 9

I cannot believe that she is lying here next to me, as I brush hair from her face. When the sun rose, it was as if a flower bloomed in my heart. I could not take my eyes off of her. Angel's arms were wrapped around my body. I'd never rested so soundly before. I planted a kiss on her peaceful face. Her grip tightened around me, so it appeared she still had her true strength as a succubus, even in a human form. During our readings together, I knew that a succubus had the natural instinct to mate, and maybe I triggered something in her human form. I was aware of the incubi and succubi shifting ability, but I still did not know the limits of the power she has. She is still young, but with time together we can figure that out.

When I open my eyes, Jason is looking down at me smiling. I knew I had to reveal my human form to him. The first time I shifted, I was amazed that I could focus myself during the transformation. It pleased me to see my human body, especially when I touched myself. A wave of excitement shook through my new form. The most sensitive area of my breasts and my core were more pleasing to me than I had realized. I decided that I wanted Jason to give me those same sensations. Jason did not disappoint me. I returned his smile. "Good morning Jason." as I placed a kiss on his inviting lips, while I felt a moan escape from mine.

Angel decides to remain in her human form, and Jason does not object to her decision. They both share a meal together, with Jason not being able to keep his eyes off of her. "If you don't eat your food it will get cold." Angel says, smiling at him. Jason feels like if he blinks she will disappear. "Oh, I know.. Hmm, I just have so many questions." as he lifts his food to his mouth chewing thoughtfully. "I understand, and I will explain all of it to you in due time." She stands and walks over to him. "Until then, let's make love again..." He raises his brow in surprise as she lets her dress slide around her frame and fall to the floor.

Angel was on her knees while Jason remained in the chair. She gave him a lustful smile. With her hands, she pulled down his trousers, revealing his already erect manhood. His eyes are wide open as Angel places it in her warm, wet, welcoming mouth. Jason throws his head back as he moans. Where did she learn to do this, and so WELL?? He becomes lost in that thought, as she moves her hand up and down his shaft. Her rhythm increasing with each motion, Jason could only brace his hands on the chair. It felt as if Angel was sucking out his soul! Waves of pleasure were crashing down on him. That's when he exploded in her mouth with a gasp, as Angel swallowed every drop of his fluids. Jason could only see her licking her lips in satisfaction, and he realized this was another method of how she fed. Angel stood from the floor and straddled him in the chair, and Jason knew she wanted more. Jason wrapped his arms around her, and beckoned her to take as much of him as she needed. They both climaxed together and shared their sweat, lust, and kisses.

Angel picks up her dress from the floor. "You know, I think you may need some new dresses. How would you feel about going into town today?" Jaran asks her as she jumps in his arms with delight. "Really? Around other humans?" She has her arms wrapped around his neck. "Yes. Since you are in a human form, you will need to see how humans live, and not just read about them." she laughs.

Jason conjures a horse and wagon with a wave of his hands. Angel is always impressed with his magic, and learning that he was a Warlock and human made her feel that she could trust him more. Angel pats the horse on its mane. This animal would have been her prey if she was in her succubus or true form. However, she enjoys the change in feeling when she is in her human form, as Jason reaches out his hand. "Shall we go, my lady?" he asked, as he helped her onto the wagon. Jason realizes that Angel is nervous, and holds her hand while the reins are in her other hand.

The town was called Blackberry Bush, with a modest population of twenty five townspeople who are very pleasant and welcoming, he explains. As they approach the town, Angel is astonished by the

112

different kinds of humans. She sees some old, some young, males and females, smiling, and talking amongst each other. It all seems so unreal to her, due to her spending most of her existence alone until she met Jason. Some even wave at her, prompting her to wave back in return, with smiles and giggles. Seeing her like that gives Jason so much joy, as they pull up to the Tailor's. Jason helps her down from the wagon, realizing she is still smiling as they enter the shop hand in hand. Angel beholds different styles of dresses as they are welcomed by the tailor. Angel picks several dresses and is delighted at the choices she has made. Jason pays for the purchases before heading to the town shops to pick up goods and supplies.

"Jason boy, Hello there..." a tall gentleman with gray hair, a slim stature, and brown eyes waves at him. "How are you Jason, and who is this lovely lady?" Jason smiles as they approach the man. "Hello Mayor Hamilton, may I introduce to you Angel, who is from the far away land of Sacred Rock." Mayor Hamilton removes his hat and bows. "It is a pleasure to meet you, Miss Angel. Welcome to my humble little town of Blackberry Bush." Angel gives him a curtsy. "Thank you, Mayor Hamilton. It is nice to meet you and visit your beautiful town." It appears that Mayor Hamiltion blushes, wishes them a good day and hopes to see them again soon, bidding them a good day as he continues his morning constitutional.

Jason and Angel return home. She is so excited about her first visit to town and can't wait to show off her new dresses to Jason. For a brief moment, she is quiet as Jason observes this.

"Jason," he looked over at her. "Thank you for a wonderful day." He kissed her hand. He is thankful for her each day that she has been in his life. After dinner, Angel twirls around in her new dresses she had picked, and asks which one Jason likes the best. Laughing, he says; "I love them all! You look so beautiful in all of them. It would be impossible to pick just one favorite." She smiles, and twirls some more across the room. "When will we go back into town? I want to see the humans again." He smiles, saying that they will visit soon. Then Jason inquires about how long Angel will remain in her human form. Angel thinks carefully and replies; "I'm not sure. I assume as long as I have enough essence to satisfy my true form, it can last as long as I am able to concentrate. Do you not like this form?" she asked sadly. "Of course, my love, I love it!" he realizes he has called her love. "I want to make sure you can continue this shift because of the risk of Hunters. They are known to frequent this territory." Holding his hand, she nods with understanding. Angel kisses him deeply, as he lifts her in his arms, heading towards the bedchamber together.

Jason and Angel did return to town frequently, to the point where the townspeople would greet her by name. While shopping, Jason overheard a passing older lady pair speaking.

"What a sweet young woman that Angel is..." Jason smiles, knowing that Angel is truly becoming accepted among the townsfolk. "Well, whatever relation she has with Mister Jason, she appears to be so happy. Such a beautiful couple they make!" they laugh. Jason seems to be taken back by their words. He never thought of what kind of relationship they had, or where it could lead further down the line. Angel happily approaches him ready to head back home, waving goodbye to the townspeople. Jason can only smile as she hums a lullaby that she only vaguely remembers from her dreams.

That night, as they lay in bed after making passionate love, Jason holds her in his arms as she purrs softly. "Angel?" she flutters open her eyes, tilting her head up at him. "Hmmm?" she smiles, and he clears his throat. "I want to know if you will be my wife?" Angel sits up to face him. "Do you mean to become your mate?" she asks, holding his hand. He starts to laugh. "Well yes, something like that. I will be your husband, and you will be my wife, in the human sense of the word." She squeals, wrapping her arms around his neck burying her face into him. After passionate kisses, Jason waits for an answer, when she finally pulls away and says "Yes!" with tears in her eyes. Never could she imagine such a thing would happen to her.

The ceremony is held in the town of Blackberry Bush. Everyone in the town attended and was honored to participate in the wedding in some way. From the Local Baker that catered the entire reception, and the tailor who made the most beautiful wedding dress that Angel had ever seen. Mayor Hamilton stood with Jason. When he saw Angel in the white flowing gown, he thought his heart would stop. She wore a crown of white lilies in her scarlet hair, which only enhanced her beauty. Angel carried a bundle of white lilies, and walked down the aisle towards her husband-to-be. The ring Jason placed on Angel's finger was actually the same ring that was her mother's. There was a slight difference, as Jason placed an enchantment on their love, to add to the ring, which appeared to already carry its own special magic. "I now pronounce you husband and wife!" Everyone cheered and threw rice in the air toward the happy couple. "Here now, I introduce Jason and Angel of Blackberry Bush." It was the happiest moment of the couple's lives, because they truly were one.

On the day that they were visiting the town, the married couple noticed a werewolf being carried through the shop district. The beast was dead. The men carrying the beast wore cloaks bearing the mark of the flaming swords. "Hunters." Jason said, holding Angel's hand tightly and pulled her closer to him. "Make way!" a Hunter bellowed to the crowd that scattered at the sound of his voice. "Mayor Hamilton, is this the beast that was seen near your border?" Mayor Hamiliton stepped towards the Hunter, timidly peering closely at the wolf. "Yes, Hunter Stephen," he nodded frantically. "I saw him when the child Elizabeth went missing." The Villagers gasp. Angel looks at Jason with so much sadness in her eyes. Angel had just seen Elizabeth a few days ago, happily running to the fields after waving at her in the distance.

Jason places his hand on her head and meets his forehead on hers for comfort. The mother of Elizabeth stands near Mayor Hamilton, shaking and in tears. He places his hands on her to steady her. "I see, well there is only one way to find out." Hunter Stephen says these words, and draws his blade. With one swipe, he slashes the stomach of the wolf. Within its entrails that spilled forth from the wolf, the body of Elizabeth can be seen. She was bitten in half and swallowed hole. The villagers scream in disbelief. Her mother cries the loudest out of everyone. "Is this your child, woman?" Hunter Stephen asks with no compassion in his voice. On her knees, the mother continues to sob uncontrollably. "Yes!" she cried, shaking as the Mayor attempted to console her. "Then I suppose we have completed our mission. Undertaker, do your damn job, and collect the remains!!" The undertaker approaches nervously placing the child in a coffin gently, like a precious babe.

The Mayor averts the Hunter's gaze, as he grunts; "And Mayor Hamilton, our fee if you do not mind." Mayor Hamilton looks at him with a shocked glare. The Hunter glares back at him. "Is there a problem, Mayor?!?" the Hunter asks. The Mayor can only shake his head in response. "Hunters! Gather that fucking beast's hide so we can properly dispose of it. Shite smells worse dead than alive!" The Mayor passes a bag to Hunter's Stephen's hand, and the Hunters depart from the town with the dead werewolf.

When they returned home, Angel was so distraught that she refused to eat. Jason held her in his arms, until she finally cried herself to sleep. It was heartbreaking to discover such a saddening fate befell the child. Jason, however, worried more about the Hunters' presence, as he felt that they would return someday. He would need to cast a double protective barrier around the home perimeter to cloak their location. All he could think about was protecting his wife and keeping her safe at all costs. Jason wanted to bring the smile back to her face. Of course, while she slept she was the most fragile. Lost in her dreams, Angel may not need Jason's protection due to her growing comfort staying in human form, but as her husband it was his responsibility. He sighs heavily, noticing that she is in a deep slumber. Tomorrow is a new day he thinks as he lies down, closes his eyes, and waits for sleep to embrace him as well.

Angel awakened surrounded by white roses in the bed. She couldn't help but laugh as she threw the roses over her head, allowing the petals to land on her face. She saw Jason at the bedchamber entrance. She beckoned him to bed. He placed his arms around her, as she did the same. Her smile was all that mattered to him. Angel gave his life purpose, and her love gave him strength. Each day thereafter, Jason surprised her with different types of flowers in bed to wake to. They shared meals together, and danced with each other as he conjured instruments. Researching was still important to the both of them as they often cuddled on the couch, studying one of the thousands of books from Jason's library. The days all ended with intense love making. It was as if they could not get enough of one another. Each climax brought them closer to the point of true oneness. They would always bring each other back from the sweet abyss, their breathing and heat from their sex completed their connection leading only to their touch to channel the electricity.

"Jason, I would like for you to be with me tonight when I leave to hunt." Jason lifts his head, he had been reading only to see her standing in her true form in the doorway entrance. He had not realized that she was speaking to him through their mindlink at the time.

"Of course, my love." he stands and takes her clawed hand into his own. When they are outside, she spreads open her wings, as they place their arms around each other's waists. Angel had begun to think about how happy she was being Jason's wife, but wondered if he truly accepted her in her entirety. She felt ashamed to even have had such doubts, but there was only one way to find out. As they took flight, Jason did not appear frightened, but why would he? He is a warlock, after all. He felt so comfortable in her arms as she sensed prey nearby. Angel landed in a clearing to ensure that Jason would have a good view. "Stay here." she whispered, and he nodded, as I began to stalk my prey. I glanced over my shoulder as I noticed his eyes calmly watching.

Angel came upon the steer, and as he observes, Jason knows that this must be the prey. Angel quickly grabs the steer, easily taking it down with her claws that she scoops into its neck. She has definitely taken it by surprise, and begins to feed on its rich life essence. Angel senses that this particular prey had just mated recently, which satisfied her hunger more fully. More prey would exist even after this one's life would end. The prey's eyes rolled white, and she knew that it was gone. She prayed to the Goddess of the hunt, and thanked it for giving its life for her.

Her eyes were red with what I believed to be bloodlust after a kill. She was even more beautiful now, growling at me as I bowed my head in respect for her. I am willing to submit to her as her mate. When I finally look back into her eyes, I see that whatever test this was I passed and we fly back home. It was amazing to see her hunt in her true form! I ask her to stay in her true form as we walk into the bedroom together.

I could not believe Jason wanted to make love to me in my true form. his cock was ready at my entrance. I straddled him as I shrieked and felt him within the walls of my body. I looked down at him, Jason was lost in ecstasy as I moved my hips back and forth. I am careful not to claw his chest, and I decided to grab the sheets instead, and work my hips faster. I am breathing heavily when I suddenly realize that Jason's body is twitching underneath me. Without warning, he flipped me over, pinning my calves to his shoulder blades! With each thrust he emits cries of savagery and intensity! I know not what has come over him but I need it more and more with each moment. Then I feel his fingernails digging into my thighs. I revert us back into our original position. When I look below, I see blood coming from his eyes, nose, and mouth!! I AM KILLING JASON!!!

Angel jumps off of his body and holds him down, and she begins to heal him with her life essence. Jason's body finally stops convulsing, and his breathing slowly comes back to normal. She shifts back into her human form and runs for water to clean him. Tears stream down her face mixing with the water as she uses a cloth to wash his face. Jason does not wake up for ten days after this, Angel stays by his side, laying with him, and kissing his handsome face. She silently begged for him to come back to her, as she held onto him for dear life. When Jason finally opens his eyes, Angel repeatedly apologies for her actions in tears.

Jason was happy to see Angel's face again and knew she felt guilty about what happened to him. He was neither upset nor had he regretted his first time with her true form. He tells her how he suspected this would be the case, as her kind can kill in this way as well. Angel holds his hand and says; "I will never do that again. The thought of losing you, I simply could not bear it." she kisses his hand. They both agreed to be more careful and forthcoming in the future with each other.

One day after the incident Jason is in the garden when he hears Angel calling for him. When he enters the room, Angel is vomiting on the floor. He cleans her up and places her in bed to rest. Angel had never been ill before. Jason goes to his study to grab the crystal ball. Could this be because she has been in her human form for too long? He places the ball over her stomach, while reciting a chant to reveal that which is unknown. The crystal ball reveals an image of a red baby. Jason then realizes that Angel is with child. "He is so gorgeous!" she says, finally able to speak with a weak smile. "He?" Jason asks with an astonished look. She nods while holding his hand lovingly. Angel and Jason are going to be parents to a son, they remarked as they embraced each other in complete joy.

CHAPTER 10

It has been an interesting life to say the least since finding out that Angel is carrying my child. As much as I would like to research further into this new turn of events, she needs me to tend to her needs regularly. Before she is even fully awake, her body is racked with nausea, which causes her to rush to the washroom. I hold her hair back as she vomits. Afterwards I assist in cleaning her, wiping the tears from her beautiful eyes. This experience is completely new and I know she must be scared. From what I have read and observed, she is experiencing normal symptoms of human pregnancy. Even though the crystal ball revealed a red skinned baby boy, only time would reveal what kind of species he will be.

I still look forward to visiting the town. I haven't been back there since discovering that I am pregnant with Jason's child. Jason is so overprotective of me, although I must admit that I love the attention. My belly has gotten bigger and Jason believes that I may be one or two moons along with our child. I wonder if my mother felt this much excitement when carrying me? As we entered town and I was greeted by the townsfolk, I noticed their looks of joy and anticipation to approach me. Jason carefully helped me down from the wagon which he conjured to be a little smaller for 'you and the baby's safety' he said. The women embraced me and squealed with excitement, as others congratulated Jason on the upcoming birth. Healer Lawerence shook Jason's hand "I see Jason, you have wasted no time in starting a family!" he pats Jason on the back. Jason beams proudly, giving me a sly wink as Healer Lawrence laughs.

"I suppose I will have to schedule home visits to check on you and the baby..." Healer Lawrence said, placing his hand on Angel's belly.

Angel gives him a nervous glance and I ask if it is necessary, as we are a very private couple and do not receive many visitors. "My boy, this is your first child! it is important for your wife to receive the proper care. Besides, what kind of Healer would I be if I was not there to bring in the newest resident of Blackberry Bush into the world?" We both smiled at him; it was apparent that Healer Lawrence was not taking no for an answer. He informed us that his first of five visits would be in three day's time. Angel and I completed our shopping and I sensed her anxiety for the upcoming visit from Healer Lawrence. The worried look had not left her lovely face even after leaving the town to head home.

During the ride I assured Angel that I was prepared for a moment like this. It was in my nature to be precautious. Angel rested her head on my shoulder, relaxing more as the ride continued. I place my arm around her waist and place my hand on her belly. This life growing within her is far too precious for me to allow anything to happen to either of them. After Angel has fallen asleep, I retire to my study. My focus is on a third degree illusion spell. I knew that the higher the degree in magic then there is the higher potential of effectiveness. My main concern as of late was how could I be a good father to my son.

"I need you to push honey" Richtor held his wife's hand. Tabitha screamed as she gave one last push. His son's cries can be heard. The Healer handed the child to Richtor. "Jason..." he whispered to his son. Richtor looked down at his wife, who had a peaceful smile across her face. With a look of horror, Richtor realized that she was dead. It is the story that was told to Jason by his housemaid Betty, who practically raised him since birth. His father never paid too much attention to him, a pat on the head, or a weary smile was the only affection ever given to him.

"He is still mending a broken heart, my boy..." Betty said, seeing that Jason was completely engrossed in his daily studies. His father was strict with ensuring he learned his lessons, or he would be punished quickly. Jason grumbled incoherently under his breath. Why should he care any longer about what his father thought?

Betty gave him a much needed hug, soaking his tears into the top of her blouse. "When your mother passed on, she took a piece of your father with her. He really does love you, Jason." The tears dried as quickly as they fell from his eyes. It seemed that all his father cared about was being at the Elder Council's beck and call. The Great Warlock Richtor, the one who slayed an entire cadre of vampires single-handedly and saved the coven. Jason swore that he would be a better warlock than his father ever was and later excelled in all magical subjects. It would never be enough, as his father eventually died of poisoning, rendering all of the accomplishments and resentment Jason had for him moot.

Jason sat back in his chair, lost in the memories of his past, when a book hit him in the back of his head. He had unwittingly conjured so much reading material that the volumes were stacked impossibly, as one faint breeze sent them all crashing down all over the room. Rubbing the back of his head, Jason hears a chuckle. He glances up, and sees his lovely wife standing in the entrance of the door. "So this is where you have retreated to. Come, let us warm our bed." she smirks, removing her night gown. The books continued falling to the floor with a series of loud thuds as he jumped out of his chair. Angel lays across the bed on her side, rubbing her belly, waiting for Jason to lay next to her. She is beyond beautiful, he thinks, as he feels himself becoming aroused simply by the sight of her. Jason opens her legs to expose her sex, unfolding her petals of her lily, as she arches her back. Her hot liquid pools between her thighs, and Jason makes sure to lap it all up as she moans his name. She grabs his hair, pulling his face closer until she erupts in a geyser of steamed satisfaction. When Jason pulls himself up to her, he realizes that Angel has fallen asleep. He smiles admiring her beauty before he finds a dry blanket to do the same.

Healer Lawrence visits Jason and Angel as scheduled, examining Angel thoroughly. He then asks her about her appetite, body aches, and how much rest she gets each night. With each visit, he prescribes her herbs and hands her a flask of red liquid. When Angel can finally find the words to ask the Healer what was within the clear flask, he looks up from his notes. "Oh my dear, that is a healing elixir. You must take that when the first wave of childbirth contractions come near. Its purpose is to ease your pain." He smiles and bids them farewell until the next visit.

Once Healer Lawrence leaves, Angel is digging into her box of belongings. She has not touched it since she came to live with Jason.

That's when she finds an identical crystal flask. The flask is the same one that Healer Lawrence gave to her. Jason stands over her, puzzled at her discovery. She says that the flask was what was left in her mother's belongings. Her mother never had the chance to drink from the flask before she burst free from her womb. Angel leans her body against the wall, and breaks down, realizing that her mother never had a chance to survive her birth. In the end her mother knew this, fearlessly sacrificing her life to her child. Angel would have done the same for her son, if need be. Jason and Angel swear together that they both will give their lives to protect him.

If it was not for the protective barrier, Jason would not have known there were villagers approaching. At first it was one or two townsfolk visiting offering baskets of food, baby clothing, and toys for the baby, however, it soon became overwhelming as more villagers arrived each day. Jason noticed Angel was becoming uncomfortable with the continued presence of visitors. When he heard a low growl from her, he firmly made a final decision about these visits. He informed the townspeople that since Angel needed her rest, that he would come to pick up any gifts that the villagers wished to offer. Although they appeared disappointed, they were understanding of the wishes of the mother-to-be.

One day, Mayor Hamilton was sitting in his study, when he noticed a letter that had arrived from the Mayor of Blood Oak, a neighboring village. As he opened the seal, he wondered what could the letter contain. Such letters from another town indicated matters of the most high importance. Mayor Hamilton read that this was a letter of request for a Mayor in-training to be sent to Blood Oak to occupy the position as the new Mayor, post-haste. Due to the recent plague infesting the town, Mayor Crowley had fallen too ill, and can no longer carry out his Mayoral duties. Mayor Hamilton placed the letter down and pondered who would be the best candidate for such an important and demanding position.

Kord Bismuth was a nineteen year old with a tall build, brown hair, and black eyes. He had lived in the town of Blackberry Bush his entire life. His uncle was Mayor Hamilton of Blackberry Bush, and inspired him to train to become a Mayor in hopes of Mayor Hamilton passing the position to him once he retired. Today, Kord was walking towards his uncle's office. "Good Morning, Uncle!" He greeted him as he entered the Mayor's office door, before he sat in the chair across from his desk. "Kord, my boy!" the Mayor said, greeting his nephew with a genuine smile. "I am glad you're here!" He passes the letter to Kord. After reading the letter, he gives his Uncle a questioning look. "Kord, I would like you to consider being the new Mayor of Blood Oak. Now I know this would not be your first choice, and that the people there live a touch more...boisterously than we do, but sometimes the needs of the people must become bigger than our own needs. This is the essence of leadership, and what makes a good Mayor." He looks at his nephew, who is now deep in thought. Kord finally stands up with a firm hand reaching for his Uncle's hand to shake. "Uncle I would be honored to become the new Mayor of Blood Oak. I won't let you down!" Mayor Hamilton rises from his chair, pulls his nephew in, and embraces Kord with a hug, "I am so proud of you, and I know your parents would be too." Kord chokes back his tears with the thought of his parents and simply nods.

Kord takes a deep breath walking out of his Uncle's office, thinking what a beautiful day it was. A great day for a journey. He lifted his face towards the sun feeling its warmth. He noticed Jason loading his wagon and walked over to help him. "Hello Kord" Jason said, as Kord handed him one of the gifts from the villagers.

"Hello to you, Jason! I see your lovely wife is not with you today. By the way, I have something for you, as well." He reaches within his jacket pocket and hands Jason a wooden baby rattle. "I made it myself and thought I would give it to you now, especially since I will be leaving the town soon." Jason held this simple, but thoughtfully crafted gift in his hands. He was filled with such a strong sense of gratitude. "Thank you so much, Kord. Hmmm, you are leaving? Why? Where, pray tell?" he asks. Feeling embarrassed, Kord wipes his hand through his hair. "I am to be the new Mayor of Blood Oak! My Uncle just told me today so I must be departing soon, I suppose." he explained. Patting his hand on Kord's back, Jason says; "Congratulations Kord, or should I say, Mayor Bismuth!" Kord blushes slightly thanking him. Jason wishes him well and thanks him again for the gift before boarding his overloaded wagon to head home. Kord waves farewell to Jason. They may not have known each other long, but he felt that Jason was a good man and was sure that he would also be a good father. Kord turns to head home himself to pack for his new home of Blood Oak.

Angel was in her garden. It was a place where she enjoyed tending to her flowers, especially when Jason was away. She looked up to the sky to see a flock of birds flying. How she missed the feeling of gliding through the air, of the wind caressing her wings. She feels a slight breeze that blows through her hair. Angel had not shifted into her true form since the night she almost killed Jason. She knew that she was denying her true self by not shifting and feeding. Angel felt so conflicted, especially with the birth of their son soon approaching. A sadness washed over her as she entered the home and started to prepare dinner.

Jason had finally returned home and unloaded the multitudes of gifts from the wagon with a wave of his hands. Each gift floated into the home and stacked neatly on the floor. Jason smelled a wonderful fragrance of food coming from the kitchen. He wrapped his arms around Angel placing a peppering of kisses on the back of her neck. She seemed focused on cooking and had not responded to his presence. He backed away and went to clean himself up for dinner. During the meal, Angel remained silent, until Jason could no longer hold his tongue. "Angel, tell me what is the matter?!," She did not answer him. In frustration, he slammed his hand on the table. "Angel!" She sharply lifted her head with tears in her eyes. Jason had never raised his voice to Angel before and had felt guilty for doing so. He walked over and held her in his arms as she began to sob.

Angel explained to Jason after she had calmed down that she wished to shift into her true form, but is fearful for several obvious reasons. Jason looked deeply into her eyes. "You can not deny yourself so I will hunt for you." She gives him a look of shock and concern, "Jason my love, you have never hunted before in your life." She walked over to sit on the couch to be more comfortable. "That is very true, but I am capable of providing food for you and our child. I mean, how hard can it be? Besides, I am a warlock!" She giggles. It was worth the comment to see that smile on her face. "Please be careful..." She kisses him, as he prepares to leave for the woods.

Upon leaving our home a thought occurred to me. What manner of beast would suffice to nourish my wife and child? Surely, it would need to be a rather substantial, robust creature. So I raised my left hand to the air and whispered an incantation; "Omi Optico" Suddenly, with my eyes closed my mind was shown the creatures in the surrounding forest. I saw bats, and while they were many, certainly their essence was too diminutive. I spotted a few mangy coyotes, who were simply too scrawny. I even observed a mountain lion, and while it was a step in the right direction, I needed something more. Then I found my quarry, grazing in the nearby meadow. I saw a magnificent ram. He was only a stretch away, but my observations with Hunters had taught me that rams are temperamental beasts at even the best of times. Trying to bring one home for slaying would probably qualify as one of the worst of times. Yet, with determination I kneeled down saying a small prayer to the Goddess of the Hunt, Artemis, and chanted, "Hermes Gale" Suddenly, a powerful gale of wild wind blew into my back, and I rushed across the stretch of trees that led me to my prey.

Sometimes when I use this particular spell, I lose control of my footing. I blew wildly towards the rear of the ram. With little else but sheer instinct, I lifted my legs and plopped right on the spine of the beast. Immediately I regretted the move, as I felt the muscles on the back of my prey tense with strength. I could feel the anger seething from the aura of this creature. I knew what was coming, but I got myself into this mess. I could only think, I am truly and utterly FUCKED. I leaned forward and desperately clung my hands to its horns and whispered; "Now, now, we are just going to go for a nice little walk to meet a lovely succubus who just wants to eat your essence! Doesn't that sound positively lovely?" Almost as if in response, the ram grunted and started bucking uncontrollably. I feared for my very life, until I decided enough was enough! "Enough is ENOUGH(see?)!" I yelled, before tensing the fingers of my left hand and swatting the ram about its nose. The ram abruptly stopped bucking, and began slowly trotting. Hmmm I thought to myself Now that's more LIKE it! This wasn't so difficult, to think Angel did not believe that.. "HEEEEELP!!!!" Suddenly, without warning, the ram accelerated to break neck speed, as though he himself had casted Hermes Gale. "WHOA, YOU SON OF A BITCH!" I cried out to him as he ignored me, and began to kick and buck again, this time as though he was much less a ram, and more of a bull.

He was tearing through the woods like a bat out of Hell, when I thought to myself; I am young, what would be an appropriate age for retirement? I looked up just in time to see us steadily approaching a tree, but it was not the tree that was most concerning, rather, it was what was perched on the tree. Hanging precariously from a weak branch was a rather large hive of some sort. How the hell did this dumb animal know my approximate height to even occur to ram me into a hive? I swear I don't know. I closed my eyes tightly as I braced myself for impact. I thought to myself two things; One, I love you Angel. Two, this is going to bloody fucking hurt. As my head smashed the hive to pieces I was most certainly right. It hurt like a motherfucker.

We were almost near my home, yet at this rate, if I did not do something and fast, my arse was not going to make it in one piece. I outstretched my right palm over the head of the ram and whispered; "Slumber" I had not thought that through completely, as he was still moving at a quick brisk pace. We were quickly approaching the wooden fence that I had built as a border for our property, and to think, we could have been enjoying a delicious rabbit right now. I'll bet bat essence doesn't even taste that bad with a little paprika... With that, I felt the ram's balance surrender to my spell as we both hurled through my fence. Yep, bats. The next meat will definitely be bats. Might even learn to make a cloak out of their hides so we could have an excuse for me to hunt many bats. No more nearly killing myself for a fucking midday snack.

We finally stopped moving. I hoisted myself off the ground, and my legs as well as arms popped and snapped promising later pains to come. I looked over at the defeated ram and said triumphantly; "Enough of this shite, you wait here. I will go retrieve some rope, don't you go anywhere! You stay right at this spot, you overgrown sheep and I'm no farmer, so you'd better not shite all over my grass. I do not need the fertilizer." Triumphant, yet definitely worse for wear after securing the beast, I stumble into the front door to my loving family.

I had been on the couch, reading a book since Jason left to 'hunt'. I will not lie, it worried me that he offered to complete such a task that could easily get him killed or at least badly injured. I could only hope he would come back in one piece. I looked up to see him covered in twigs, sting marks, and dirt. I couldn't help it. I let out so much laughter as my dear husband stood there, looking as if he had come back from a battle. He stood there frowning; "This is not funny." I held my belly roaring again with laughter. "My love, please go see yourself in the looking glass." I continued to snicker as he left the sleeping prey and headed to the bedchamber.

I didn't appreciate Angel laughing at me when I entered our home. I mean, I could have died. I walked into the bedchamber still hearing her chucking in the other room. I stood in front of the looking glass and caught a glimpse at my reflection. A piece of hive was stuck to my face, as a hornet lay underneath. It stung me several times, shite! shite!!! I thought as I crushed it between my fingers. Staring back at my reflection I can't help, but laugh as I remove a branch from out of my trousers. Angel hears me, and also continues to laugh some more, as I entered the room and sat next to her on the couch. She helps me remove the remaining twigs from my hair, God, how I love her with all of my heart, I think, before tickling her in retaliation.

Jason drags the ram near Angel as she begins to shift into her true form, which takes her longer than she thought. This is most likely because she has not shifted in six moons. Angel begins to feed from the ram's life essence, with eyes full of bloodlust. It was a good thing that Jason had tied the beast as it started to jerk around as she started to feed, until it no longer was moving. With her eyes closed, Jason decided to take the beast to the kitchen to strip its flesh, knowing it would make a good meal. While he was fileting the meat, a thought occurred to him. He placed the spine, horns, and head in front of him. With his hands over the items he began to recite an incantation, and fashioned the bones into a hammer. The weapon would be used when he hunts for Angel. With pride and confidence, he holds it in his hands. Jason thanks the ram for its life as nothing has gone to waste. He smiles, finishing cutting the meat until he hears Angel yell "Jason!!"

I remember hearing their voices, knowing them as Mommy and Daddy. Mommy has such a sweet voice. She tells me how much she and Daddy love me. She sings to me at night before she falls asleep.

When she cries, I cry with her. I want to tell her not to cry, Mommy. While Mommy sleeps Daddy talks to me, always making me giggle and wiggle. He always kisses me, as I can feel it. I wish I could speak to them. Then I feel a change in Mommy and, I say; "Mommy?"

Jason runs into the room with his new weapon in hand. He kneels in front of Angel. Her hands are on her belly and through their mindlink, she says; "The baby spoke to me." Jason is not sure how this is even possible, as she connects him to the mindlink, and he hears his son for the first time. "Daddy?" as Jason places his hand on her belly. They both cry with joy at hearing their baby's voice. He tells them that he has always heard their voices, and is happy to speak to them finally. Jason suggests that this is because Angel is in her true form, and his speech has developed at such a high rate because of his warlock blood. The baby is able to tap into it and conduct speech through his ancestral magic. Jason remembers the gift that Kord gave him, and shows Angel the baby rattle. The baby kicks with happiness and Angel can only continue to cry. For the rest of the night they all continue to talk to each other until slumber takes hold of them all.

On the day of the birth Jason casted an illusion spell to ensure that when Healer Lawerence delivered the baby, he would see him as a normal human. Even if that was not true, as long as the baby was healthy, that was all that mattered to the expecting parents. Angel had drunk from the crystal flask that was given to her by Healer Lawrence. She knew that she would have enough strength to deal with the pain, as Jason successfully hunted prey for her in order to feed them, this time with less wounds. She was so proud to have Jason as a husband and mate.

"Angel I need you to push, I can almost see the head!" Healer Lawrence instructed her as her legs were braced open while she clutched Jason's hands. "You're doing great, love" Jason says, as he wipes the sweats from her brow. "Almost there Angel, give us one last push!" She feels Healer Lawrence pull the baby from her birth canal. They hear the baby's first cries, as Healer Lawrence wraps the baby in a blanket. "Congratulations, you two are parents to a healthy, beautiful baby boy!" He hands the baby to the waiting mother. The baby continues to cry as the parents see his true form with a red complexion and little wings.

128

In addition, the baby had two little horns on his forehead, and a little tail. Angel and Jason kiss him as he shifts into a human baby, ceasing his crying. "So what will you name him?" Healer Lawrence asks while cleaning his hands. In unison they both say; "Richtor."

CHAPTER 11

Since the day that he was born, Richtor has amazed his parents. At only three moons old he was able to control his shifting and establish a mindlink with them while in his true form. While visiting the town, Richtor saw an apple and was able to levitate it towards him. Thankfully, Jason was able to cancel the spell before anyone saw it. It only appeared to any outsiders that the fruit fell from the cart. Angel and Jason felt that it would be best to limit their time in town, at least until Richtor had control over his powers. With his increased potency in the use of magic, Jason was always concerned with attracting the attention of Hunters, which he wanted to avoid at all costs for the sake of his family.

At home, Angel was standing in her true form, Richtor was also in his true form as well. He opened his wings, and began to lift himself off of the ground. Angel beamed with pride at her son, who was learning to fly before crawling. Jason walked in with his new prey in hand. "Now this is a sight to behold!!" he says with a chuckle. "Look Daddy!" Ritchor screamed, and flew up to the ceiling. "I can go high!" he said, before finally spinning upside down in the air instead. "Richtor, that's enough for today..." Angel smiles. "Awww Mommy!" the infant whined. She growls softly, and he quickly lands on the floor pouting. "It's not a good idea to go against your mother, lad." Jason states, patting his son on the head and placing the prey before the both of them. Angel and Jason decided that besides breastfeeding Richtor, they both would feed together in their true forms. It would help him to understand his incubus side, as well as bonding with his mother.

After dinner Angel prepares Richtor for his bath, for which he gives her a hard time. He shifts and flies all over the house, while his

131

mother gives chase. He enters his father's study with Angel close on his tail, he hides behind his father's chair. "Daddy help!" he says giggling, Angel is also in her true form with bloodlust in her eyes. "Every night with this Richtor!" she growls as he whimpers; "I'm not sleepy yet, Mommy." Jason cannot help but to chuckle. Angel growls again at Jason who straightens his back to her backlash. "My love, I mean, really! That is quite enough. I don't recall this serious side of you during the Ram incident!" he snickers out as she shakes her head. "A little help here, and no excuses." Jason brings his son to his lap, as Richtor sucks on his clawed thumb. "Son, it is time for bed..." then he whispers; "Slumber" Normally, he does not like to cast a spell on his son. This however, would not have ended well if he had not intervened. Richtor shifts back into his human form, as does Angel. "Sometimes I just don't know what to do with him," They look down at their sleeping child in Jason's arms. "But he is worth every trouble." kissing him on the forehead. Jason hands him to her and she begins to sing him a lullaby before laying him down to bed.

Jason arches his eyebrows as he notices Angel leaning against the entrance of the study. "I know that look love." he closes the book he was reading. Angel walks over to him and sits in his lap, with his arms wrapped around her she sighs before saying; "I was thinking about my mother. I wonder if she was here, maybe she could give me some advice on how to be a good mother to Richtor." Jason responds by giving her a tight squeeze. "Angel, you are a wonderful mother to our son." she leans her head to him. "I just wish I knew more about where she came from. I know the cave where I was born was not her true home." At that moment, a thought occurred to Jason as he looked down at Angel's ring.

Books began flying everywhere in the study. I knew that Jason was having one of his 'frenzied episodes', as I duck when a book comes too close to smacking my head. I walked out slowly, deciding to allow him some time before explaining what he was up to. I go to the looking glass in our bedchamber, change into my nightgown, and start brushing my hair. When Jason finally enters our bedchamber, he has a map and a small crystal ball in his hands. We both sit on the bed, and he begins by telling me that with a location spell, he can find my mother's birth place. Jason opens up the map and asks me for my wedding ring. I remove it and quickly hand it over. He smiles, and places it on the map. He closes his eyes and when he opens them they are white. He starts to recite a chant in an unknown language to me. The object darts across the map and it stops at a location. the town of Blood Oak.

"Blood Oak?" Jason says, coming out of his trance and snaps his finger. "That is the town where Kord Bismuth is the new Mayor! He was the one that had given us the baby rattle for a gift." he finishes explaining. I can't believe it! I can finally find some answers. As Jason places the ring back on my finger, he kisses the palm of my hand. That night we made passionate love as if the world was coming to an end. I whispered; "I love you, Jason" as he fell fast asleep in my arms.

It's a sunbaked afternoon on a humbled spring day. The whirl of the wind carried with it the scent of flowers, wheat, and pollen that ensures that life will continue. It is on such an afternoon that a steady rhythmic clopping can be heard accompanied by the whistle of the wind in the air. It is here that we find young Kord Bismuth, riding his noble steed Zenith. Filled with an unbridled optimism, he holds fast to the reins, gently yet firmly guiding his horse to his destination. The quiet little village of Blood Oak, which is currently in desperate need of both a new Mayor, as well as an increase to the male population. "Just you wait, Zenith. We'll set up farming, live off the land, and work towards the good of the people. You being my faithful friend, you'll have all the oats that I can fit in your feed bag. Sounds good?" Kord asked, while patting his stallion upon his head. Zenith gave a horse smile, and whinnied in reply.

Meanwhile, in Blood Oak, things were getting worse with each passing day. Arthur has been utilizing placebos to medicate those in serious medical need, including the now recently departed Mayor Timothy Crowley. The mysterious plague has claimed yet another victim. The undertaker can be seen shivering under a heavy blanket, as the chill of the plague now visits his doorstep as well. The blacksmith's widow has since taken up her late husband's tools, and has decided to continue the trade, much to her father's disapproval. Suddenly the village gates(a new addition added by the current Healer to discourage the presence of outsiders) opens, and in the gate struts a beautiful horse, and on its back an earnest young man with ambition and a good heart.

Kord Bismuth has arrived in Blood Oak, and approached the town square, where the centerpiece was a gallows with a series of podiums and levers.

Hmmm... I won't be having any use for this. I will NOT be a Mayor who leads his village with fear and death. I will have this dismantled as soon as possible, Kord thinks and shakes his head in disapproval of what he has seen, when he notices a... less than modestly dressed woman in a VERY low cut dress.

"Pardon me, madam. I am Kord Bismuth. I am to be the new Mayor of Blood Oak. Might I inquire as to how I might gather the townspeople, that I might introduce myself?" he asked politely. "Why salutations, young sir. I'm Cassandra, I run the tavern over yonder. Pray tell, will you be moving here with your...wife?" she mused in reply to the handsome figure before her. "Erm, no ma'am. I am not married. I haven't found the right one yet, however my eyes are always open. Take care!" He said, with a wink and a smile. Sadly that interaction didn't bear much fruit, so Kord began the slow but necessary process of door to door introductions.

After several hours of canvassing, Kord happened upon a small cottage just at the base of a great hill. The front door was made of a rich oak with a fancy 'G' carved into the front. He approached slowly, beginning to feel the weariness in his legs from the lengthy travels, and dismounted Zenith. "Wait here old fella. I'll be back momentarily." Kord knocked upon the door. After some waiting, there was no answer. Twice he knocked, three times, yet still, there was no answer. Kord had resigned that there was nobody home, yet just as he was about to head back, one heard the unmistakable sound of shouting. While Kord was a fairly educated man, it did not require his substantial intellect to know that the cries were coming from inside the home he had just knocked on. Immediately, Kord sprang into action as he banged on the door as hard as he could, but still to no avail. Then he heard it, a shrill scream of a woman distinctly crying out "HELP ME!"

With a determined look on his face, Kord paced backwards a few steps, got a running start, and tensed his shoulders with all his youthful might. He collided with the door, loosening it from the hinges, causing it to fly open. What he saw on the other side would unnerve even the strongest man. Before his eyes was a twisted, crooked, misshapen form. A truly old and decrepit man on top of a woman, who was significantly… less decrepit. In the corner slumped to the floor, and shaking in pure, understandable horror, was a beautiful, tender, full figured marvel of a young lady. After a quick recovery from the ghastly sight, Kord steeled his resolve, and with bass and all the authority of his newly appointed station, stomped his foot down and cleared his throat. Startled, the ragged old ruffian scrambled to his feet, trying haphazardly to fasten his trousers in a feeble attempt to feign his modesty."How DARE you intrude thus, young sir? This was a private affair between adults!" The elder man yelled, his feathers clearly ruffled by Kord's timely intrusion. "Well, yes sir, I can see that. I also heard the distinct sound of a woman in sheer horror, screaming for help. So like any good samaritan, I led the charge to see what was the matter, and if I may be of any assistance." Kord said, straightening his burgundy peacoat.

"Just who are you supposed to be, anyway? I had been led to believe that the few remaining males of this village were either old, ailing, or barely entering infancy." The old man asked, clearly agitated, narrowing his gaze at the young Mayor to a laser-like focus. "Certainly introductions are in order, as that is precisely the original purpose of my visit. My name is Kord Bismuth and as of today I am the new Mayor of Blood Oak." Kord thoughtfully rubbed his chin while glancing over the room. The young blonde lady at once stood in the corner, but never moved from that spot. While the woman, who was just moments ago beneath the skeletal frame of the old man, was settling herself and attempting to look decent, all while her head sunk low with shame.

"However I'm afraid that does not answer the more immediate concern of what has transpired here, and are you ladies quite alright? Also, not to stick my nose where it ought not to be, but isn't that a young child crying I hear?" I inquired, and indeed it was, and as though the sound had just now occurred to the blonde, she spun and ran towards and up the stairs without so much as a pardon. Kord glared at the old man whose fists were clenched tightly with white knuckles, determined to receive his answers. Suddenly the scowl and anger on the man's face gave way to a cocksure smile. He replied; "While I must admit to some embarrassment, I am quite pleased to make your acquaintance. My name is Arthur Nesbit, that is, HEALER Arthur Nesbit. I was simply calling upon the madame of the house. This is Ms. Candace Goodwind. I am afraid you have stumbled in on two old friends, caught up in the comforts of carnality. What you mistook for the muffled, mortified screams of help, was actually the simple throes of passion and lust. As our lovely Mrs. Goodwind has been without a release since the the passing of her late husband, the FORMER Healer, Vincent Goodwind. She may no longer be accustomed to the physical presence of a man within her, ahem… jewel. Furthermore, dear Candace has a tendency of crying out to the Gods above at the peak of her, um… climax, as it were."

Not buying the fertilizer that Nesbit was selling for even a second, the Mayor turned his attention to Lady Goodwind. "Ma'am, is this true? There was a third party, and a crying child. You yourself have tears in your eyes…" he interrogated. "All a simple misunderstanding, my good lad, forgive me, MAYOR, sir. I'm sure Candace will introduce you to her son and housemaiden in due time." Nesbit said, resting his yellowed hook-like claws onto Kord's shoulders. "Now, I'm afraid I must be leaving! As I'm sure you will soon be made well aware of, the needs of the people in this village are quite plentiful." Nesbit placed his top hat on his head and grabbed his cane. He took the handle of the busted, still locked door. He stopped, and turned to Kord. His eyes narrowed to the appearance of snake eyes. "After all there is a plague out there, don't you know, BOY?" and with that he slammed the door, and departed.

A hush fell over the room, as Kord thought to himself: indeed, I'll just bet there's a plague. A big, withered, rotten plague named Arthur Nesbit. Slowly the energy in the home began to settle down, as Kord turned his attention to poor Candace. She seemed quite relieved to be Nesbit free. "Are you alright, ma'am?" he asked, passing her his handkerchief to wipe her running makeup. With a sigh, Candace rested her head in her hands and smiled.

"Yes, I'm quite alright Mr. Mayor, but please, Candace will do. Ms. Goodwind, if you must, but not ma'am or madam. Please don't age me any faster than life is already doing." She laughed and Kord gave her a warm smile and hugged her gently. "Candace it is then. Not to change the subject but there was another lady who had captured my notice. I do believe she fled to check on the child?" Candace's eyes stretched open and suddenly she exclaimed, "Oh!!" That's right, please Mayor, pardon me!" With that she sprang up the stairs leaving a perfumed fragrance in the room. Kord found himself a rocking chair, and relaxed himself, pleased that he had been able to be of assistance.

After a brief wait, Penelope slowly descended the stairs with a sweet demure smile on her face. "Hello, Mayor Bismuth, I apologize for not formally introducing myself earlier. Circumstances were...complicated, to say the least. My name is Penelope. I am the housemaiden for Ms. Goodwind, as well as the previous village baker's daughter." she said, blushes forming on her full, soft featured face. Kord felt his heartbeat beginning to pick up pace. Truly, he was awestruck by her beauty. "Please, just call me Kord, and I completely understand, fair Penelope. I hope you're alright. That said, may I ask what is the story with Arthur Nesbit, anyway? He seems to be quite the dubious character." Kord asked with a look of concern on his face.

"Everything your instincts have told you is absolutely correct, Kord. Arthur Nesbit is a cruel, sadistic, and perverted evil man. Since he has become Healer of the village, the only thing he has healed is his coin purse. He has chased every woman in the village, and I am no exception." As Penelope continued, Kord could see the despair welling up in her eyes. "Fear not, milady. There's a new Mayor in town, and from this moment forward you and all the citizens of Blood Oak are under my personal protection. In fact, I think I'll pay that lecherous cretin a visit, since his is the only home in town I have not yet visited." So with that, Kord embraced Penelope, who beckoned for a kiss, yet with some internal struggle, he resisted. "Uh, I.. really must depart. I shall return to call on you both another time." Kord said and took his leave with a determined look on his face.

It was time to visit the craven bastard. "Let's go, Zenith." Kord said, as he mounted his steed. He began trotting uphill, towards the estate of Healer Arthur Nesbit. As Zenith made the journey, thoughts of home filled Kord's mind. He missed his uncle, but there was nothing waiting for Kord in Blackberry Bush. Again, his heart began racing as his thoughts shifted. This time images began swirling in his mind of a beautiful blonde mane of hair. "Penelope..." Kord whispered under his breath, as Zenith finally arrived at the Healer Arthur Nesbit's opulent estate. Equal parts amazed and disgusted, Kord dismounted, looking in awe at the expansive, extravagant estate. Wow. This is a complete and total waste, Kord thought, making mental note of how many emaciated young villagers he saw on his way here. With a deep breath, Kord made his way up the massive staircase to the door of the mansion. Slowly, all the suffocating luxury Arthur surrounded himself with truly made Kord begin to feel ill. Nonetheless he extended his arm to use the brass knocker on the door. it banged with a resounding 'Klong!!'

Slowly, the massive gold painted door moaned aloud, nerve rattling creek, as it spread open its maw, revealing the familiar, small, twisted figure behind it. Not waiting for a proper greeting that would likely never come, Kord cleared his throat and spoke up. "Healer, I would have words with you." A cruel sneer spreads across Nesbits's face that eventually gives way to a crooked, almost toothless smile. "Why, but of course. Do come in! Come, come!," Arthur said, pulling the door all the way open. "Yes, welcome into my parlor, said the spider to the fly..." Nesbit muttered under his breath, sending a chill up Kord's spine as he passed, entering the great hall of the manor.

The walls of the great hall were massive, filled with grand works of art that young Kord could only imagine had come from around the world. All except for one, in a sparkling, golden, gem encrusted frame, there was an oil painting depicting a battle between armed men and women in armor, and a legion of demons.

The image was graphic, with copious amounts of gore and viscera as far as the eye could see. In the center of the painting was a rather embellished rendition of Arthur himself, clad in armor, driving a broadsword through the chest of a large, gruesome, crimson, winged demon.

Almost as if on cue, Nesbit chimed in; "Do you like it? I had it commissioned after I had this home built. It's meant to commemorate my ultimate victory, slaying the demon who once wandered these very halls." he lied with a proud, confident smile. "It's uh, it's truly... something..." Kord replied. Immediately, Kord's thoughts shifted to Penelope and he felt his hands tighten into fists. "You know, Healer, you have obviously been blessed with inexhaustible wealth, opulence that could surely benefit all of the people here, were it shared... Have you ever considered this?" Kord asked, barely restraining the agitation in his voice. "While I'm certain that much is true, what I have is only that which I have earned. Surely it is not my responsibility to line the pockets of the entire downtrodden village? I am responsible for their health, not their wealth." Seeing that his breath was wasted on the current topic, Kord appeared annoyed at this point. "Fine, but also I wanted to discuss what happened earlier. At Candace Goodwind's-" "Oh, that!! Hahaha!!!..." an interrupting Arthur laughed, dismissing the obvious concern on Kord's face. "Yes, yes, that misunderstanding. It was embarrassing, to be sure, but these things do happen. Best just to put it behind us and move forward. Leave it behind us..."

At this, Kord straightened his posture, and his tone became firm. "No, Arthur. I know the truth. I know what you are. You're a predator of the weak. A scoundrel and a ruffian with undeserved, ill gotten gains. I don't know the full extent of your misdeeds in this village, but I have come to let you know that it ends today. You will not cause the darkness in my village to spread and cement its roots any further. I will protect my village!" Kord declared. The smile on Nesbit's face twisted and distorted its leathery creases into something that could only be described as a garish sight from nightmares. "How DARE you? You insignificant, delusional BOY! Do you know who I am? I am the savior and the lifeblood of this meager little hamlet. It is less than NOTHING without me. You speak of the good of the people? I AM the good of the people!! I am their hero! It was I, not you, who saved the people from the demon who infiltrated in their midst, just as it is I who is the only one safeguarding the people from this darkness! While YOU were still wet nursing at your mother's tit, you insignificant little SHIT!! My TRASH is their treasure, my PISS is their poultice, my SHIT is their sustenance! If I DEIGN to spit upon them, it is as though The Gods have dropped blessed rain upon a dying CROP!!!

Yor village?! I AM this village! Know your place, you ignorant, insolent cur, and be mindful of how you speak to your betters! Have a care, I will have you know that those who have stood in the way of what I wanted, my enemies had a tendency of not lasting very long around here. You have your little title, but that's not power, BOY.

Power is money and influence. You've been here less than a day, and you have already made a dangerous enemy. Now get out of my home, before you make things worse for yourself!" Arthur said, with his face blood red with anger.

Kord turned with haste and opened the door. Preparing to step out of the door, he stopped.

"Oh and Arthur?" Nesbit lifted his still frowning face. "If you go near Penelope or Ms. Goodwind's home again and I see or hear of it? I'll kill you myself. Also referring to me as BOY? Let this be the last time you make that mistake. I am your Mayor, act like it. The gallows in town square will be dismantled, as I found it distasteful, yet perhaps there is time enough for one more execution. Take care..." With that Kord made his way down the stairs, mounted Zenith and left thinking to himself. Power means nothing if you're too dead to use it.

The day I was to depart for Blood Oak was difficult for me as I had never been separated from Jason or Richtor for this long. I've decided it would be best to fly there in my true form, and shift into my human form once I've reached my destination. Jason was more concerned with Hunters, as there seemed to be an increased presence of their activities as of late. Richtor, on the other hand, was begging me to take him with me, as he flew into my arms in his true form. "Mommy, Mommy, please take me with you!" he cried, burying himself in my bosom. "I can protect you!" my heart ached at the sound of his words. "My petite(little one), you have to stay and protect your father. Can you do this for me?" With tears in his eyes, he nodded. Richtor flew back into his father's arms wrapping his arms around his neck and sobbed into his chest. Jason pats his son's head in comfort, while walking towards me.

"I should be coming with you." I can only shake my head to respond. The night before we laid in each other's arms knowing that the day was approaching that I would have to go on my journey. Preparing was the hardest part for both of us, especially with considering Richtor's tender feelings. Enough words were spoken between us as Jason placed a kiss on my lips. I returned his kiss and kissed my little one on the head before whispering that I loved him.

It was a clear sunny day as Angel felt the wind beneath her wings. So much was going through her mind. Was this the best decision to make? What if she did not find the answers she was searching for? Her heart was yearning to be back in the presence of her husband and son. Shaking her head to clear her thoughts, she decided that she had to learn the truth; this would not be all in vain. With a sigh, Angel continues her course to her mother's birthplace Blood Oak.

CHAPTER 12

It was nightfall when I finally reached the town of Blood Oak. The stench of rancid death and decay was pungent in the air, even after I shifted to my human form. I peered over the area which was empty, save for a lonely woman who was on the ground sobbing pitifully. As I approached her, I saw she was holding a swaddled bundle in her hands. She was plaintively wailing, to the extent that her sound carried on the winds, causing a sting in my heart. The woman must have noticed my presence, as eventually she looked up at me. The woman bore the mark of death, and dark circles painted her eyes and chalky pale skin, which I'm sure once was flushed with color at some point, as her wrists and hands were still a copper hue. "My baby..my baby is dead!" she continues to wail more intensely as her grief quakes her body. My attention was drawn to what I realized was now her dead baby's body. My heart ached for her. My hand reached into my satchel for the crystal flask containing the red healing tonic.

Jason encouraged me to take this along in case of emergency. I kneeled down to her, and placed the flask into the young woman's hands. I stared at her eyes "Drink this concoction, and begone from this Godforsaken place of death. Never look back, just go and live." her eyes are wide with surprise. I walk away, leaving her there to decide her own fate. I am not here to save anyone in this town, but I saw the loss of hope in her eyes. Now, she has a choice.

April turns her head back as the beautiful stranger leaves, clutching the gift she had given her tightly to her bosom in place of her baby. She was alone in her quarters when she gave birth to her baby. Mayor Crowley passed away a few days prior. She did everything in her power to avoid Healer Nesbit, but he consistently stalked the halls of the manor after the Mayor's death. Alice would hide away in her room until one day she felt the pain radiate throughout her body. Alice screamed and cried as her child escaped her womb and was born into this hell. She lay there bleeding, thinking that she may die. When she was finally able to move she saw her child, a son, HER son. There were no cries coming from the child, as she noticed that there was no breath coming from his tender little body.

All Alice could do was sob as she wrapped him in a blanket. Alice cried and coughed blood, the plague had taken her child, and soon she would inevitably join him. Alice looks at the flask, opens it, and drinks the concoction. She leaves her son at the undertaker's door, trusting that he would give her son a proper burial. Alice gathers what belongings she has, and leaves Blood Oak once and for all.

Angel approaches the town tavern believing that she will find more information there from the drunken local patrons. The only patrons within the tavern are the barkeep Cassandra, who wears a low cut dress revealing her massive bosoms. She is serving a tankard of ale to a woman who appears to be very lithe, laughing at something the Barkeeper has said in jest. The woman innocently grazes her hand across Cassandra's bosom, which then lands on her arm. Cassandra just smiles as she takes the silver coin from the woman. In a far corner is the undertaker, who sips his drink alone. He knows that the plague runs its course through his body, and that his wife is waiting for him at home. He contemplates his final thoughts of his life, procrastinating his husbandly duties, while considering a woman of the night's services. There have been plenty of them in town as of late, partly due to the females having so few men to support them. Angel takes a seat, when Cassandra approaches with a tall mug of ale.

"You are new here in town, so the first ale is on the house. Welcome to the Bronzed Cock, my humble little establishment, where any vice is for sale, but the Mayor only knows about the ale! Ha ha ha!" She sits the drink in front of Angel and goes back around the bar. Angel starts to sip her drink which she is obviously not used to. "I tell you, I may have to close the tavern tonight. Can't afford to get shipments of new ale. That old cheap bastard Nesbit takes up one of my six stools for half a day, nursing one fucking drink!" the buxom barkeep says to the thin woman. "He has brought nothing but misery since he became the new Healer." The thin woman replies, circling the rim of her glass with her finger, while giving Cassandra a seductive look. "He lives on the ashes of the old St. Peter property where that girl supposedly carried that demon child. Funny thing is, they let that old cro magnon talk the people into forming a mob and burning down the home, when I don't recall them EVER finding any proof to back the accusations..." Cassandra avoids her eyes, cleaning out one of the ale glasses. Angel listens carefully as she continues to ramble. "It is a shame, maybe that is the reason why this plague fell among this town. I mean, The men are nearly gone and yet Arthur Nesbit somehow still lives after 'killing the demon' supposedly."

Angel decides she's heard enough and leaves the tavern, having gained the information that she sought, and begins her way to Arthur Nesbit's home.

Angel in her true form soared the skies above the hills of Blood Oak. Seeing more upscale homes, she lands on a branch of a tree, and scans the area. Suddenly she begins to see images coming to her mind, seemingly from the land itself. She sees her mother dragging what appears to be her injured father. The images leave her as quickly as they come, and she braces herself on the tree branch. Breathing heavily, she hears a scream coming from the direction of a decadent mansion. A young woman dressed similarly to the one she'd met near the village entrance could be seen running and stumbling out of the front door of the estate. Holding her dress, which appears to be ripped, Angel glances at the door seeing a badly aged, physically malformed, ugly man. "You fucking Bitch! How dare you! I hope your family dies a painful and slow death! You'll never get a tonic from me, y'hear? NEVER!!!" he shouts along with other lewdities regarding her mother and a riding crop, while holding his trousers poorly with one hand.

Arthur, enraged by the young maiden's unwillingness to barter for treatment, stormed into his great hall, slamming his door shut. He only begins stepping towards the stairway to his wine cellar, when he hears a knock on his door. "Who the hell would be coming to my home at this fucking hour?" he grumbles. In truth, Arthur was merely agitated, as he was interrupted before another evening of intoxication and necrophilia, which is how he spent most of his nights, of late. When he opens the door he beholds a beautiful sight! It was a young woman with golden silken hair, green eyes, and delicious creamy skin that made his mouth water. "Hello my dear, and what can I do for you?" leering at her young supple body, Arthur was aching to touch her. With pleading eyes she says; "I'm sorry, I hope I'm not intruding. I was told I could find the great Healer Arthur Nesbit at this location. I do apologize for coming to you at such a late hour, but I am desperately in need of your... 'healing services'." Tears are welling in her eyes. "It's my two younger brothers, they are suffering from the plague..." the tears now begin to stream down her lovely face. "I beg you sir, to please help them." A wicked, tight lipped smile spreads across his hollowed face. "Poor sweet flower, please, come in" as he opens the door, deeply breathing in her scent as she walks in. "Let us go to a more comfortable area in my private chambers."

Angel saw that the door was slightly ajar, as she slowly snuck into the manor. Angel becomes overwhelmed when her eyes fall on the center painting of the great hall, which depicts a great battle, and a knight slaying a demon. Bloodlust fills her eyes and body as she realizes that the demon illustrated in the painted mural is her father! If this is a historical gallery, that must mean that Arthur Nesbit slayed her father! A low, rumbling growl can be heard erupting from her chest, and she begins to stalk her prey. His corroded scent leads her closer to his guest room door, as Angel slowly opens and is taken aback, witnessing a horrid image. There, the withered man was stroking his cock. All that could be heard was the jingling of the excessive gold rings on his fingers and bracelets on his wrists. There were bracelets on his arms and several melladions around his neck. The sound echoed in the room. It appeared as though he was struggling with so much weight, while he continued to please himself. With his eyes closed, he said; "So my lovely, it seems that you have finally regained your senses and have returned with a change of heart." As his eyes open, his visage twists in horror and shock with the image of an azure, winged demon standing at the entrance of his doorway.

The sheer horror of what he saw immediately caused his member to shrivel and soften in his now limp wristed hand. He felt an odd sensation filling his mind, as he took notice that the demon's eyes began to glow. With a hiss she spoke, although speaking isn't exactly the most accurate way to describe it, more like she inserted a verbal message forcefully and directly into his mind. "You are...the one they call 'Nesbit', yes?" she asked, only to be met with whimpering, sniveling, and no reply. Arthur fell to his knees, precious adornments of gold and jewels rattling as he trembled with fear. She continued "You are...the hero of Blood Oak, and a great slayer of demons, Yes??" Arthur began to feel a pool of warm wetness spreading beneath him. In horror, he looked downward, realizing he had both urinated and defecated all over himself. He looked up at the red eyed beast before him and suddenly he became oddly emboldened by his indignity. He slowly struggled to pull himself to his feet Then, standing in his filth with his chest puffed out, he began his tirade.

"I'm not sure who or what you think you are, but I am not just anyone. You are addressing HEALER-" she spread her wings before he could finish. "Your armor, put on your armor...Prepare yourself, demon slayer. Be ready and draw your mighty sword, yes..." she interrupted, baring her fangs and exuding wave upon wave of bloodlust. Arthur promptly forgot his train of thought, lifted his trousers and began to flee down the decadent halls of his manor. "No, no, NO!!" he cried, running for his life with more urine trailing behind him. "You defiled the flesh of the mother of my mother. You have lusted for my mother, and instigated treachery against her. You participated in the murder of my father.. I have tiptoed through the catacombs of your mind, and you are a weak, sick, depraved waste of life." As Arthur looked behind and saw the demon steadily keeping pace with his plodding steps, he saw a slight beacon of hope when he found himself at the base of his stairs. He turned to run up his stairs to his master bed chambers, but soon found himself overwhelmed with exhaustion.

Angel stopped at the bottom, carrying something large and unwieldy. "I found this around the corner, on display. Is this what you wore when you 'slayed' my father? Only fitting you should wear it for our destined battle, Yes?" She asked, and dropped something at the base of the stairs, which hit the floor with a loud clunk. It was a part of the coat of arms that Arthur had never worn, merely had on display, and yet another part of his heroic facade. Again, Arthur strained and pushed himself until he made his way to the top of the stairs. Words continued to force themselves into his corrupted mind. "Having trouble moving? It seems the jewels and luxuries you once coveted have proven to be weighing you down. Fear not, for I shall assist. Yesss…" she said.

Suddenly a set of claws dug deep into Arthur's shoulder. A hollar of pain escaped his mouth, then dried and faded as the demon effortlessly lifted him and tossed him through his bedchamber door and onto his bed. Arthur laid there, whimpering and defenseless, not unlike a newborn baby. "I-I know who you are…It wasn't me! It wasn't me! It was Hummmm…" He pleaded, until Angel clasped her clawed hand over his mouth. She did an odd thing next, as she lowered his trousers. "No more, Nesbit. I can smell the blood on your hands. I can taste the rot in your soul. Blood once spilled, can never be cleaned. Truly, you ARE Blood Oak's hero, and now you shall receive a hero's reward. Yesss?" Angel climbed over Aruther's body and with reluctance allowed him to enter her depths, shallow as his reach may be. She fed upon his essence as the pervert quivered and moaned. He did his best to resist, but even his very willpower was being drained from his body. Then, it was his memories being consumed. He slowly forgot the events that took place in his life as this demon winded her hips, straining to feed the wet mouth of her hungry cave on Arthur's far less than ample manhood. He wanted to beg her to stop. He found himself feeling not pleasure, but excruciating pain, however it was far too late. Soon he forgot the St. Peter's family, or rather his memories were stolen as she consumed them. A sad smile came upon his face, as Angel moved faster and faster, up and down. Arthur saw her full breasts heave in the moonlight that entered through his bedroom window. Then a tear rolled down his cheek as he had what was his last pure memory, that of a young boy, working the fields alongside his father, consumed along with the rest.

Angel climaxed and leaned forward, crading Nesbit's drooling, empty head in her arms and pointed a finger into the air with her pointed claw. Arthur muttered one last final phrase; "Marianne, I'm sorry…" and Angel swiped the claw across the throat of the old fool, spilling blood that was such a deep, dark red, as to almost appear purple. Thus, Arthur Nesbit, Healer Arthur Nesbit, the TRUE demon of Blood

Oak was no more than a memory. Angel clutched the fresh corpse with a mischievous gleam in her ruby eyes. She dragged the body down the massive stairway, stopping only to glance at a familiar sight to curl her lips with pure satisfaction. Outside the manor a figure could be seen standing in the moonlight. In the dimly lit sky, the clouds parted and a single solitary beam of light pierced the sky. Within that light, another figure appeared on the scene.

The graceful being had the appearance of a naked woman, but with large, white, feathered wings sprouting from her back. Truly however, the being was not male nor female, but an angel. As she descended, the lone figure in the darkness looked up with a slight sense of hope. "I am the angel of Death. I have come to take you to your great reward… Arthur Nesbit." The lone figure stepped forward from shadows, now illuminated by the light, only to reveal Arthur Nesbit. "Yes, yes, I knew you would come for me. At long last, I am ready for your embrace." Arthur said wearily. The angel tilted its head slightly before reaching out and wrapping her arms around him gently. "We will have far to travel, so I hope you've not left any regrets." the angel said softly. "I am ready. I am ready to be reunited with my darling Marianne once more!" Arthur proclaimed with a smile.

The angel straightened it's head, released Arthur and stepped back. "No Arthur…" it said and then came a rumble of thunder, and the thick black clouds had closed, snuffing out the beam of light. The angel became visible only by the luminescence from the moonlight. "Your wife was a benevolent soul who truly made your life heaven in this bleak world. You however, have become a hateful, cantankerous, old cudgel who spent your time shunning the friendship of the good people of Blood Oak. You coveted all that was youthful and life preserving. You forced yourself upon the young, vibrant women, and even laid with the flesh of one long deceased to satisfy your sick urges. In the process you have violated the law of the Gods. As such, you created an illness borne of a curse. One that you spread with every young woman you bedded, and with every night you continued the sordid affair of decaying flesh. Truly you were an evil man, sadly. It did not have to be so."

As the angel spoke, it seemed as if its wings had turned black and folded over its body, only to take the form of a robe. "So what is to be my fate?" Arthur asked, the sound of trembling resonating in his voice. The angel's flesh then melted away, revealing only bone. Her once beautiful face became a garish skull with snakes slithering in and out of the eye sockets. The angel raised its left hand and a burst of flame shot up from the ground. When the burst dissipated, in the angel's hand was a long black handled scythe, its hook shaped blade gleaming in the night, as lightning began to fall. "For yourself, Arthur Nesbit, there is only despair. There is only oblivion." The angel's voice became a low, raspy croak. The angel swung the scythe's blade and ensnared Arthur Nesbit's body through the chest cavity. At the same time, the wide swing sliced open a large chasm. The chasm in the ground began to spread rapidly, as the sound of heavy rain joined the lightning descending upon the ground.

"No Arthur Nesbit, there is only... HELL!" the angel declared slowly, beginning to laugh. Arthur looked up and saw hellfire in the eye sockets of Death. The chasm finally stopped spreading as it had become a gaping hole in the ground, a pit. "No!! Marianne, Zeus, someone SAVE ME!! Reaper, please have Mercy!!" Arthur screamed. "I am not the judge, The time to plead for mercy and forgiveness at this moment. Now let's be on our way!" The angel said, and with that it hopped into the pit with Nesbit falling in behind it. The only sound that could be heard faintly over the thunder and rain was a long scream and a laugh. One that faded in the passing wind. As suddenly as the pit to hell opened, suddenly it slammed shut, signifying the closing of the darkest chapter in Blood Oak's history.

It was early the next morning when Kord was suddenly awakened from his new estate's comfortable bed and well deserved rest. The loud booms, stomps, and bangs woke him from his peaceful slumber. When the newly appointed Mayor opened his eyes, he saw the Barkeep Cassandra's massive breasts heaving as she took each labored breath. Her raven black hair was flowing through the breeze of the opened window filling the room with a gloriously seductive scent that uncontrollably caused Kord's nature to rise. With a groan the Mayor asked; "Cassandra? What is the meaning of this sudden intrusion?" he blushed at the realization of the full erection he was now sporting. This fact did NOT go unnoticed by the sweet smelling entrepreneur before him.

"Mayor, the entire village has gathered at Healer Nesbit's manor! You must come quickly! Although…" She said, and narrowed her gaze at the young Mayor's throbbing manhood before biting her lip.

Then as if suddenly realizing something of great urgency, she shook her head further, filling the room with her scent. "There's no time! Much as it pains me to say, we have to get you dressed! It's an emergency!!" With that, Kord sprang up from his bed, and immediately dressed himself right in front of the barkeep. In a panic, he asked, "Is it Penelope? What is the matter?" Cassandra simply grabbed Kord's peacoat and said; "No time! You'll see when you arrive, Mr. Mayor sir!" She led the charge down to the stable, where she had taken the liberty of already prepping Zenith's saddle. Kord mounted his steed and with one hand guided Cassandra by the hand and lifted her to ride side saddle behind him. As Zenith went full gallop along the path to Nesbit's manor, he immediately thought of Penelope and Lady Goodwind. Had they been attacked or worse? It did not take long for Zenith to approach the massive home, and the gathering of citizens before it.

What Kord saw was beyond the imaginations of even the most deviant of mentally deranged humans. From horseback, Kord could see Arthur Nesbit on display. He was hanging from his upper floor window, equipped from head to toe in his coat of arms. The Mayor was speechless, his mouth agape, yet without an utterance as he took in the details of the scene. Arthur was hung by his small intestine, which was also wrapped around his throat. The breastplate of the armor was spit down the middle. His chest cavity, ribcage, and abdomen had been completely opened, his vital organs were left on display. His lungs were spread outside his chest, raised to give the impression of wings. Below his hanging body smeared in blood was the massive painting covering the front door. On the painting, was blood, the blood spelled out the word

'JUSTICE'. An elderly woman spoke up; "Well, that makes two freshly dead old men." the crowd turned their attention to the source, the undertaker's wife.

"As you all know, the Undertaker was afflicted with the plague. He suffered for a long time, but last night his battle ended. I know due to his profession he was not popular, but he was my husband and he was a good man. I will miss him for the rest of my days." she said, before sobbing uncontrollably. Kord tugged at his collar and with a solemn look, declared; "I am sorry for your loss, We will set services for both of these men and do what needs doing. Firstly, who among you will aid me in the retrieval of the body?" The crowd fell silent. "No one? So be it then." Kord said, and dismounted his horse. With all the commotion, it seemed that no one noticed a winged creature soaring through the clouds. Angel had found her answers and she was going home.

Angel's only thoughts were that she was looking forward to being in the arms of her husband and son. She had stopped to hunt for prey to replenish her energy, before continuing on her trip home. All of the events of Blood Oak had left Angel emotionally and physically spent. Justice was finally served and now she could find peace at home with her family. As she landed closer to the house, she reached for a mindlink with Jason. However, there was no reply. She suddenly felt a tightness in her chest as she drew near. Her heart began to beat faster with each step she took towards her front door. She was calling out to Jason so loudly that the sound of her voice echoed in her mind.

Then Angel smelled blood, and felt a lump forming in her throat.

CHAPTER 13

I
t had been one moon since Angel had left home for her journey to Blood Oak. Jason missed her terribly, and Richtor would cry for his mother every night. Jason would hold and rock him to sleep, humming the lullaby that Angel always sang to him. He would then dreadfully drag himself to their empty bed yearning for her touch. All Jason could do is look forward to her returning to them. It was the only thing that gave him any peace of mind as he drifted off to sleep.

The alarms went off in his head when he felt their presence: HUNTERS. Jason ran to Richtor's room and was thankful that he had put him to rest for an afternoon nap. He had no time to use an illusion spell in order to hide his presence from them. Besides, it would not be safe to do so. Jason calmed his breathing and focused, there were four Hunters approaching from what he could tell. At least three had a strong aura. If it came down to it, he could take out at least two of the Hunters with his new weapon, grab Richtor, and flee using Hermes Gale. Jason estimated that their chances of survival would be roughly forty five percent, but he had to give it everything he had, no matter the cost. All he could do now is be patient and wait for the right time to strike. Jason soon heard the banging on the front door. The Hunters had arrived.

"I don't fucking understand why we have to come all the way out here. It is hot as shit!" a medium build Hunter complains, adjusting his sword. "Because arsehole, we go where the magic leads us to kill the demons." a blonde Hunter next to him responds by elbowing him and rolls his eyes. "Yeah, yeah, yeah, this shit better be worth the damn pay!" the medium build Hunter says before spitting on the ground. "WILL YOU BOTH SHUT THE HELL UP! I AM TRYING TO

FUCKING CONCENTRATE!" an item hums in what appears to be the lead Hunter's hand.

"APPRENTICE!" he yells at a young boy carrying the Hunters' excess supplies, and struggling in the process. The lead Hunter huffed thinking why in the hell would he out of all the Hunters be assigned to this emaciated boy? When the apprentice finally reaches them, he appears out of breath. The lead Hunter glares at him, completely annoyed. The other two Hunters snicker in union, when they see the lead Hunter shifting his gaze to them, they immediately stop and stiffen their postures in attention. The lead Hunter grabs his sword from the apprentice, who gives him an apologetic look. As they all approach the small home, the Hunter bangs on the door.

Jason walks to the door and opens it to see a towering man forcefully enter his home. He gulps at the size of the man. "What is your name?!!" The Hunter's voice thunders, as the other three Hunters enter the home behind him. "My name is Jason." not allowing his eyes to leave the man's own. "Oh, and who else resides here with you?" he clutches the hilt of his sword, and Jason visibly notices this. Clearing his throat, he answers; "My wife and son." The Hunter licks his lips which makes Jason feel increasingly uncomfortable. "Where is she?" The Hunter asks, looking around hoping to catch a glimpse of female skin. "She is away visiting family, and my son is resting." Jason replied with his fists clenched, as he saw the lust in the Hunter's eyes. "What is the meaning of your unannounced visit, Sir? Jason asks. The Hunter raises an eyebrow. For such a small stature of a man, he certainly appeared to be very bold. "I'm asking the questions here!" The brutish man takes a step closer as he feels the object hum in his trousers. "I think you know full well why we are here..." as the Hunter smirks in Jason's face.

In a flash, Jason conjures his weapon in his hand and swings it at the Hunter. The Hunter is taken aback by surprise as the staff grazes his head, knocking him back and causing a spurt of blood to run over his eye. The other two Hunters circle Jason, their swords drawn to attack. With one stroke of his hand Jason casts a spell of suspension stopping the blonde Hunter from swinging at him. Jason uses the end of his weapon to block the other Hunter's sword, giving him a quick kick to the stomach. The Hunter falls to his knees and coughs up blood from his mouth. Jason now focuses his attention on the lead Hunter who appears to have recovered from the initial blow. Holding the weapon in his hands tightly, Jason whispers; "Hermes Gale" and rushes towards the Hunter. Suddenly Jason feels the sharp blade enter his body, and stumbles backwards, attempting to hold back the blood that is spilling from his chest. His breathing becomes heavy as he falls to the floor on his knees.

"You are stronger than you look, but I am a Hunter. apprentice!" The Hunter notices that he is in the corner of the room. His knees trembled while he witnessed the bloody chain of events. "Get the fuck over here! You better not have shitted yourself!" he yells as the apprentice walks over. He notices that the blonde Hunter is now moving as well, as the other Hunter is slowly pulling himself off of the floor. The Hunter grabs him by the shoulder, "Now you see this apprentice? This was a warlock, and a strong one to boot." The Hunter pulls the sword from Jason's body, watching as the pool of blood well around him. "But as you can see, it only takes a Hunter's final blow to end his fighting spirit." He smiles as the apprentice nods his head. "Now, you will go and find his child." he draws a small blade and hands it to the apprentice. "End its fucking life."

Jason whispers; "No, please not my son!" as tears stream down his face, mixing with his blood. He has no strength left to move, nor magic left to draw from. He watches as the apprentice walks towards Richtor's room. He begins thinking of how useless and weak he was. Even with all the magical prowess he had possessed, he could not protect his loved ones. As his breath is shortened and eyes become heavy. Jason's last thoughts were how he would miss Angel, his beautiful wife, along with his son, they were his everything. He tried to remember her lovely smile which made his soul shine as if touched by the sun. It was the only comfort he had left and that knowing his son may be joining him shortly. Under his breath, Jason whispered his final phrase, 'Altor Patronus' and a faint glow left his hand, marking his passing.

The apprentice walks in the child's room, he hears the other two Hunters curse and kick the now dead warlock. He shakes his head to focus on his task, for this will be his first kill. He looks over the sleeping child appearing so peaceful and innocent. His hand is trembling causing him to hold the handle grip of the blade tighter. Standing over the child, he is unsure if he can do the deed. He looks over and grabs a nearby pillow, placing it over the child's face, hoping to smother it and then stabs it. The child awakens and with eyes wide the Apprentice sees its body change. Richtor began to glow mysteriously, as his heavily bleeding wound closed. He began to fight under the apprentice with his claws and tail. He continues to thrash and growl, the apprentice has no choice at this point and drives the blade repeatedly into the baby demon's body. Panting, the apprentice lifts the pillow from the demon's face, it appears again as a human and is no longer moving. He sees that the demon cried as he holds the blood stained blade.

"Apprentice!," the lead Hunter calls out to him, as he walks out of the room to join them. Spotting the blood on the Apprentice face and the blade, the two Hunters cheer for him. "About fucking time!" The medium build Hunter says while patting him on his back. "You finally popped your cherry!" as the other Hunter nudges him. "When we get back to the Hunter's Camp, you can officially become a full fledged Hunter!" the blonde Hunter says, running his fingers through his blonde hair. He was looking forward to leaving this bloody place, as he never had the stomach for the sight of blood. The lead Hunter places a hand on the young boy's shoulder. "You did a good job." noticing the boy's paleness and weak smile. He has now known that feeling of the first kill and the uncertainties of his actions. It is a Hunter's duty, and something they all must face. This path is not one easily walked. It will either make you stronger, or kill you slowly. No wondering whether the youngster will fit in the former or the latter, however he has made his choice and with that they leave the home heading back to the Hunter's Camp. As they departed though, none bothered to notice the earlier glow that surrounded Richtor intensifying. When the glow faded, the body of the baby...was gone.

The scent of blood was so strong that I almost choked as I entered our home. My eyes fall on the sight of Jason's body. I rushed to him, holding him in my arms. "NOOOOOO!" I scream as I am still in my true form. I embrace him in my wings, cradling him, as I can detect four essences of Hunters. I sensed the one that was the strongest which ended the love of my life. I growled with the revelation. The other two

Hunters were slightly weaker, and the last as I sniffed the air. I headed to Richtor's room, after gently laying down poor Jason's body. My heart is racing, seeing sprays of blood painting the walls matching a pool on the bed. I wail in grief that my son is dead! I search the room feverishly for any trace of my child's body, yet there is none. I panic. There is so much blood, but I can detect a hint of the fourth Hunter. My son fought for his life to the very bitter end. I am so proud as I gather his blood soaked blanket.

Angel wraps her husband's body with their son's blanket, lifting him tenderly. As she is on her knees she continues to sob uncontrollably. When she can no longer shed any more tears, she carries him to her garden. Her beautiful garden where she felt so much peace, this would now be the final resting place for her beloved family. She began to dig into the earth, remembering how she once buried her mother in the same fashion. Once it was deep enough, she placed them in the ground and stood over it wishing this was just a dream, but instead it was her worst nightmare. With the earth between her claws she covers her husband's body with each clump of dirt. Her heart becomes heavy with unbearable sadness.

Angel shifts into her human form. Cleaning herself, she changes her clothing. She then grabs her husband's staff and her son's rattle. Angel uses the staff as a marker for the grave, and hangs the baby rattle on one of the horns. She remembered Richtor playing with the rattle and levitating it all over the house. She chuckles thinking how he had scared Jason into thinking that it was a rattlesnake. Angel falls to her knees and holds herself in front of the grave, feeling alone and empty.

The clouds parted as the angel of Death descended from above. The angel's body glowed of pure holy light only to be seen as a white pair flowing wings. Witnessing the scene in front of it, the angel outstretched its arms. "Departed soul come forth." Jason appears in front of the angel with a thin beam of silver light leading from his hand to somewhere far off in the distance. Jason turns to see Angel grieving for them. "I wish I could comfort her, tell her I love her one last time. She doesn't even know-" The angel of Death shakes its head. "I am sorry, but this is not possible. Your path has ended in this life. Wave your last goodbyes because you will never see her again." With one swift motion they departed into the hereafter.

Angel lifted her head from her hands, believing she heard Jason's voice in the wind. Turning around she realized that there was no one there, only her. Angel left the gravesite in a daze and began to walk into the forest. There was nothing for her; the loss of her family left a hole in her heart. A pack of werewolves noticed her scent and began to stealthily stalk her in the forest, waiting until she stood in an open clearing. The wolves stared at this odd woman whose arms are stretched out and face towards the sun. It didn't matter that she would be but a light snack for the five of them before reaching their destination. They circle her growling and barking at her. It appeared as if she did not notice them with her eyes still closed. One wolf leaped at her, but stopped just short of her, as her eyes opened, appearing blood red.

Angel shifted into her true form and before the wolf could react, her hand was around its throat. It let out a yelp as her claws dug into its flesh, and with one twist of her wrist, she had snapped the wolf's neck. The other four wolves stopped in place, incensed at what this creature had done. Two of the other wolves growl, approaching her more cautiously. Angel hisses at them in an attack stance, as one approaches from behind slashing her wing. She was able to swipe at it with her tail, sending it flying back into a tree. With her back turned the other wolf charges at her and latches onto her hand with the wolf's mouth. She lifts the entire wolf's head off of its body. The wolf's head rolls on the ground closer to the last two dead wolves.

Angel does not wait for the next attack, and leaps into the air. One of her clawed hands slashes one of the wolf's eyes, blinding it. With her other hand she rips into the belly of the other wolf. Its entrails spill from its body as it falls on its side, dead. Angel begins to feed from the blind wolf as it whines, as it is no longer able to see or fight. Her wounds begin to heal, she had never tasted such a rich essence, surely this prey would be worth killing.

Angel's back is still turned as the wolf that flew across the field charges at her. In a mid-leap, an axe landed in the wolf's chest. Angel turns to see who had thrown the weapon at the now deceased werewolf. A man approaches the wolf on the other side of Angel. He is a large, burly man with brown hair and a curly long brown beard. He withdrew the axe easily with his rippling muscles. He gets some blood from the wolf on his plaid shirt. Angel hisses at him, which makes him take a step back from her. She drops the dead wolf from her hand and it lands at her feet.

"Are you alright?" The man asks. Angel is still consumed with bloodlust, and does not respond.

"You have to be cautious, these woods are not safe. I do not know what you are, but I could not let you be slaughtered, outnumbered like this." he says, as Angel stares at his axe. "Oh you take a fancy to this? I am a woodsman. I make trade in selling lumber, and I happen to know these woods are plagued by werewolves. I crafted my axe with silver that kills them, that is, unless you are facing a Silver Wolf. Then, silver does not not immediately slay them, but beheading with an axe works no matter the material, But still, you must be cautious."

The Woodsman turns his back to Angel, continuing to ramble on. She attacks the woodsman with no hesitation, as he falls forward on his face. She slashes into his back as he tries to throw her off of him. She takes her claw and slashes his throat, as he looks up to her. The woodsman croaked out his last words with blood gushing from his open wound; "I was... just an innocent man... who saved you..." Angel thinks of her husband and son. They were innocent, too. Who tried to save them? She roars as the woodsman draws his last breath. Angel stands, breathing in all the carnage that lay before her. She realizes what she wants more than anything. Revenge. The Blood of the Hunters who took away her husband and child would not mend her heart, but it was as good a start as any.

Healer Lawrence quickly approached the home of Jason and Angel. He was concerned when he saw the Hunters heading towards their home looking determined. Damned Hunters, always leaving fear and trouble in their wake. Nothing good ever comes when they are around, he thinks. Please God, let them be okay as he walks into their home. "Jason... Angel, are you home?!?" he stops in his tracks as he notices the excessive blood on the floor. Where are the bodies? he wonders. He continues to search for Jason and Angel. In the child's room there is more blood on the bed, but there is still no body. Scratching his head for the love of God, where is this family?

Healer Lawrence walks towards the back and sees an odd, hammer-like object, with what appears to be a baby rattle. As he approaches closer, he suddenly realizes that he is standing in front of a grave. "Oh God No! I can't believe this!" he cries, and starts to dig up the grave.

As he continues to dig he finally discovers a body wrapped in a blanket, which is revealed to be Jason. Healer Lawrence can not help but cry at the loss of the father and husband, but where is Angel and the baby? Did the Hunters take them? Were they killed somewhere else? There were so many questions swirling in his mind. He wiped his tears and reburied the body. He says a prayer for the soul to find peace. As quickly as he arrived, he left the home heading back into town. He had to speak to Mayor Hamilton immediately. Healer Lawrence was out of breath when he finally had reached the Mayor's office. "Lawrence, for the love of God, are you alright, man?" the Mayor asked as Lawrence made his way to a chair to sit. After he calmed his breathing, the Healer explained everything he had discovered at Jason and Angel's home. Mayor Hamilton looked shocked and saddened. He and Healer Lawrence went to the town bell. The Mayor rang it to summon every townsperson to the square.

"My dear townspeople, I have distressing news." the Mayor says, choosing his words carefully. "It is with a heavy heart that I have to report that Jason was discovered dead. Healer Lawrence has informed me of this tragic news, and that Angel and the baby are missing and presumed dead as well." Gasps and cries can be heard from the townspeople. A villager shouts; "There were five werewolves found dead in the forest west of the border, among them, the local woodsman was found dead!" There are wails and exclamations among the townspeople now, frightened that this has all occurred so close to their town. "Please calm yourselves, people. Everyone, just go to your homes until further notice, until we can investigate all of these incidents!" Mayor Hamilton declares.

A tan broad shoulder man with long red hair and medium height steps forward from the crowd. "This would not happen if we had a Sentinel in our town! Matter of fact, I Silas will train to be the new Sentinel of Blackberry Bush!" He has big feet, and almost stumbles over himself. Not wanting to create more of a scene, Mayor Hamilton says;

"Now, there will be none of that. We are a quiet town, and have no need for such a dark taskmaster." Silas looks at the Mayor with disgust. "Well if we did, then none of this would be happening! I am leaving this town and I will become a Sentinel!" and with that, he departs. The townsfolk begin going to their homes with uncertainty and fear of what fate has befallen their town of Blackberry Bush.

CHAPTER 14

The nightmare is always the same. I am placing the pillow over his head. I have the dagger in my hand, as I begin to stab him repeatedly, refusing to stop until he stops moving. Once I remove the pillow, his eyes open, pitch black as he changes into a demon. His claws dig into my chest as I am screaming, and then his fangs bore into my neck. "NO!" I wake up screaming, sweat soaking through my night shirt. Every night I awaken from the same nightmare. It's the blood and pain that I remember the most. I place my head in my palms. I can't stop trembling as I remember those black eyes burrowing into my soul. Yet no matter how I rationalize my actions, there will be no peace for me. I clutch my stomach and run to the nearest tree to vomit the contents of last night's dinner. As I walked back to my sleeping area I noticed that the lead Hunter was sitting up with an annoyed look on his face. "What the fuck!? This fucking shite again with you!? Well, since you're up and can't keep anything down, make your sorry arse useful, and go hunt us up some breakfast for the morning!" He shakes his head and lays back down to sleep.

I grab what weapon would be most useful to me, a bow and arrow. The one and only thing I am good at hunting with, I never want to wield a blade again. Besides, I'm better suited to archery. It is a skill that I've been naturally gifted at since I was a child. My father had no time to teach me anything, he was more concerned with women and drinking.

"Boy, you know you're nothing but a piece of shite" my father would say, often followed by a swig of his drink. "What are you going to do with your life, eh?" I'd continue to eat my meal. I never answered, as there was never a right answer for him. He'd stand up as my thought was that he would mercifully pass out very soon anyway from the drink. "I know what I'm gonna do for you, boy..." the stench on his breath caused bile to fill in my throat. "Let's go. I know where you will fit in nicely." and he grabbed me by the shoulders pulling me out of the door. My father changed after my mother died from illness, that was when I had to deal with his daily routine of beatings. These stopped once I would no longer cry from the pain he afflicted as he said he was 'toughening me up'. Honestly, I felt too numb to feel the pain any longer. What was my purpose for being here?

We arrived in front of a Hunter's Camp. I noticed this, as the flag of a flaming sword insignia was blowing in the wind. "I need to see Hunter Dean right away." my father says. A man dressed in a cloak of the same flaming sword insignia, obviously a Hunter, looked at him. "Who the fuck are you?!! Why in the Hell would he want to see a lowlife shite like you?!" The Hunter looks at my father, sizing him up with disgust. My father pulls out two silver coins. I guess he didn't have enough time to waste it on women and drink. He hands them to the Hunter. "Tell him my name is Robert Herstick. He will know who I am." The Hunter smiled devilishly, pocketing the coins for himself. When he returns, he says; "Follow me..." we are then led to a larger tent, and walk in.

Hunter Dean sits behind a desk reading some scrolls. "What do you want, Herstick?" He says without looking up from his papers. "Oh Dean my boy, it's always good to see you!" exclaims my father. The Hunter glares at him. "YOU WILL ADDRESS ME AS HUNTER DEAN!" his voice booms as my father is taken aback. "Of course, of course, my apologies Hunter Dean." bowing his head in respect, while he fumbles with the brim of his hat in his hands. "I don't want to take much of your time, but this is my boy, Sebastian. Now, let me say that I know he doesn't look very strong. He's a hard worker and a good shot with a bow, though. Just the other day, he brought home a buck for dinner, and you know those bastards are fast. So, I was wondering if you could make a Hunter of him?"

The question hit me like a blow to my stomach. Hunter Dean walks over to me, sizing me up and laughs. "There really is not much to this boy!" he states as he rubs his chin thoughtfully. "I know, I know, but here..." my father passes a small bag of coins to Hunter Dean. "This is six silver, all I have. Please make my son a man!?" he pleads with him. I can't believe that my father was selling me to the Hunters, worse yet, paying them to take me! Worse still, he stole MY money that I earned hunting three days ago to do it!!! My fist was balled in anger. He had treated me like shite and now this. Hunter Dean looked at me again after taking the coins. "Well now, welcome to your first day as an apprentice." and with that, my father left without ever saying another word to me.

My father's betrayal made me push myself harder in training everyday, even though I failed at many of my tasks. It was in hunting that I excelled among my peers. I was assigned to Hunter Aubrey, who was harsh, but strong and wise. Along with him was a medium build male Hunter Oscar, and his blonde friend, Hunter Sean. Oscar and Sean would constantly tease me and nicknamed me "Half Pint." "Come on, Half Pint, pick up the fucking pace! You're always lagging behind!" he'd say while pointing me out to the others. Sean laughed, always knocking me on my back with his hand, causing me to drop the supplies I was carrying. "Oh sorry, Half Pint. Guess you'd better be more careful next time." This was to become my new life, a life that I never asked for, nor was I given a choice.

Sebastian found his prey, a boar resting at a nearby tree. With his bow and arrow ready, he shot it clear and true through its head. Only a squeal can be heard as it dies. He walks over and begins to hogtie the beast. Drawing out the arrow, he sighs with a thought that this is the only killing that he has ever felt comfortable with. Pulling the beast over his shoulder, Sebastian turned after hearing a rustle come from some bushes. He rushes back to the camp area, where the Hunters are still asleep. He places the boar in a safe area where no other beasts can poach it. Tired from his task, he finally rests himself, so maybe there will not be any more nightmares awaiting him, if he's lucky. Maybe. From the bushes a pair of crimson eyes stare at the sleeping camp.

The next morning the men awoke, stretching their bodies preparing for the long day ahead. It would be another three day journey before they reached the Hunter's Camp. Oscar was the first to notice the boar, and cut it down from the safe area. "Now that is some fine fucking meat! Not a bad job, Half Pint!" as Sean snickers, admiring the animal as well. "Enough with that shit today!" Hunter Aubrey groans, looking forward to ending his journey with these fools. "Apprentice, go fetch some wood to start a fire so we can cook this meat. Oh, and don't drag your ass. I want to start traveling soon." Sebastian leaves the group in search of wood with an axe in his hand. "That fucking kid is going to be a Hunter, eh? Huh, what a damn waste!" Oscar shakes his head, while saying. "Well, he did kill a demon..." Sean began to flay the flesh from the boar. "So he says it was a demon, but we don't fucking know. He could be lying for fuck's sake." Just then Hunter Aubrey punches him in the face. "Watch your damn mouth, Oscar! We are a brotherhood, and he is our brother! If you're calling him a liar, you are calling me a liar as well. So am I a liar!?!" Towering over him with his fist balled. "No, no Sir, I believe Half Pint." he nervously replied. "Also, stop with that Half Pint shite, either call him apprentice or by his name! That goes for you too Sean! He will be a Hunter soon, so we start treating him like one!" The two nod their heads as neither of them want to be targeted in his sights.

Suddenly, Oscar hears a rustling from a nearby bush. He pulls himself from the ground, and approaches where the sound is coming from. He draws his sword as he hears the sound again. Angel leaps from the bushes before he can react, slicing his throat with her claw as blood gushes forth from his jugular. As he pulled one hand back he realized that there was nothing left but blood there. Angel had gouged out large chunks from his neck, therefore he could no longer consider screaming as he fell to his knees. He felt his body grow cold quickly before everything faded to black. Hunter Oscar fell forward landing on his face, dead. Angel quickly kneeled in a three point stance, and with a sudden burst of speed, dashed behind the blonde Hunter. Sean did not realize this until the fear jolted through his heart as she escaped his sight. There was very little in the way of warning before the pointed tip of Angel's tail was thrusted through the back of his head, skewering him. When she pulled her tail back, his inner meat was still attached. His body did not even yet have a chance to fall, as Angel turned her attention to the last Hunter.

Hunter Aubrey stands prepared for Angel's attack, but then he hears a voice in his head. "You are the one who killed my beloved mate!" she grumbles, hissing at him. Aubrey realizes it is the voice of the demon before him. Gritting his teeth, he says; "Foul demon I ended his pathetic life! How he spawned a child with you at all is a sinful act! Unholy Creature! Now, you will join your wicked family in the 13 Hells!" He charges at her. She ducks safely from the swing of his sword and grabs his arm. Angel gives a ferocious yank, and rips his arm off of his body. The Hunter screams in pain and anger, still holding the sword in his remaining hand. Angel is faster than an average Hunter as she is blessed with having harpy blood within her veins. She smiles wanting to take her time with him as he continues to swing his sword, missing her each time. Angel finally catches his wrist with her clawed hand as she kicks him in the stomach, savagely tearing the other arm from his body.

The Hunter falls to the ground and begins to laugh. "GO AHEAD AND KILL ME, BITCH! MORE OF MY BROTHERS WILL EVENTUALLY FIND AND KILL YOU!" Angel smiles,

"Well until then, allow me to send you to heaven, before I send you to hell!" She kneels in front of him and pulls down his trousers exposing his manhood which is slightly erect from battle. She licks his shaft which brings it to full attention. Angel straddles him as he begs her not to. "Don't you want to feel the inside of this vile creature?" she whispers as she guides him into her weeping hole. She grinds up and down on his considerable girth with her slit, listening to his delicious screams mixed with his moans. The blood from where his arms once were pumped out more on the ground with each of her movements. Angel feeds on his life essence as he finally coats her walls with his seed. Angel looks down at the once mighty Hunter whose face has literally exploded with blood.

Horror and joy washed over his dead face, as she stayed on top of him absorbing his liquids. When she removes him from her entrance, she then rips his member from his body before shoving it down his throat. A last insult to injury as she smiles, looking at her lovely handiwork.

Sebastian is heading back to the camp area carrying wood in his arms. He had to go deeper into the forest to get the driest wood for a good fire. As he approaches the area, he drops the firewood and witnesses the gruesome scene before him. The Hunters, all slaughtered!! Before him stood the demon, her eyes blood red. "OH NO!" he screams, turns and begins to run as he hears the growl of the demon behind him. He briefly stops, and as he does, he notices that she is nowhere in sight. Panting, he tries to catch his breath, when the demon is right before him. She grabs him by the throat, pressing him hard against a tree. He struggles to breathe. "You are the one who killed my son??!!" she hisses through clenched teeth. "I'm sorry, I'm sorry." he chokes out at her. "He was my only child, my precious miracle!! You stole him away from me! You FUCKING HUNTERS!" she screams in his head. Angel then begins to feed from Sebastian, but what she sees are images of Richtor's last moments.

This Hunter carried the memory of her son, fresh in his mind. But why? She hears Richtor calling for her. "Mommy! Mommy!" His last thoughts were of her, she realized as tears stung her face. She drops the Hunter to the ground. "Thank you, thank you for sparing my life." he says. Angel rakes her claws across Sebastian's eyes, tearing his retinas and blinding him. Sebastian screams in pain.

"You don't deserve death. I want you to live and remember what you did. I took your sight so your only thoughts will be on the demon that scarred you as you have scarred me. Choose another profession, and pray that our paths never cross again." Angel leaves him while he continues to cover his eyes, howling in pain as she shrieks in the distance.

In a clearing in the woods, some mysterious figures gather by a tree next to the mouth of a large cave. One of the figures laid a severed human arm onto a long flat rock before the tree, which has claw marks on it. The figure then turned to the group. "There, the werebear should be satisfied with that offering, let the meeting commence." This figure reveals himself to be the Rogue Alpha, Issac with his dark hair, piercing grey eyes, and tall stature as his aura illuminates his high position. He was the former Alpha of the Golden Claw pack of werewolves, whose previous Alpha (his father) mysteriously was poisoned. Alpha Issac ruled the pack along with his mother, who was known as the Luna. His sister was his Beta or his second-in-command.

Every wolf bent to his every whim, so when it was discovered that he was having an incestuous affair with his mother and sister, no one challenged him.

There was disgust and shock among the pack. It wasn't until the Alpha King, who ruled over all the werewolves stepped in to address this, as well as other accusations that Alpha Issac murdered his father, that the pack would dare to hope for some manner of justice. Alpha Issac had two choices; death, or banishment from the Golden Claw pack forever and becoming a rogue. He chose to become a rogue, and it did not take him long to establish a new position among other rogue werewolves.

Alpha Issac's Beta stepped forward from the shadows. "What is your report?" he asks as she bows her head to the Alpha in respect. "Rogue pack A was assigned to attack the town of Blackberry Bush, and was discovered dead." A hushed murmuring is heard from the other members. Alpha Issac growls and all become silent as the Beta continues. "They were viciously killed as their wolf bodies were torn apart and slashed. A large human male was found among them, also slashed. It would appear to be the work of a vampire, but the scent is completely off, and entirely different." Issac holds up his hand. "Enough!" the Beta bows and returns back to her spot.

"These activities are very concerning, especially at a time when I am in the work of expanding my territory." He mindlinks with the warrior who discovered the dead bodies of the werewolves, and marvels at the work the creature created. Such precision and strikes that Issac knew that this could not have come from a mere vampire. Issac felt himself becoming aroused from the bloody images. He cuts the mindlink. "Simply beautiful..." he whispers as he closes his eyes. Ending the meeting, he returns to the rogue encampment, his scouts greeting him with a bow. Fear is what governs his new pack. If there is no loyalty, then death is imminent.

Alpha Issac enters his tent, where his Omega she-wolf awaits him. Omegas are low status wolves whose only purpose is to serve, whether that be a King, Alpha, Beta, Delta or Gamma. The Higher the rank, the stronger the wolf, and a human must be equally strong to handle such a wolf, especially during the shifting into a wolf form. Issac's wolf was named Maximilian. They both shared the same goal to be the strongest and become the Alpha King. This required him to expand his pack and take over other werewolf packs. He smiled as the she-wolf rubbed his chest. "You're thinking about that creature too, eh?" his wolf asks, stirring in his head. "Yes I am truly intrigued by the scene of the slaughter." feeling as the she-wolf laps at his neck. "So, we are in agreement of what to do next..." smiling at his wolf's thoughts. "Yes." He then grabs the she-wolf by her wrist, jerking her to the ground. She is on her knees in front of him, looking at him with those innocent brown eyes. She reminds him of his mother, those damn eyes, raven hair, and sweet red lips. It was the reason why he chose this particular Omega. How he craved for his Luna, lover, and mother.

"Issac we can't do this!" as his mother Rebecca tried to break free of his grasp. "Your mate is dead, mother. You are the Luna in this Pack," he states coldly. "which means by right you belong in my bed." She gasps; "How can you say such a thing? What about your father and sister? We are family!" she pleads. "Don't worry about my sister," he smiles devilishly. "She will warm my bed as well, and can not defy my will." Holding her close to his body. The Luna shed tears for the son she once loved and looks at the monster that now stands before her. He tears the dress from her body, as she attempts to cover herself. Rebecca feels only fear and shame as her son pushes her onto the bed, ravishing her breasts, suckling on her nipples as he once did as a baby.

Now he is a demon trying to set her on fire, and all she can do is close her eyes, hoping that it will end soon. He hovers over her body, ignoring her tears. She will learn to love him as a mate. He nudges the small skin between her neck and shoulder, while he marks her with his canines. She gasps in pain, and eventually pleasure, as he claims her body as his.

Issac awakes with the Omega lying at his feet. He is truly never satisfied, but ambition runs through his veins, as it must for any Alpha. After the Omega cleans and dresses him, he mindlinks with his Beta. "Bring two of my best warriors ro me. I will be going to the forest near Blackberry Bush, myself." There is some hesitation from the Beta. "but My Alpha-" "Do not question me!" his voice echoes in the Beta's head, causing her to whimper. "Do as I command!" with that two of his warriors are already approaching him in their wolf forms, bowing to him. Issac shifts into Maximillion. "Took you long enough." he says to Issac who chuckles. All three head to the border of Blackberry Bush, Maximilian sniffs the area, which is now clear of the dead bodies.

"Scout the area to ensure that there are no other creatures around. I do not want any interruptions." Bowing their heads they respond; "Yes Alpha!" and run in the opposite directions. The Alpha tracks an unfamiliar scent. It is sweet like fresh fallen rain, but the rain is actually blood. It was definitely a demon, he surmises as the scent lingers in his snout. This will be imprinted in his memories. He feels that it will not be the last time this scent will cross his path.

CHAPTER 15

I t had been three moons since Angel had massacred the Hunters. Since then, she has flown to an unknown territory. Her wings were tired, and she decided to walk for a while. Angel was covered in blood. Some was from prey she had viciously killed, as well as the viscous fluid from those Hunters. She lifts her arms and smells herself."For the love of the Goddess!" she exclaims, scrunching her nose. It is obvious she needs to bathe soon. Angel notices a lake on the other side of a grassy field. Flying was not an option temporarily, so she decided to walk across the field, but suddenly she loses her balance and falls. As she pulls herself up, she notices movement where she had walked from. A large figure slowly rose, sporting a head, limbs, and body parts that were composites of other body parts of various flesh. Even its face seemed sewn together out of the flesh of many human faces. He was massive, easily two feet taller than the largest man that Angel had ever seen.

Angel hisses and growls at the strange creature and buries her claws deep within its chest. The wound instantly closes as Angel exclaims; "What in the hell are you?" The giant takes a step back. "I am sorry that I startled you my dear," it bellows. "I found myself here before for lack of anything better to do. You have my apologies." Angel continues to stare at the now closed wound. "Again I ask: what are you?" "I am nothing, because I am not alive. Neither of us look common, yet I imagine you at least know what you are." he explains. "Well, I know little, but I am not living for any purpose. I do not exist." Angel is amazed that this creature can understand her without bleeding from its orifices. It appears very intelligent, as well as polite. She is amused by this odd creature. Noticing her smile, the creature says, "You have a lovely smile. May I ask your name?" "My name is Angel, and what is yours?" she replies as she reaches her hand out to the creature. A puzzled look appears on its face. "I have no name to offer." It reaches its hand out to her anyway in return. "Then I will give you a name that is fitting. Legion, your name is Legion." A smile spreads across his face. "I will not be alone because I am Legion now." and with that, he follows her to the lake.

Angel removes her clothing as she enters the clear, blue water. Legion watches from the lakeshore as she bathes. She begins to wash the blood away from her hair, skin, and body. So much blood was collected that she had lost count on just how many she had slain. Her dress was as filthy as she, so she washes it as well, putting it back on still wet. She turns back to see Legion watching her. What an odd companion this is, she thinks. In the time that passes, Legion continues to travel with Angel, even as she soars above him. She does not fly too far ahead of him, and mindlinks with him to communicate. The loneliness seems to be lost with Legion conversing with her on various topics. He appears to be very learned, most likely because of his own travels or something else. Angel stalks nearby prey and informs Legion that she will be needing to feed soon. As she stuns and feeds on the prey's essence, she sees Legion approach. Angel drops the prey to the ground as Legion's mouth stretches and swallows the prey whole. Angel stares at him in fascination when a part of the prey, an antler, forms on his shoulder. What an amazing being Legion is, she thinks and decides to walk with him instead of flying.

Angel and Legion notice that the weather has become colder. Snow begins to fall, as it covers the ground in white. The wind also becomes much harsher. Angel wraps her wings around herself, but the coldness still starts to take its effect on her. Legion picks her up and carries her in his arms. His body warmth soothes her as the cold doesn't affect him. As they travel farther, Legion notices a tall and majestic looking tree, which appears to have a door. "Angel, I will make sure to protect you from this changing element." Legion says as the door slowly opens. Standing there is a gray haired older woman, who appears to be blind. "Who goes there? Braving such a storm?" She reaches her hand and touches Legion's arm. "By the Goddess! Please come in!" she beckons, appearing to have some familiarity of the being in front of them. "I am sorry to intrude, but my friend needs warmth, and I can only give a little of what she requires." Gently Legion lays Angel near a roaring fireplace. Angel shifts into her human form as she has fallen into a deep slumber.

The woman places a blanket around her body. "No need to worry, she is exhausted and has shifted to protect herself. It is in her nature to do so." Legion is shocked by this old woman's knowledge of Angel. He did not even know this about her. She laughs, "Where are my manners? I am Glenda." Legion reaches over to her to shake her hand. She seems surprised by this action.

"I am called Legion. It is a pleasure to meet you." he says. "Is there something the matter, Glenda? If I may call you Glenda?". She shakes her head. "Oh no Legion, there is not, and yes you may call me Glenda." she said. "You should rest as well. When your friend wakes we will speak further." as she retires for the night into another room. Legion pulls himself in a corner where he has a good view of Angel. He closes his eyes to enter a dreamless sleep.

I awake in a strange place and realize that I was in my human form. I notice Legion resting in the corner as he begins to stir. I look around to see an old, gray haired woman, whose eyes are white. She gives me a gentle smile. "Good morning! you're awake and well rested, I hope?" she reaches her hand out to me. "Hello, I am Angel." she nods her head. "I know who you are, I foresaw your coming and the bringing of the Golem to my door." We begin to sit as Legion joins us. "Angel, are you well?" Legion gives a concerning look. "Yes Legion I am. Thank you very much for taking care of me." I placed a hand on his arm. "This is so amazing!" the woman gasped, "Oh, in my old age I have gotten so forgetful. My name is Glenda, I am the last witch of the Nocturnal Assembly coven. Please forgive my rudeness, but Legion you have exceeded our expectations." I am confused by Glenda's words, as it appears she has knowledge of the both of us. Glenda stands and goes to bring tea for Legion and myself.

"Let me start from the beginning in order to clear things up." she says, pouring herself a cup of tea. I look over at Legion and begin to sip my tea as she begins her tale.

"The witches of the Nocturnal Assembly coven were well known in the Northern territories. The High Priestess protected her sisters with all the power she had, and continued to share her wisdom with them. This was a peaceful coven, and was prosperous, withstanding many threats. The most deadliest of these threats were Hunters, who attempted to kidnap witches for their own wicked personal gains. The High Priestess thought very hard on how she could continue to protect the coven, in the case of being depleted of her power, risking her life and being in a vulnerable state. On the outskirts of their border, she gathered remnants that were left behind from many Hunters that escaped during their recent attempt to ensnare the witches. Along with her sisters, they casted an incantation of resurrection to summon a Golem."

"The purpose of the Golem was to guard the borders from all intruders, especially Hunters. Other than that, the Golem had no other purpose as it had been created with no soul. In the beginning, the Golem did its job well, stopping all Hunters from entering the territory. The High Priestess was proud of her creation, and would visit it to observe how it would act towards her. Even though she was happy to be in the presence of her sister witches, she yearned for male companionship. The Golem was the closest thing to a 'male' that had ever been around, you see a High Priestess' powers come from her virtue. The Golem may not have been a man in one sense, but it had the equipment of Hunters, who in turn were men. To the High Priestess, it made sense to be in his presence since she no longer required her powers. The High Priestess had witnessed her sister witches leaving to encounter males during the mating season. They would return with a female child, hence increasing the coven. How she envied them, desiring to share such pleasure with a man. Besides, with the Golem there protecting the coven, she could continue to remain in her position as High Priestess. So she had decided at that moment that she would give herself to the Golem. She unfortunately did not realize that she was being watched. A band of Hunters attacked during their sexual encounter, while holding down the Golem. They took axes and chopped its body into pieces. The High Priestess witnessed this vicious onslaught on the Golem, but she was too weakened to save the Golem or herself. The Hunters massacred all of the witches of the Nocturnal Assembly coven, but one survived..." Glenda finished her tale as Angel and Legion stared at her in astonishment. She smiled, "Well barely survived, they did take my sight, but it was a small price, I say." She walks towards Legion. "You survived as well," she said, touching his face. "by absorbing dead bodies, you were able to revive even without a spell, and gained strength as well. Do you remember anything?"

"No Glenda, I am nothing and I only carry basic knowledge from what I have consumed." she laughs. "Well that is to be suspected, but it does not, Angel." she turns towards her. "Thank you, as I told you before I've seen you in your succubus form. Yes, I know about your kind." Angel looks at her, knowing how powerful witches are, having read about them during her life with Jason and Richtor.

How she missed them, as tears streamed down her face. Glenda opens her arms and engulfs her in an embrace. "Angel, I know your pain and loss. Let it empower and give you strength. Forgive those who caused it, and find purpose in life." Angel begins to feel a warm energy within her body as she continues to close her eyes. Angel remembers the love she received from her mother, Jason, the people of Blackberry Bush, and most of all her son Richtor. In that moment, she feels overcome with peace, as she falls from Glenda's arms, and Legion catches her."Glenda, what has happened to Angel?" Legion asked, looking down at Angel's fragile form. "Well Legion, I casted a healing spell which put her in a state of rest and made me a little tired too." She flops on the soft cushion of her armchair. "You can lay her in my bed and then we can continue to get to know each other." She smiles while Legion goes into the other room with Angel in his arms.

Angel and Legion remained at Glenda's home for five days, until the storm passed. During that time Angel wondered where she and Legion would be journeying to next. "Glenda, do you know of any other creatures that are in this territory?" Angel asked. Glenda lifts her head from the game of cards that she was playing with Legion, which she had taught Legion how to play. "Well, there are not many creatures that come this far North, due to the cold." She places a finger on her cheek thinking. "I have heard that there were werewolves who travel in packs through this area, more than I would like to recall. I am thankful that Hunters have not come to my door. I did cast an illusion spell, but

I was surprised that Legion was able to find my home. Then again, he is full of surprises." she replies as Legion places his card down. "Gin, I win again!" Glenda pouts and Angel can't help, but laugh as Glenda inspects his cards, accusing Legion of cheating.

Legion innocently declares that he won fairly, and doesn't understand why she is so upset. He suggests Glenda have some tea to relax. Angel is literally in tears from laughter, holding her stomach as the events continue to play out. Angel is thankful she has crossed paths with Legion and Glenda. The Gods do work in mysterious ways.

Once the storm has passed, Angel prepares to depart with Legion and shifts into her true form, stretching her wings. "Angel, may I have a word?" Legion asks, stepping outside. Angel nods with a smile. She was not anticipating this conversation, but sensed it was coming. Legion was apologetic as he explained that he would not be going with Angel, but would be remaining with Glenda. Angel gives Legion a hug. He truly was becoming more than a soulless Golem. He had now become her friend, and she promised that she would visit them someday and gave Glenda a hug and her thanks. Angel took flight, and headed further North, feeling grateful for what she was leaving behind.

A battlefield of bodies was soon laid before her, werewolves in both wolf form, and those in their human forms. It is a familiar scene that Angel had come across often after she had left Glenda's. The loss of life was great in this territory, but she took advantage to feed on those who were still on the brink of death. She is a succubus after all, and it was her instinct to feed whenever the chance presented itself. She enjoyed the life essence of what she realized were rogues. They were a treat as a big meal. Angel always feels so giddy thinking about them after feeding. Maybe it is because she is somewhat of a rogue herself, with no family left to speak of. Their life essence becomes a part of her, giving her their strength so that in a way, she does not feel alone.

Angel lands on the branch of a tree. She has not traveled very far, when she sees another battlefield before her. This time she notices a carriage, which is turned onto its side. Angel hears a cry coming from the inside of the overturned carriage. A rogue werewolf emerges from the forest. Angel realizes it has heard the cry as well. It charges towards the carriage at full speed. Angel flies over to the carriage and lands, positioning herself where the wolf can clearly see her. It stops startled at the sight of her and begins to growl. Angel kneels in full attack stance and spreads her wings, hissing at the wolf. The wolf leaps up at her, bracing to attack. Angel in mid-flight grabs its neck and with her other hands snaps its neck in half. The wolf's body hits the ground dead, as she shrieks in victory. The cries could still be heard inside of the carriage.

Inside, she finds a dead woman holding a crying baby. She reaches inside to pull the child out, who appears to be injured. It is a boy, and a pup from his scent, meaning both parents are werewolves. He had black hair, deep blue eyes, and his breathing was becoming shallow. Angel's only thoughts were of her own son Richtor, as she holds this child in her arms. She can not bring herself to end his life. Before death can claim him, Angel does the unthinkable. Angel gives the child some of her life essence, unsure if she can save his life. His cries stop as she looks at him, the child now sleeping peacefully. On his right hand, there appears to be a blue birthmark in the shape of her pointed tail. Angel lifts her tail to compare it visually to the birthmark.

Angel smiles, as at least the baby will live to see another day, even if he will not be with his mother, she thinks. Holding him closer to her, she decides at that moment she will care for and protect him as if he was her own. She looks down at the woman who was his mother. "I promise I will care for your son and protect him with my life. You can rest in peace." as she says a silent prayer. Angel opens her wings and takes flight. She noticed that the blanket that the child was wrapped in bore the insignia of a red moon. This must be the symbol of the child's pack. The child's father must be worried, if he lives. It probably would be best to bring the boy back to him. She would then figure out what to do from there.

Angel uses the scent of the child to find his pack, as she continues to fly she soon notices a flag bearing the red moon insignia. Before she crosses the border, she lands to shift into her human form. The boy remains asleep and is breathing normally now, which is a good sign. She needs to play it safe for now, and being in her human form will show that she is not a threat. Angel crosses the line into the pack's territory and immediately hears the howling of werewolves. Cradling the child closer to her, she realizes that she is being watched. There are blurs of wolves seen in the forest beside her as she walks towards a wooden gate entrance. A man approaches her as well as several werewolves, which close in from all sides. She feels his energy. He was no normal werewolf that she had ever crossed. This was the aura of an Alpha. Angel holds out the sleeping child to him. "Bring me the pack Healer!" he yelled, never swaying his eyes from her face. He is a tall man, well built with black hair and blue eyes. Angel noticed a scar over his eye, as he continued to stare at her.

A man came running toward them dressed in Healer's attire. He appeared as a much older man than the Alpha. She holds out the sleeping child to him. He takes the child from her arms nervously; she can't help but to give him a little smile. It takes all of her will not to follow him. She remains in place; she has encountered many werewolves in her travels, but never an Alpha. His aura was illuminated with so much power that simply breathing it in was intoxicating. "Guards!" quickly two men came to his side with bowed heads. "Take her to the dungeon until further notice." the Alpha commanded, his eyes remaining fixed on her the entire time. "Yes Alpha!" they say in unison, as they placed shackles on Angel's wrists and escorted her to the dungeon.

It has been a few days since I'd arrived in what I'd learned was the Red Moon pack's settlement.. I hear this from the guards in passing speaking to another guard during a shift change. "I heard they found Luna Elizabeth dead among several rogues and some of our own warriors." My back is facing them as I lay on a cot listening. "Prince Alex's scent was there, as well as an unknown scent that the warriors could not track." I smile, so that's the body's name, and it appears that the Alpha is his father. "Well, it doesn't matter because he is home now." the other guard says. "So, how is the delicious looking human doing?" I hear him smacking his lips, "Asshole, don't even think about it! We have orders, and she is not to be touched." one guard says. "Yeah, yeah, I know. Get out of here, I'm here to relieve you." I hear a door slam, and feel the guard's eyes on my body. He opens the cell door and is standing over me as his breathing is labored. "Stand up woman!" he orders me as I roll onto my back. Enjoying the view, he hungrily gazes at my heaving breasts. "Mmmm, I wonder how tasty you really are..." he says, licking his lips as I notice his growling arousal. Before he can place a hand on my shoulder, I quickly punch him in the stomach, which instantly knocks him out as he falls to the ground. I take his keys, removing my shackles and locking him in the cell, which I will not miss.

The first thing I will need to do is mask my human scent. I've learned to do this when I am stalking my prey in my true form, and came to realize that I can do this as a human as well. I am not sure if I can take down a pack of werewolves. I carefully hide myself in the shadows of the castle to not draw further notice. It appears there is a buzz of activity going on, which is a plus in my favor. I sniff the air for Alex's scent. I hear his cries coming from behind a closed door. As I turned the knob I thought I caught a whiff of another scent in the room, but as I entered, it soon vanished. I scan the room where I only find Alex laying in a bassinet, his little hands reaching up out of it. I walk over and lift him into my arms and he briefly stops crying, but then begins to wail even louder. Then I realize that he does not recognize me. I shift into my true form, remembering to continue to mask my scent. He looks up at me with those beautiful blue eyes, smiling and cooing at me. I rub my face on his chubby cheeks as he reaches for my horns. He is a strong pup, as he attempts to place his mouth on them. I can't help but to laugh.

"So, this is who you really are..." a husky voice comes from the shadows. I hiss, holding Alex close to me as I see the Alpha standing behind me.

CHAPTER 16

"Such a beautiful creature you are..." the Alpha says, stepping closer in the moonlight. "I hope I did not startle you." he walked over to light the candles, causing him to gasp when he caught a full view of Angel. She was still holding Alex, who was desperately trying to get her attention, reaching his pudgy fingers towards her face. Angel has not moved since noticing his presence. It is not fear that has her paralyzed, but rather the sheer awe that this Alpha can mask his scent and considerable presence. This could be trouble, she thinks, yet she will not allow fear to cloud her judgement. "Do you understand me, my pet?" he smirks at her. She is annoyed by the nickname which he apparently has thrust upon her. Angel established a mindlink with him. "Yes..." his eyes became wide "By the Moon Goddess, you can mindlink, and with such a lovely voice as well..." he chuckles.

Angel soon heard another voice laughing. "Don't be rude Xander, you should introduce yourself." the Alpha says. "Stupid human you haven't either, all you have been doing is drooling over yourself." Angel can not believe she is overhearing a conversation between the Alpha and his wolf. "Okay, okay, calm down. My name is Alpha Ivan of the Red Moon pack. That pup you hold tightly to your breast is my son, Prince Alexander, the heir of the pack." The other voice then speaks; "I am Xander, the Cursed Wolf of Death." Angel notices that Ivan's eyes have become black, indicating that the wolf has taken possession of his body for a brief moment.

Alexander cries for Angel, becoming impatient that her attention is being drawn away from him. Angel smiles and coos at him. "He has always been a rather attention seeking pup, even with his mother. It always seemed that I had to compete for her attention." he scoffs and takes a seat in a chair. "She was the Luna for the pack only. A Mother to her son, but nothing more. I did not want a mate, but rejecting her meant losing my status. That I will not allow." He is deep in his thoughts, then looks up at her. "You are the reason for Alex's change of scent. It's not noticeable by the average werewolf, but as the Alpha, I know." Alex begins to whine, until with a touch of her hand, Angel compels him to sleep and he immediately gives her a sweet yawn.

"Ivan, she is full of surprises!" Xander chuckles while Ivan joins in. "We are going to have so much fun together, right my pet?" She narrows her eyes at him and gently lays Alex back in his bassinet.

Ivan is still smiling at her when two warriors rush into the room and draw their swords. "Alpha!" he lifts his hand and they become silent. "Do not speak of what you have seen, If either of you utters a word, you both will lose your tongues." They fall to one knee, bowing their heads and quickly leave the room. "Now, where were we, my pet?" as he begins to pour the two of them some wine. "Enough with 'my pet'. I have a name." Angel blurted, well beyond the point of annoyance. "Well, you have not told me your name, so I thought of a more suitable one for you. Your presence in my private quarters has piqued my interest." Ivan playfully quipped as he looked amused.

"Alpha" Angel hears a third voice chime in. "Is everything well?" Ivan responds; "Yes, Beta Austin. I will link with you later." "Yes, my Alpha." the voice responds as Ivan cuts the link to him. "Your name. What is it?" he asks, leaning forward. Angel hesitates before answering. Should she trust him with such information? He seems like a smug asshole, she thinks. Roaring laughter is then heard. "She called you an asshole!" Ivan frowned at his wolf "If I'm an asshole, then you are too!" the wolf growls in response. Angel had not spoken those words. It was obvious that they could delve deeper within her mind without her realizing it. Angel decided she would remember that in the future. "I am called Angel." she says. "Angel" they both moaned in unison, it was Ivan who spoke next. "I want to hear you speak your name aloud. I want to hear it with my ears." Angel smirked this time. "If I spoke to you, you would die." she said through the mindlink. "I would love to see that..." Ivan mocks with a curiosity gleaming in his eyes. Angel opens her mouth for a brief second, but closes it shut when she remembers that Alex is in the room. No, she could not put him at risk. "I see," he says looking over at Alex. "You have changed my son somehow. I could just kill you, but there has been enough loss today. Don't you agree, my pet?" Angel growls as he continues; "No matter, the fact is that you saved his life and it appears that you two have a connection." Angel finally says; "I want to be his protector. I will make him a strong Alpha of the Red Moon Pack." She waits for his response. "You will remain here as a human. My pack is not ready for what you are. I will have to mark you temporarily, to ensure you will not be touched and will be protected only by me." The thought of being marked does not sit well with Angel, but for Alex she was willing to agree.

Alpha Ivan stands up as does Angel, standing in front of each other. Their body heat makes this moment more intense with each passing second. He brushes her scarlet hair from her shoulder, nudging his nose between the soft spot of her shoulder. Licking and sucking at it, Angel begins to purr as he places his hand on the small of her back. "This will hurt for a moment, but then there will be naught but ecstacy, my pet." She ignores his last word, and falls into the ecstasy of his kisses. Suddenly she feels the pierce of canine fangs on her neck. Gasping, she sees his eyes are black looking at her as he bites down. The pleasure sends a wetness between her thighs, clenching her moans, she grabs onto his waist.The wave of pleasure was sending her over the edge, she had never been overwhelmed this way before. Ivan retracts his fangs and licks the blood to seal the mark, his eyes blackened with lust. Angel could see the droplets of blood in the corners of his mouth. She glanced at the mark. It was in the shape of a crescent moon. Angel wanted more. She needed more. She could tell that he sensed the bloodlust in her as well.

Angel falls to her knees and pulls down his trousers, she is surprised at the monumental size of the Alpha's manhood. How could such a member be this long, and still have so much girth? She began licking his shaft, worshipping it with her tongue. He moans gratefully as she sucks the mushroom head, licking the pre release from the tip. Placing it entirely in her mouth, she feels it all the way in the back of her throat and a little further still. She began bobbing her head up and down, increasing her speed with each thrust he gave her in return. Angel wraps her tongue around his cock as it pulsates in her mouth. She digs her claws into the back of his thighs, it is more than he can bare. The Alpha climaxes in her mouth as she feels the ample load of his seed in her mouth. She swallows faster as more flows into her. It fills her belly as she licks the remaining reward from her lips.

As she rises to her feet, she notices that Ivan is not moving, his eyes cleared a glassy white. Angel leans her head to his chest, his heart is still beating, so obviously he is not dead. Angel assumes that because he is an Alpha the effects of a succubus are handled differently than with a human. Before turning towards Alex, she decided to pull up Ivan's trousers. His monstrous cock was distracting, to say the least. Angel looks down at the still sleeping boy. If she left with him she could mask his scent, but there was a high chance that she would be hunted by the pack. At least the mark would warn her of their presence. There were more than a few werewolves here that knew her scent as a human, as well as her true form. Could she really risk this? Angel was deep in thought when she heard a growl, slowly turning around she saw a huge black wolf. The wolf had one green and one blue eye with a white scar over his eye. He bares his fangs and growls at Angel. This must be Xander The Cursed Wolf of Death standing before her.

"I can't believe she is giving us so much pleasure." my human moans. "I want to claim her for our own..." he continues to moan. "Don't be stupid, you're not thinking with your right head, as usual." I roll my eyes. "She is just another conquest, an interesting one at that, but that's all." Something doesn't feel right. "Ivan, make her stop... Ivan, can you hear me?" he isn't responding to me. "Fucking human..." I sigh and watch her stand, realizing what she has done. Sneaky minx, well at least she pulled up his trousers, I snicker. She turns away, approaching the pup. So, that is her true goal. I begin to take over the body, hearing the bones and ligaments cracking, as my claws begin to extend. My head and snout became oblong, and my black fur started to cover my body. She looks surprised at my appearance. I chuckle. "Now we can play, my pet." I snarl as I slowly move towards her. I realize she does not want the pup to be hurt and thinks carefully about her next move.

She truly is a beautiful creature as she crawls to me with her head bowed. So submissively she approaches as she rubs her head and horns against my fur and licks my snout. I moan as I have only dreamed of such affection, but have always feared. Angel is not afraid of me. She crawls towards the large bed and when she stands she lets her dress fall to the floor. Seductively she lays on the bed as I walk towards the front to get a better view of her. Laying on her back, I am able to see all of her lovely shade of azure flesh. Her eyes are the same color of red as her hair. I can only be mesmerized by her movements as she places a finger in her entrance. She pleasures herself, making my mouth water and my cock harder still.

When she climaxes, the scent of her juices fills my nostrils. My pet gets on her knees and lifts her tail, exposing herself to me. "Come to me and take me..." she says, that's all it takes for me to crawl up to her. The bed sinks and creaks as I step up onto it. I sniff and lick her womanhood with my tongue. She shivers with excitement, she tastes amazing to me, so sweet that I cannot compare it to anything I have ever tasted. Then I lap at her backbone, working up and down her back. She meows in response. I lower myself aligning with her entrance, as I feel her heat. I have been with many she-wolves and even my mate, yet none have ever truly satisfied me. It is why I chose to be alone, and Ivan chooses that as well. With us having a shared bond, I know he wishes for love and companionship. However as his wolf, it is not my fate nor his, as we are entwined souls. Angel looks back at me arching her back, she rubs my fur between her clawed fingers. She is different, as I thrust myself in her and she grabs onto me I push myself deeper.

I feel lost inside of her, as I feel myself filling her womb. Our groans and moans fill the room and I'm surprised that the pup has not awakened. I am not sure how much longer I can last as I climaxed inside her. As I stop moving, she pushes herself further on my cock, as if she is draining me. I removed myself from inside of her and collapsed onto the bed. I feel myself shift back into Ivan as I drift into a deep slumber, satisfied.

Angel laid exhausted on the bed. There was so much of his release still inside of her womb, that it would take some time for her to absorb it. She closed her eyes feeling the raw, new energy that was now becoming a part of her being. When she was finally able to move, she felt energized and then she felt a sudden jolt of pain. She fell to her hands and knees. It was nothing like she had ever experienced before. Angel struggled to get back to her feet, but she was soon met with darkness. She had passed out from the pain.

When Angel finally awoke, she looked around to realize that Alpha Ivan and Alex were still asleep. She placed her hand on her head, when she noticed that her claws had grown in size, as well as the ones on her feet. Pulling herself up from the floor, she walked over to the looking glass. With a shocked look on the face, staring back at her was Angel, but she had transformed. Not only had her claws grown, but her horns, wings, and tail as well. Her horns were longer, and the points were curled slightly at the base of her mane of hair. Angel stretched her wings that were much larger and more defined, she was looking forward to feeling the wind under them. When she looked at her tail, she felt spikes along it and the pointed tip was sharper than before.

This was amazing, Angel thought and it was all because of the essence of that Alpha. Angel could not hide her smile, wondering if her human form was affected by this change. As she shifts, she notices first that her breasts have grown in size. Her hips were more shapely, and her behind was more ample. This would be a little problem, for the dress she loved would no longer fit her. The bigger problem was the Alpha, who would most likely have a hard time keeping his hands to himself. She sighs brushing a strand of hair behind her ear. For now, she would worry about it in the morning, as she walks over to Alex, admiring his sweet face. Lifting him into her arms, she carries him to bed with her. Angel slides her body under the cool sheets, with Alex close to her side. For the first time she is welcomed by sweet dreams, nestling Alex's head to hers.

The next day Angel awoke to the sound of someone speaking or rather rambling without pausing. She opens her eyes and sits up, and she notices that Alpha Ivan is no longer in bed. Turning her head she sees where the noise is coming from that has disturbed her from her sleep. A young woman with shoulder length brown hair and dark green eyes is holding Alex in her arms talking to him. "And that's how all the King's men saved the Princess–" She stops, realizing Angel is awake as she rocks Alex in her arms as he giggles. "Oh, Good Morning! Please forgive me, I am Penny, your handmaiden, and an Omega." She bows her head as Alex attempts to free himself to get to Angel. "Alpha Ivan has appointed me to be at your beck and call, helping when needed for little Alex." she explains, and hands Alex to Angel. His arms wrapped around her neck as he gave her a squeeze. He is content and nestles his face in her neck, smiling at her. Angel takes his hand with the birthmark and kisses it. He giggles as she kisses his forehead as well.

"Alex seems so happy with you!" Penny says. Angel looks up at her. "I am happy with HIM, actually..." Angel responds. Penny smiles the biggest smile that Angel has ever seen. "There is something I need, Penny." Penny stands to attention like one of the pack warriors. Angel can only giggle. "I need a dress suitable to fit my... 'ample' frame." Penny blushes as she happens to notice that Angel was naked as she continued. "I will need a dress with the back out." she thought it would be best in case she ever had to shift into her true form given the change in size of her wings. "Of course, of course, I do know of some she-wolves who...who are not my size." Penny blushes again. "But your size, I can find you a dress, a perfect dress, well, nothing is perfect, but to suit your needs!" This rambling continues for a while, to the point that even Alex looks at her with a confused expression. Angel places a finger to Penny's lips. "Thank you." Penny looks at her with tears welling up in her eyes. No one has ever thanked her for anything before in her life. She bows politely. "Lady Angel, I will bring it to you quickly." and hurries out of the room.

Angel smiles, saying to Alex; "She seems like an odd Omega, don't you think?" Alex just giggles in response and puts his hands in his mouth. Angel wraps her body in the bed sheets, as it is the only covering she has at the moment. She lifts him in her arms and throws him up, catching him as he falls. Her strength has also increased, she finds. She continues to play with Alex, who is enjoying their time together. After some time has passed, Penny returns to the quarters with a sad look on her face, with a lovely dress in her hands. Angel is holding Alex's hands as he stands up on the bed.

"Penny, is something the matter?" Penny's face was flushed from crying. "No! Uh, Yes!"

She takes a deep breath in. "Today is the day we send our fallen Luna Elizabeth to the Moon Goddess." she says, as the tears stream down her face. Angel knows grief all too well, and she feels for this she-wolf.

"I'm sorry, I'm sorry." Penny begins to shake her head. "It is not my place as an Omega to break down in front of you." Angel stands up with Alex in her arms, as she walks over to Penny and wraps her arms around her in a hug. She hears Penny gasp and begin to sob uncontrollably. Angel comforts her the only way she knows how, and even when Alex pats her head, Penny lifts her head wondering who this beautiful human really is. Penny jumps back from Angel, "I'm sorry, I'm sorry." she really does go from one extreme emotion to the next... Angel thinks. She will have to have patience with her. She looks down at the dress that Penny is holding in her hands. "Is that for me to wear?" Angel asks Penny innocently. "Oh, Yes!" she exclaims. "This will suit you for today's occasion, being that you are known as the Savior of Prince Alexander. Your presence is greatly needed, especially now." She holds the dress out for Angel, it was a dark blue dress with precious stones embroidered in the waist and sides of the hemline. It tied from the neck, which would leave her back out.

"Is it to your liking, Lady Angel?" Penny gives her a concerning glance. "Yes, it is." Angel says while Penny smiles. "Then, may I prepare your bath? I will have to prepare young Prince Alex as well afterwards." Penny asks nervously. "No, I will bathe Alex myself. You may wash my hair, if you like?" Penny was shocked that she was given a choice. She happily followed her and Alex into the washroom and ran their bathwater as Angel prepared Alex and herself to sink into the warm relaxing water. Penny gently washed Lady Angel's hair while listening as Lady Angel hummed an unfamiliar song to Alex. Penny took particular care to massage Angel's scalp and hair.

Once they were dried and dressed, Angel stood in front of the looking glass while Penny held Alex in her arms. All she could do was smile at her reflection, as she barely recognized herself. Penny had brushed her hair and made her feel as if she was royalty, which was a new experience for her that she did not think she could get used to. There was a knock on the door as Alpha Ivan entered, when he saw

Angel, he appeared stunned at her appearance. The warrior next to him began blinking several times at the sight of Angel. Alpha Ivan clears his throat. "I have come for Alexander." Penny's head was bowed in his presence. Angel decided that out of respect she would do the same. Once he gathered his son, the warrior approached Angel. "I am Austin, the Beta of the Red Moon pack. I will be escorting you to the Last Rites of the pack's beloved Luna." Angel could tell he was fighting back his tears, a sign of a true noble. Even in the sea of sadness he remained strong in her presence. Angel nodded, accepting his hand with Penny following behind them.

They walked through the castle halls and it was clear that there was a wistful longing that Luna Elizabeth left behind. There were many pack members in attendance. The Beta had brought them close enough to the front where she could feel their eyes on her. The Luna was laid on a wooden platform, where she was dressed in a white gown with her blonde hair flowing over her peaceful face, as her fingers lay folded on her chest. Alpa Ivan approached her with Alex in his arms and placed two white roses on her chest before giving her a light kiss on the forehead. Alex looked at his mother as though he did not recognize her, placing his thumb in his mouth. He began searching for Angel until their eyes met. They then walked away, as the pack Priest approached.

"My brothers and sisters, let us pray to the Goddess of the Moon. Please embrace our Luna, who has left this mortal coil far too soon. Please show her your eternal love, as she blessed this Pack with her son. Watch over her, and protect those she held dear, that in time we all will be nearer."

All that can be heard is howls and cries. The pack Priest lights the wooden platform on fire. This is how the Red Moon pack sends their pack members. Angel hears Alex's cries as she makes her way to him, with the Beta and Penny following. Once Alex sees her, he reaches his little arms out to her. The Alpha gladly gives his son to her with a bothered look on his face. Angel is relieved that he is back in her arms, and takes comfort in his scent. Alpha Ivan intensely stares at Angel, both wolf and man remembering the night they shared together. With Angel sensing the lust in his eyes, she ignores his gaze.

"Alpha!" a massive sturdy frame of a man approaches with a powerful and angry scowl on his face. "I don't like it, she is not one of us, and I have been around a long time. Outsiders in dark times are an ill omen. I warn you brother, if you do not cast her aside now there will be untold amounts of death and misfortune among the pack. Yet of course, you lust for this wench, so you will do what you decide, as is your right." Alpha Ivan's jaw tightens. Angel takes a second to take in this rude man's appearance. His hair and beard are greyed to a silverish hue, his beard flows down to his belly and hair is in a ponytail flowing to the back of his knees. His eyes are an eerie but wise silver, and his very presence emanates power, possibly more than she has ever felt in any other creature thus far. "Elder Wolf, this woman has saved my son's life. I suggest you mind your tongue when you speak to your Alpha!" Ivan raises his voice slightly, to which the Elder Wolf scoffs back a little. Alex growls at him in an attempt to protect Angel. It is Beta Austin that breaks the silence. "My Alpha, we should all retire and commence to the third meal banquet. The pack members need your strong presence during this dark time." he bows respectfully.

They all enter the Dining Hall, as the pack members stand at attention when the Alpha enters. "I, Alpha Ivan, would like to welcome Lady Angel to the Red Moon pack. She will be caring for Prince Alexander, my son from this day forth. There will be no one who will speak ill or hurt her, so is the Command of the Alpha." Angel realizes that he has used his Alpha voice, which no pack member can ignore. The entire pack says "Yes Alpha!" all in unison, and they commence to eat their meal that was prepared by the Omegas of the pack. Angel's attention is on Alex, who happily eats his food, taking time to look at her and share his food in a manner befitting a baby. After the meal, Angel notices that Alpha Ivan is speaking to his Beta, the pack Healer, and that cranky Elder Wolf. She approaches them and after giving Alpha Ivan a bow, she turns to Beta Austin.

"Beta Austin, I would like you to find a suitable room for Alex and I to share. All of his belongings should be moved into the room as well. Lastly, I need it to be an adjoining room for my handmaiden Penny." Beta Austin's eyes darted to Alpha Ivan who had a stern look on his face. "There is no need for you to have such a room. You should remain in the Luna's room." he says casually. "With all due respect Alpha, I am not your Luna nor will I ever be. There is no need for me to sully that room." The room is quiet as everyone awaits the Alpha's response.

Angel knew what she was doing, his actions on this day of the Luna's last rites would either sway his pack to remain loyal to him or overthrow him. With that knowledge, he would not wish to risk his status. This would ensure that he would remain out of her bed, especially with Alex and Penny being so near. Alpha Ivan sighs and waves at his Beta to complete this task.

"Elder Wolf," he raises an eyebrow to her as she starts to speak. "It matters not if you care for my presence, but I would make a better friend than an enemy." Before the Elder Wolf can respond Angel hears Penny's voice behind her. "Oh My Goddess!" as Angel turns around, she sees Alex walking towards Angel. She hears murmuring from some of the pack members.

"Alexander is taking his first steps!" Angel feels so much pride in her heart as she watches him. In a brief trance, she sees a flash of Richtor taking his first steps. She smiles as he makes it to her, grabbing her legs. Angel lifts him into her arms. Angel kisses his birthmarked hand and forehead. Beta Austin returns as she calls out to Penny, who quickly comes to her side. "Good night to you all, we will be retiring for the night." They leave together as Beta Austin leads them to their new quarters.

EPILOGUE

C old is a state of mind to some, yet as the pitch black sky blots out the peeking moonlight in the village of Blood Oak, thick clouds can be vaguely seen forming in the sky above. A light drizzle is falling that threatens to become a massive torrential downpour. It is on a night such as this that we find the buxom barkeep, Cassandra having recently closed the Tavern for the night. She was set to walk home, but lost herself along the path thanks in some part to her having a few stiff drinks before locking up. Stumbling her way through town, she barely noticed the drizzle, save that the chill in the air triggered the natural needs of her body. So on this relatively quiet night, all that could be heard is the sound of the Tavern keys jingling to the cadence of Candace's heaving breasts, along with the heavy clopping of her wooden clogs as she fled expediently down the cobblestone road, seeking a place to relieve herself. Then serendipitously, she tripped over a rock and due to the very short dress she happened to be wearing she felt a sobering rush of stinging pain as she skinned her knee.

Slowly she felt an unusual burning sensation as she looked and realized she was now bleeding down her shin. "Fucking rotten luck!" she cursed as she scrambled to her feet. Then something grabbed her attention. She looked and realized she had landed on a bed of grass and not just anyone's grass, this was the property of the late Healer Arthur Nesbit! "Well, that's one problem solved, then! At least I know where I can handle my own needs." she said, making a slightly more cautious dash to the back of the estate. Finally she reached her objective, and with an accomplished smile, she proceeded to lower her undergarments. Before her was a golden tombstone encrusted with rubies and emeralds.

On the front was an engraving that read: 'Here lies Healer Arthur Nesbit, a loyal pillar of the community, and a friend to all who shall be missed'. "Friend!?" Cassandra chuckled to herself. "That's one R too many, old bastard!" she said squatting over the decadent headstone. "Well Old Man Nesbit, never let it be said that I never did anything for you. You were a cheapskate who only bought one tankard of swill a day, and nursed that one drink for Half a day just so you could gaze freely at my lovelies. Well tonight, you make sure you sip slow!" she laughed and began to offer liquid gold to match the solid gold beneath her. Suddenly a rumble could be heard, and the rain fell slightly heavier.

Most unsettling of all, Cassandra swore she could FEEL the rumble as well. To her great relief, she had finished her business. She rose, pulled up her undergarments, and proceeded to skip the rest of the way home. She hadn't been gone long when a bolt of lightning struck right in front of the headstone where she had 'watered' the earth. It made a small crack in the ground. As Cassandra, soaked from the rain, opened her door to enter her home. A powerful gust of wind blew under her dress, exposing her modesty to the only soul awake nearby, a stray cat. She laughed at the vague humor of the situation. Her laugh slowly got louder, until she heard another more sinister laugh in the air joining her own. It was a voice she had believed to be long gone. She rushed indoors and slammed her door shut...

...It was the unmistakable laugh of Arthur Nesbit.

On the outskirts of Blackberry Bush, it was midday. The trees and slowly setting sunlight provide plentiful shadows. It was here that one could find a young lad, snaking about an old home, searching for clues... and memories. The boy looked to be aged 8. While that was not his true age, for our purposes that age will do nicely. The home was a sad sight from the outside, with vines and weeds threatening to claim this land back to the earth that the home was built on. Oh, but indoors, indoors was a veritable cornucopia of evidence of neglect. There were layers of dust thicker than quilts, and cherried wooden floors from long abandoned bloodstains. Shaking his head in disappointment, the lad started toward the rear exit of the home, when he came across the door to a great library/study, left carelessly ajar. "No. This was your passion. I was never given a chance to grow and find my own." the boy said to a flickering light source in the otherwise black home. I said the boy snuck in, I never did say he was ALONE. Exiting the decayed cottage, the sunset was meeting its peak over the surrounding hills, not unlike two lovers meeting in climax. The boy found a simple gravesite, left relatively unmarked, save for a peculiar ram skull staff with a handcrafted wooden baby rattle hanging from one of it's horns. The light source from earlier grew into a full on familiar glow, yet the cascading embers of dying sunlight left no sign of the boy, save for a silhouette. "No. It is obvious that no love remains here. A house without love can never be home." the boy said, as the silhouette seemed to sprout wings, horns, and a tail, then proceeded to fly away. "Don't worry, Dad. We'll find a new home..."

"...and Mommy too."

To be continued in

THE

BLOOD
OAK

CHRONICLES:

Book II: The Pack

CPSIA information can be obtained
at www.ICGtesting.com
Printed in the USA
BVHW070621250621
610261BV00001B/25